ESCAPING MEMORIES

A LUCKY TOWN NOVEL

BOOK 1

AMANDA SIEGRIST

Every part of this material was human created, including all written words and the cover.

Note: The towns Lucky and Mulhene are fictitious towns in Minnesota, as well as Fortune County. The Twin Cities are real. I also describe the Twin Cities as 'the Cities.' Born and raised in Minnesota, that's what I've always called it.

Cover Designer: Amanda Siegrist
Photos Provided by Andreiuc88/Nina Buday/Shutterstock.com
Edited by: Lisa Edward at More Than Words Copyediting and Proofreading Services

ALSO BY AMANDA SIEGRIST

A happy ending is all I need.

Consequences Novel

Dark Consequences

Cruel Consequences

Fatal Consequences

Haunting Love Novel

Third Time's the Charm

Thirteen Days Gone

One Mistake Too Late

Holiday Romance Novel

Merry Me

Mistletoe Magic

Christmas Wish

Snowed in Love

Snowflakes and Shots

Holiday Hope

Sleigh All the Way

Lucky Town Novel

Escaping Memories

Dangerous Memories

Stolen Memories

Deadly Memories

Forgotten Memories

McCord Family Novel

Protecting You

Trust in Love

Deserving You

Always Kind of Love

Finding You

Dare You to Love

Mona & Mason

The Paranormal Chronicles, Volume 1

Perfect For You Novel

The Wrong Brother

The Right Time

The Easy Part

The Hard Choice

Psychic Love Novel

Exploding Love

Captured Love

Slaying Love Novel

Won't Let You Go

Doomed Love

Deadly Crazy

Evidence of Sin

Finding Redemption

Obsessed Hope

Short Stories

Paint By Murder

Follow Me, Sweet Darling

Sleighville Novel

Dashing Through the Fear

Here Comes Chaos

The Last Noel

Standalone Novel

The Danger with Love

Conquering Fear Novel

Co-written with Jane Blythe

Drowning in You

Out of the Darkness

Closing In

Her past is a deadly puzzle she must solve...

before it's too late.

1

SIGHING HEAVILY, he closed the folder wondering why life had to be so cruel. Innocence, beauty, and a sweet abundance of happiness ripped from the little girl before she had a chance to live. Ten years old. Too young to have died.

"Knock, knock, Sheriff. I hate to bother you, but her uncle's here." Deputy Thomas Bolton pushed the door open a bit and stuck his head in.

"Thanks, Bolt. I'll be right out," Logan replied with a nod.

Bolt nodded back and popped his head out of the door. Logan placed a tiring hand on the folder, stood up, and walked out of his office to handle what he never thought he'd see in this small town. He grew up in Lucky, lived most of his life in this great town, only venturing out a few years in Minneapolis as a beat cop. That's where reality slammed into him, sending him home to his tranquil sanctuary.

He saw death, hatred, abuse, cruelty, and just too many other things he wished to forget. Living in that ugliness had weaved a misery inside himself he didn't like feeling. Peace, small-town happiness, the random idiocy, petty squabbles. Now *that* he could live with.

When he walked into the sheriff's office just days after moving back, asking for a deputy position, Sheriff Bob Overly had jovially accepted him into their family—a tight-knit place with only two deputies, and Charlotte, the queen of the front desk. Five years later, at the age of thirty-three, Logan found himself in the sheriff's position when Bob retired, and the small county of Fortune graciously voted him in. He hadn't even put his name on the ballot, but the county took it upon themselves to do it for him. Or more like Charlotte had without his permission after he heard a few whispers around Lucky. The county had loved Bob as their sheriff, and two years into his term, they loved him as well.

Running a ragged hand over his face, he released a calm breath and pasted on a friendly smile as he turned the corner to the front area. The walk from his office, located at the hallway's end, wasn't far enough. The dreadful conversation he was about to have plagued him, it made him wish he could walk right out the door.

"Mr. Thomas, I'm Sheriff Caldwell. I'm sorry we have to meet under these circumstances," Logan said, holding his hand out to shake hands with the man.

"My niece...where's her body?" He choked the words out, barely speaking above a whisper.

"She's currently at the clinic, sir. We're a small town here in Lucky. We don't have a coroner's office or a hospital. Thank you for coming so quickly."

"Does an autopsy need to be done? I want everything to...what the hell happened, Sheriff?"

"Would you like to talk in my office, Mr. Thomas?" Logan gestured a hand toward the hallway he just came from. Not that Charlotte would judge the man as she sat behind her desk, but sometimes privacy was called for.

"No. I want answers, Sheriff. Then I want to get the hell out of here with my niece," Mr. Thomas said, his voice becoming stronger.

"I've never had a problem with your brother-in-law, Mr. Thomas. No calls of service to that residence. No reports from the school of anything unusual. I want you to know if I had come across any of that, it would've been taken care of. Unfortunately, nobody in town suspected anything. There's no need for an autopsy. I witnessed most of it myself. Early this morning, we received a report of shots fired at their residence. Mr. Baxter was standing on the porch when I arrived, the gun pointed at his head. I saw your niece Brittany lying in the front yard with multiple gunshot wounds to the chest. Before I could even utter a word to Mr. Baxter, he shot himself. Brittany was already dead, Mr. Thomas. If you would like an autopsy done, I can arrange that," Logan said, looking the man in the eye the entire time. Talking about a death, any death, especially the death of a child was difficult. He was no coward. Looking the man in the eye was the least he could do.

"No, that's fine, Sheriff. I should've known something was wrong. Her mother...my sister...dying last year. Brittany struggled with her death. I never really cared for Baxter, but he was her father. It's not like I could just take her home with me. She never said he was abusive, but I knew she was unhappy. I should've known something like this would happen. I should've."

Logan placed a comforting hand on his shoulder. "It's not your fault, Mr. Thomas. I wish I had known as well. But the sad reality is, how could any of us have known? You can't blame yourself. Think of your niece with happy memories.

That's what she would want. I can walk with you to the clinic if you'd like to see her. I can help with the arrangements for her funeral. You tell me what you need, and I'll help."

"I'd like to walk myself, Sheriff. You've done enough. Throw some fire on Baxter's body and let him rot in hell. That's the only thing I need you to do." Without waiting for a response, he turned around and stomped out of the building.

"Damn! You dealt with *that* on a daily basis in the Cities. I don't know how you did it, Logie," Charlotte said with awe.

Logan looked over at her. "Char-Char, I never dealt with *that* on a daily basis. If I did, I would've never lasted five years down in the Cities like I did. Did I see death? Yes. But that just now, that was hard. This is my town, and I can't believe this happened."

"Must you call me Char-Char?" Charlotte said with a sliced tone, even as she smiled.

"Must you call me Logie?"

Charlotte pierced her eyes in a measuring manner, then laughed. "I sure do love you, Sheriff. You can't prevent all tragedies. Just like you told him, it's not *your* fault."

"It's my job to keep the county safe, to keep it in peace. And I feel like I failed today." He looked at the door where Mr. Thomas had walked out wishing he had never walked in to begin with.

He loved this small town with all his heart, and now it was tarnished with a horrible memory. Lucky, MN, population 381. Rarely did a newcomer move in and announce, "This is it. This is the place where I want to be." Most people, if a chance presented itself, moved out. This town provided nothing for advancement, only peace, friendliness, and a sense of community. If that's what a person wanted, they stayed. If they didn't, they hightailed it out of town without a backward glance. He suddenly wanted to do that.

"Why are you still here? Leave already," Charlotte said with annoyance.

"You are the bossiest woman I know, besides Kat. I thought I was the sheriff here."

"You are the sheriff. A damn fine one, too. But if I recall correctly, which I have an excellent memory, your vacation started today. You shouldn't even be in the office standing in front of my beautiful face."

"I need to be here. A little girl died today. I'll leave when I know Mr. Thomas needs nothing else from me."

"I don't know how you survived in the Cities. You're such a damn softie," Charlotte said with a grin.

"I don't know how I did either, Charlotte." He glanced one more time at the door with Mr. Thomas's forlorn look imprinted in his mind. "I'll be in my office if anyone needs me. Let me know right away if Mr. Thomas needs me for anything. And I mean anything, Charlotte. Don't you dare take care of anything for me without asking."

Charlotte placed a hand on her chest, feigning innocence. "Me...do that? Never."

Logan shook his head, laughing, as he walked back to his office.

SHE SAW the sun dipping down into darkness and wanted to scream to the heavens to stop the movement. The light was her freedom. It would show her the way out. She had suffered the darkness for far too long. She didn't want to suffer in it anymore.

A twig snapped.

Turning her head slightly, she saw nothing in her vision, peripheral or otherwise. Focusing ahead, she tried to run faster through the woods before he caught up to her. He had to be in pursuit. She didn't stick around to find out if he heard her finally get the door open. She just ran and never looked back. And she decided, as another twig broke, she wasn't going to look back now either. Going back into that room was not an option. Seeing the darkness, living in the darkness again, was not an option.

A branch hit her cheek. A soft cry echoed around the brisk night as she stumbled. Correcting herself before she went head first into the ground, she continued to run. Her feet would give out before she stopped running. She would stop for nothing, or she would die. She knew it with every breath in her body. If he found her, he would kill her.

Stumbling again, over a small log this time, she thankfully managed to stay afoot. Each step brought her further away from the madness, yet brought the sun ticking down from the sky, cloaking her in a darkness that threatened to paralyze her. She couldn't decide what was worse—difficulty seeing with the dark wrapping her up into the deep abyss. Or getting caught by the man who had been her daily terror for so long she couldn't remember what day it was.

Another sound ricocheted around the towering trees, louder than a twig breaking. Swiveling her head, unable to stop herself, she saw nothing. It didn't matter. That movement was her undoing. Her foot stepped into a hole, plunging her forward and messed with her rhythm. With no time to correct herself, she fell hard to the ground. Dirt and leaves coated her body as she rolled, waiting for the momentum to stop, to get up, get back in her fluid pace of escape.

But only the raging speed of rolling increased. She knew

she hit trouble, hit her last thread of life, as she tumbled down the hill.

LOGAN SHUT THE TRUCK OFF, his hands lingering on the keys as he stared at his cabin. He loved this place. The town provided peace and a sense of home, but nothing could compare to his cabin. Nestled nicely fifteen miles out of town, deep in the woods with nothing but wildlife and the fresh outdoor air surrounding it, this place was his haven. If he truly wanted peace, this was where he came.

Another heavy sigh left his body. How many times had he done that today? Too many. What a shitty way to start his vacation.

Mr. Thomas had come back red-eyed and distraught from the clinic. Logan had taken over from that point on. He had arranged for the transport of Brittany's body to Mr. Thomas's hometown. He had filled out all the paperwork, made all the calls, and provided Mr. Thomas the relief that nothing would be left undone.

He had also made a call to Mr. Baxter's family, offering the same helpful gesture to them as he had for Mr. Thomas. It wasn't their fault that Mr. Baxter was a bastard and killed his own daughter. Even with a few reminders of that to himself, he couldn't shake the malicious feeling Baxter deserved nothing. No sympathy whatsoever. But in the end, they declined his help and his sympathy. They were ashamed, embarrassed to know what their son had done. The guilt had poured out in every word they spoke, just as it had in Mr. Thomas's voice.

Rubbing another hand over his face, he resisted the urge to slam his hand against the steering wheel. Wallowing in pity, if that's what he wanted to call it, wouldn't change the facts. It wouldn't bring her back.

He yanked the keys from the ignition and opened the door. This was his safe haven. The place he came to find peace. Allowing the day's tragedy to fester would only ruin that. He had to move on. Brittany wasn't coming back. He needed to accept it.

He grabbed his bag from the cab of his truck. How could he move on? How could he live with himself? He was the sheriff, damn it! It was his job to see these things. To see the first signs of trouble and stop it before it turned into the ugliness he walked away from.

Strolling to the cabin door, the cool night air swept through his hair and a little toward his heart. Nothing like a bit of the woods' peacefulness to calm his soul. This was what he needed. A week of fresh outdoor air, mingling with nature and putting that horror behind him. Even though his vacation officially started the moment he left the office, he had his phone strapped to his hip just in case a call came through. He was the sheriff, after all.

He had left Deputy Derek Graham in charge. He trusted him with the authority. Not to mention, Derek had the most experience within the department. The county should've voted Derek as the sheriff, not him. Except, Derek hadn't wanted the sheriff's position. He had kindly congratulated Logan on the win and breathed a sigh of relief. He liked deputy status and had no desire for anything else, even playing active sheriff while Logan was on vacation. Logan wouldn't let him argue, reminding him that he had the most experience.

Logan climbed the steps to the cabin, glancing around to appreciate the wilderness at its finest. A small disappointment swept through when he saw no wildlife—one of his favorite parts. How many times had he come up here with his father and seen a deer walk through as they sat on the porch? Too many times to count. A beautiful memory, each and every one. Rabbits, foxes, and even a few coyotes had walked by as well. It was always a sight to see. Why couldn't one of those gorgeous creatures cross his path now? Something else to take the horrible sight of the little girl's body out of his mind. He needed something to erase it all.

Another small breath released as he made the last few steps to the door. The knob twisted with ease. It never crossed his mind to lock it. Nobody ventured up here. His little cabin was hidden from the world. Just as he liked it. He had formed the habit of locking his door in town, something he developed from the small stint in the Cities, but not here, there was no need. And if a wandering stranger felt the need to take refuge while Logan was away, then so be it. As long as they left it in the same state he had, he didn't mind.

He dropped his bag to the side and fumbled for the switch on the wall to his left. This was becoming ridiculous, the tension, the guilt that wouldn't go away. He knew this cabin like the back of his hand. Why wouldn't the pain go away already? Charlotte was right. It wasn't his fault. He couldn't have known that Mr. Baxter would kill his own little girl this morning. But he should've. That was the problem.

No light illuminated the cabin when he flicked the switch up, and he cursed under his breath. Figures. Nothing wanted to go right for him today. That would make it easy. And nothing about this day had been easy.

Heading to the kitchen on the right, he maneuvered to his left, walking around the table that he knew sat in the way, and bee-lined it to the cupboard below the sink. Grabbing the handle a little harder than necessary, he nearly fell on his ass when the knob flew off.

"Are you...kidding me?" He threw the knob to the floor.

He grabbed the other doorknob, opened it with less force than the first one, and shuffled around. The first smile of the day lit up his face when he found the box that he knew would have light bulbs. Triumph zapped his bones as he opened the lid. Just as swiftly, a nasty groan escaped. Completely empty.

Tossing the box, perhaps even landing near the damn knob he threw, he slammed the door shut and ran a haggard hand over his face—no big deal. There were light bulbs in the bathroom as well. This wasn't a bad sign of his first day of vacation. His first clue would've been the loss of the sweet innocence he had the misfortune to lay eyes on.

Already adjusted to the darkness, he hustled to the bathroom down the hallway to the right. He didn't bother to turn on the light, because really, the way his luck was going, it wouldn't work anyway.

Wrong choice. He stumbled as he collided with something solid.

"What the hell?"

Before he could process anything, he went down in a heap of pain as the woman lying on the bathroom floor kicked him in the knee.

A painful moan escaped before he barely managed to dodge another kick issued by the woman. "Quit kicking me."

"Get out," she screamed as she kicked again, nearly hitting him in the crotch.

He managed to scramble back, jumping up with a quickness he learned from the many years of running track in high school, and groaned as his knee almost gave out. The woman's leg geared for another shot at him. Instead of jumping back like she probably expected him to do, he jumped forward, landing on top of her. Her head hit the toilet's bottom with a soft thud as he pressed his weight over her body and pinned her arms to her sides.

"What the hell is the matter with you?" He inhaled a ragged breath, trying to find the strength to get through this ordeal. How much worse could this night get? The soft body beneath him made him sick to his stomach. He didn't want to hold her down, but he also didn't want to experience any more excruciating pain in his knee.

"Get off me!"

"No. You attacked me. For no damn reason, I might add. Who are you?"

"I don't have to tell you. Get off me."

Logan inhaled a patient breath. "I am not releasing you until you tell me who you are and what the hell you're doing in my cabin."

"Your cabin?"

"Yeah. I'm trying to start my vacation out right, and it's been shit from the get-go. I can't take much more. Now, I'm going to repeat it one more time, nicely. What are you doing in my cabin?"

"Nicely? You're pinning me to the floor. I wouldn't exactly call that nicely."

Her body trembled. The wrenching sickness in his stomach increased. This was not his idea of a great vacation.

"Well, you attacked me first. How can I be that nice if I have no idea if you're going to kick me again? Are you going to kick me again?" He tried to relieve a little more of his weight off her but still maintained a good grip on her arms. The last thing he wanted to do was hurt her, regardless of the fact she had been kicking him.

"Are you going to hurt me again?"

"What are you talking about? I never hurt you to begin with. You kicked me first."

"You're hurting me now. Your hands...they hurt where you're holding me," she whispered in a painful breath.

He immediately let go of her wrists without issue, but made no move to lift his body off hers. Some answers first, and maybe a little more reassurance she wouldn't kick him again. "I'm sorry. My intention was never to hurt you. Now, please. What are you doing in my cabin?"

"I don't know."

"What do you mean?"

"I don't know."

"Work with me here. I don't want to hold you down, but I want answers."

"Why should I tell you anything? Get off me. Maybe I will."

Logan leaned down. A few faint scratches littered her cheeks and forehead. If he had to guess, she was in her twenties, but it was hard to confirm his suspicions with the lights off. "You'll tell me. I'm not getting off you until you do."

"Who made you the boss?"

"I'm the sheriff. Doesn't get much bossier than that. Now, who the hell are you?" Logan's tone issued no argument.

"I don't know."

"I swear..."

"I don't say that to be smart. I truly don't know. I have no idea where I am. I found this cabin and the door was open..." she paused as tiny tremors flowed beneath him. "I don't know who I am. I can't remember anything."

2

LOGAN JERKED FROM THE ADMISSION, rushing off her and back toward the door. "Let's start over. I hope the bathroom light works. I can't take much more."

He found the light switch with ease and flicked it up. The bright lights briefly pinned his eyes in a glare until he adjusted them enough to get a good look at the woman.

Sitting up against the toilet, her arms wrapped tightly against her stomach, he tried to hide his flinch. Her hair was matted, twisted in knots and snarls with a few twigs and leaves mixed in. As he originally thought, scratches, nicks, and a few smears of blood covered her face. Her clothes, if one could call the rags she wore clothes, hung from her body loosely. He assumed at one time, the dress may have been a bright white, but now it was dark gray with holes sprinkled around, the edges tattered. Her legs were tucked underneath her, not providing much of a view. He didn't need to see. He could discern enough from what he already saw.

"I'm not going to hurt you. I swear. I'm Sheriff Logan

Caldwell. We're in Lucky, Minnesota. Do you know the town?" He figured the best thing at the moment would be to keep his distance. Get her calm. The fear in her eyes tore his heart up. Yet, he had felt her bravery, heard it in every word she said.

"No."

"What's the last thing you remember?"

"I don't know."

Logan ran a hand through his hair. "What's your favorite color?"

She burrowed her brows in confusion. "I don't know."

"You remember absolutely nothing? Where you're from or anything at all about yourself? Am I understanding you clearly?"

"Yes."

Logan nodded, at a loss for words. He'd seen plenty in his life, but he had never come across this before. Memory loss—of everything.

"Can I come closer? Can I take a look at some of your injuries? I want to make sure nothing requires immediate attention."

She leaned back, trying to ward off any potential touch. "I'm fine."

A small corner of his mouth turned up with amusement. "Fine, huh? You're covered in scratches, bruises, blood, and who knows what else. You don't look fine to me. I said I wouldn't hurt you and I mean it. Jumping on you before was only to protect myself. I didn't mean to hurt you if I did. I just want to help. Let me help." His last words came out rough as he ran another hand through his hair. Just once today, he wanted to feel like he could help.

"Why do you care? Just leave."

"Let's get something straight here. I'm not leaving. This

is my cabin, and if anyone's leaving, it's you. Not to mention, I'm the sheriff. It's my job to help people. I already managed to fail this morning, so I'm not failing now. If you won't let me look, then I'll just call the damn doctor."

He turned to leave when she sputtered, "Please don't."

Glancing back, she stood gingerly, barely managing the feat without cringing in pain, and took a seat on the toilet. A laugh wanted to escape, but he held his face as neutral as possible. Laughing at her wouldn't go over well. Had she known the lid was already down? He imagined it would've given her additional pain to fall butt first into the toilet.

"Maybe it's best if a doctor has a look. I'm no doctor. The fact you can't remember anything is very concerning."

"I'm embarrassed as it is. If you want to look to make yourself happy, then look. I don't want to see a doctor. I won't," she said firmly and went back to wrapping her arms tightly around her waist.

"Don't be embarrassed. I'm sure it's not your fault for whatever happened to you," Logan said, stepping closer to her, limping a little as he did. Ignoring the refusal to see a doctor seemed wise, as he needed her to stay calm and cooperative.

"I could've asked for it."

Logan knelt in front of her. A strange urge overwhelmed him. Before he could stop himself, he placed a gentle hand on her cheek. "Nobody asks for this. Have you even looked down at your body? I'm afraid to see what's underneath this rag."

She turned her head away at his touch.

"I won't hurt you." He gently reached for her arm, almost prying it away from her waist. There was no masking the cringe this time when he saw the deep bruises circling her wrist. The scratches, nicks, and tiny abrasions covering her body said nothing like the bruises covering her wrist.

When he made no move to do anything else but stare, she glanced at him. "What are you doing?"

"Trying to wrack my brain who would restrain a beautiful, innocent woman like you," he replied, in a barely audible voice.

"I'm not beautiful."

He reached for her other arm, gently holding that one as he looked at it, the same deep bruises marring that wrist as well. "Beauty isn't always what you see on the outside, sweetheart."

"I...I wish I could remember who I am."

"I wish you could, too. I would love nothing better than to jack the bastard up who hurt you like this."

"Is it normal for the sheriff to jack someone up?"

Flickering a quick look at her, a corner of her mouth tipped up, shining a bit of happiness to the day for once. "No. But I've had a shitty day. I think I deserve to give a little ass-whooping, sheriff or not."

She made no response except to lift her mouth a little higher. He offered a weak smile in return as he went back to perusing her body. Uncomfortable just whipping off the rags she wore, he ventured a look at her legs. He found more bruises of varying sizes with additional scratches and abrasions. Trailing downward, he saw blood peeking between her toes. He let go of her arms and reached for her foot. Another grimace was impossible to hide when he saw the tender part of her foot bleeding with cuts and bruises, a few pebbles and splinters still embedded on her sole. He gently lowered her foot, knowing he didn't need to see the other one. It would look the same.

"What do you remember?" He held up a hand to stop

her from speaking. "And I don't want to hear I don't know. How did you find my cabin?"

"PLEASE, TALK TO ME," he whispered as he lowered his hand.

Did that mean he was finished looking for injuries? After the initial terror had left, she had enjoyed his touch somewhat. He had been gentle, calming the pain that littered her body. Even thinking of when he straddled her body when she attacked him, he had been gentle, keeping his heavy weight from crushing her.

"I don't know..." She put her hand up this time to stop him from interrupting. "It's so easy to say that because when you don't know your own name, what else can you say?"

"Just take your time. We'll figure this out. I need to know what you do remember. Or is kicking me in the knee the first thing you recall?" he asked with a short grin.

"I'll have you know, you kicked me first."

"I did not."

"Yes, Sheriff, you did. I felt a shoe wedge in my leg, jolting me...and I kicked you back in defense."

He sighed heavily. "Okay, I concede. When you put it that way, I kicked you first, but that was an accident. I'm sorry if I contributed to any additional pain you may be experiencing."

"You didn't." She smiled weakly, appreciating the tender tone of his voice. So soothing, calming her even further. "The only thing I remember is waking up in the dark and trees towering over me. My mind was blank. I could barely function because I just felt this blinding terror. I had no idea what was going on. I got up and just started walking. After a short while, I saw this cabin. The door was unlocked...and...and I don't know. I just stumbled around until I fell. I guess I blacked-out or something."

"That's good. That's a start. We'll figure this out."

"You sound so sure."

"Well, I have to be sure. Otherwise, I might freak out. You don't want to see that, do you?"

A small sound, almost like a laugh, escaped her lips. "I can't picture you freaking out over anything."

"Hmm...well, I have my moments," he said with a small chuckle. His smile dimmed as he glanced at her wrists. "It looks like you were restrained. We should still get you to the doctor. You have a lot of small injuries that I can see. Probably more that I can't."

Fear, a fear so deep she had no idea why it pulsed through her veins. A doctor? She didn't want to see a doctor. Pulling her arms around her chest, she cowered away from him. "Please, Sheriff, please. I don't want to."

"Hey, it's okay. It's okay," he whispered, grabbing her arms and gently loosening her grip until they rested lightly on her lap. She shivered from the light caress as he wrapped his larger hands over her small bruised hands and gave another heavy sigh.

"You're hurt. In a lot of places. Your feet...I have no idea how you even walked. What happens...what happens..." he cleared his throat, unable to finish the sentence.

She stared again, fascinated at his hands. She could stare at his hands all day, the sheer size of them, the softness that wrapped around her fingers. So relaxing. They looked large when she stared at them earlier, but now she knew how truly large they were. "What happens, what? What are you trying to say?"

"What happens if you were touched in an unwanted manner?"

The fear jumped out of nowhere. His grip tightened, dispelling the shivers. "You mean raped?" she whispered, just barely.

"Yes," he whispered back.

Suddenly, she stopped shaking. A tremendous amount of fear swarmed around her, but not that kind. "I hurt in a lot of places, Sheriff. But not there. I can't explain the reason, but I don't think that happened to me."

"But you don't know—"

"Please, Sheriff. I don't want to. Please."

"Can you call me Logan? Sheriff sounds so official," he said, offering another gentle smile.

"Well, you're asking questions in the official capacity."

"True, but I'd still feel better if you called me Logan. Why don't you want to see a doctor?"

"I don't know."

"That's becoming your favorite saying. Can you pick a new one?" he asked with a light teasing tone.

"You say doc...ter and my insides cringe with fear," she said with a shiver. If she had to start kicking him again, she would. No doctor. Never.

"Are you scared of me, too?" He almost pulled his hands away when she grasped his hands with a painful squeeze.

"You have a very gentle touch. Even when you manhandled me."

"I did not manhandle you. I was trying to thwart any further kicking, but I'm glad I didn't hurt you because that was never my intention."

"I'm sorry for kicking you."

"Don't be. You have every right to defend yourself." He looked down at their hands. "Well, if you won't go to the...you know where...then let me help you. We need to clean these wounds. I don't want you developing an infection of some kind. Just let me help you somehow."

"You really have this need to help."

"I do. Today, more than any other day."

The sadness in his voice. The pain in his eyes. What put it there?

"Why?"

"It wasn't a good day."

She nodded, knowing she wouldn't be able to coax the answer out of him. It didn't matter anyway. He let the doctor topic drop. "I don't think I can stand in a shower," she said lightly.

"No, I imagine you can't. I'll start you a bath. I'll grab you a towel and some of my clothes for now. When you're done, I can help put salve on some of these wounds. How about that, sweetheart?"

She nodded. His soft touch and soothing words made it unnecessary to say anything else. A deep smile, the first one of the night, punctured his face as he gently released her hands. He turned the water on in the tub, found the right temperature, then turned the plug closed.

He gave her another smile and dipped outside of the bathroom, coming back a few seconds later. "Here's a towel. I'll let you take a bath. Just holler if you need me. Do you need help...getting in?" he asked as he hung up the towel near the tub.

"No. Thank you, Logan."

He started to walk out when he turned around. "Light bulbs. The living room light is out." A quick look underneath the sink had him smiling as the other box of light bulbs sat neatly waiting for him. "Bathroom's all yours."

She didn't move a muscle. When he finally closed the door, he couldn't stop seeing the fear in her eyes. Would she be able to make it into the tub without a problem?

A huge gulp of air did nothing to relax him. Perhaps occupying his time by changing the light bulb would help.

No memory, bruised body...those wrists.

He pulled his phone out, switched the flashlight function on, and placed it on the table for enough light to see what he was doing. A loud scraping sound filled the room as he dragged a chair underneath the light fixture hanging in the middle of the room. A sharp pain attacked his knee as he stepped onto the chair.

Quickly completing the mundane task didn't help him forget about the woman in his bathroom like he wanted it to. What the hell happened to her? Where did he begin to start helping her? Useless. That's how he felt. Still unable to help anybody. What kind of sheriff was he?

Two more twists and the screw would be secure. Suddenly, a scream erupted. The screwdriver dropped from his hand as he scrambled down the chair. Shoving the door open, he jerked back a step. His mystery woman was on the floor, naked and crying.

"Hey, honey, are you okay?" Ignoring the despair that wanted to consume him, he helped her sit up and tried not to stare at all the wounds covering her body. So many it tore at his heart.

"I managed to get my dress off. It hurt to raise my arms, but I did it. When I went to stand, my feet gave out." Her words came out in broken pieces as the tears streamed down her face.

"I'll help you. It's going to be okay. I promise." Not the

way he planned on helping, but he couldn't take it anymore. Gently scooping her into his arms, the world suddenly shifted. His heart immediately pounded with an emotion that he was unsure of. A painful breath left her mouth. "I didn't make the water too warm, but it might sting a little. Some of your wounds are fresh."

She nodded into his chest, grabbing a fist full of his shirt. "I'm scared."

"Please don't be. I won't hurt you, I swear."

"That's not what I meant," she whispered, refusing to release the grip on his shirt.

Damn, she needed to let his shirt go. Holding her like this—she just needed to let him go so he could put her in the tub. "What did you mean?"

"I don't know."

"We gotta work on that, sweetheart. This 'I don't know' business," he said with a soft laugh. "Let's clean you up."

Bending onto his knees awkwardly, she grabbed him tighter. "You have to let go so I can put you in the bathtub. I won't look."

"You already saw me when you busted in the bathroom," she whispered into his chest.

"No, I saw bruises, scratches, and a horrible amount of pain. I know you're naked, but the only thing I feel and see is pain. Let me help. Let go."

She slowly released her grip. He sighed in relief and carefully lowered her into the water, hating the small cries that left her lips. As soon as he had her fully in the tub, he turned off the water. Good thing she screamed when she fell, not only to help her with her injuries but also to turn the water off. It had come close to overflowing.

"I'll be right back. I forgot to get you a washcloth." He left briefly and came back in with a few washcloths. "Here."

"This is embarrassing, but will you help? It hurts to move," she whispered.

"I can...or I can call—"

"No, Logan! Please, I trust you. I'm not sure I have it in me to trust anyone else right now." She grabbed hold of his arm resting on the tub's side and held on tightly.

Damn the fear. How could he take that away from her? The fact she trusted him already filled him with an emotion that words couldn't describe. She had no reason to trust him—or anyone else. No memory, bruises everywhere. Why should she trust anyone at the moment? But she trusted him. His heart filled with an aching wonder.

Not a pleasant task ahead of him, but he figured it would be far worse for her. A lingering fear swam in the depths of her eyes as she waited for his response. Her lower lip trembled, her eyes round with panic. He just wanted to scoop her back up and hold her until the fearful tension went away. The last thing she needed was to feel nervous. But shit, he was a little nervous himself.

"Of course. I said I would help."

He covered her hand that held his arm in a deathlike grip, squeezed once, then slid his fingers underneath and lifted, almost having to pry her fingers from his arm. Instead of returning her hand to the water like he had intended, he found himself raising it to his lips. A sweet, gentle kiss that finally managed to wash away a bit of her fear.

"You're safe now. I won't let anyone hurt you. I'll do everything in my power to help you in any way I can."

"Thank you, Logan," she said, barely above a whisper.

When he was all done, his mind was as frazzled as his nerves. He grabbed the towel hanging from the hook and threw it over the toilet. Disappearing from the bathroom for a few seconds, he walked back in with another towel hanging over his shoulder. Without a word, he leaned down and scooped her into his arms.

"Oh, my, Logan. You're getting all wet. You could have waited for the water to drain." She shivered in his arms, the water soaking him to the bone.

"I'll dry, honey. It's only water." He set her on the toilet lid and quickly wrapped the other towel around her. "Let me go get some clothes. I completely forgot about that. I don't know where my brain is right now."

Walking back in with a pair of sweats and a large T-shirt, he grabbed the salve from the medicine cabinet and knelt in front of her. "I'm going to ask just to be sure, but do you want me to do this as well?"

She nodded. The bath hadn't been so bad. While he could've enjoyed looking at her naked body, all he had seen were bruises and pain. Now, having to touch her body some more, it was almost starting to get to him. As bad as it seemed, he wanted to touch her in a totally different way. An intimate way. That just made him sound like a jackass.

Here she was, in pain, no memory, and he was thinking such horrible thoughts. Yet, she hadn't pulled away or cringed once as he washed her body. Even now, as he covered her wounds, she didn't pull away. If anything, she leaned a little closer. Helping her only. He had to keep that in mind. There would be no other touching of any kind.

A few embarrassing minutes later, since he had to move the towel a few times, he had dosed her with salve over every inch of her body. He grabbed the sweats. "All right, one leg at a time, darling."

"You keep doing that." A shiver rippled throughout her body as his fingers brushed her skin, guiding a pant leg on.

"Doing what? Am I hurting you?"

"No. I mean, calling me different names...honey...sweetheart...darling."

Did he really? He hadn't noticed. "Well, I don't know your name. You don't know your name. I don't know what else to say, I guess. I'll stop if it bothers you."

"It doesn't bother me. It's just strange. What happens if I never remember? Should I let everyone call me that?"

"That's your call. We can think of another name to call you until you remember." He grabbed the T-shirt and carefully pulled it over her head. She did the rest.

"And if I never do?"

"You will. I will help you remember."

"Because you're the sheriff and you like helping people."

"Yeah." He grabbed the towel from underneath her shirt that he had kept wrapped around her as he dressed her. "Done. That wasn't so bad."

"Says you. You weren't naked the whole time, or in pain," she said softly, a small crinkle forming on the corner of her lip.

"You're absolutely right. I should've done it naked. Maybe that would've helped," he replied with a slight grin back.

"And the pain part?" she asked with a slightly bigger grin.

"Oh, I felt the pain, honey. Any man worth his salt would feel the pain." His words were tender as he lifted a hand to caress her cheek. He stood up, put the salve back in the medicine cabinet, and turned to her with compassionate eyes. "Are you hungry?"

"I don't know."

He raised a brow, a smirk filtering in. “Your belly has no idea if it’s hungry?”

“I guess I could eat.”

“Good. Let’s fill you up. You look like you need it.” He didn’t wait for an answer as he scooped her into his arms. “You smell much better. I have to say I’m a damn good doc...nurse.”

She chuckled into his chest as he carried her out of the bathroom.

3

SHE WATCHED as he moved around the kitchen in a graceful form. He never hesitated when reaching for something, clearly knowing where everything was located. She supposed most people probably acted like that in their own home. Living in one place, day in and day out, you just remembered where you put things. She couldn't even remember her own name.

He had a natural rhythm to the way he moved. Measured, yet smooth as he reached for a cupboard handle. Confidence in each mannerism as he grabbed a utensil or opened a drawer. Or the softness in his movements as he closed the fridge.

Soft—just like his hands. He had been so gentle as he cleaned her. She had been captivated watching him lightly rub the washcloth over her body. She found it easier to linger on his gentle touch than the excruciating pain covering her body. And to her shocked mortification, she had enjoyed it. Not only had he cleaned her of the dirt, grime, and blood, he had sent a tingling sensation throughout her body. The way he had held her to his chest, so gentle, so sweet, so carefully. She wanted him to hold her again.

He had tenderly laid her on the couch, given her a small smile, and left the room down the hallway. He came back with a pillow and blanket, then proceeded to the kitchen to make her food.

It was a tiny cabin. One big main room connected the kitchen and living room as one, and a short hallway led to the only bedroom and bathroom. She smiled inside, grateful it was so tiny. She enjoyed watching him.

She wanted to rest her head against the pillow, but she couldn't turn her head away from him. He fascinated her, making her wonder if he treated his wife or girlfriend as gently and sweetly as he did her. The thought he had someone waiting for him pierced her heart with a deep aching pain.

Forget thinking like that. There were bigger things to worry about. Like who the hell she was.

Before she knew it, he slid something onto a small circular plate and walked over to her. "Now, my mom's always a stickler about eating at the table. She says it's a proper family thing to do. But I'm going to let that fact slide for tonight," he said, giving her a wink as he handed her the plate.

She gingerly smiled. "This smells divine. Grilled cheese. Who knew a grilled cheese sandwich could smell so divine?"

"Well, I'm just thankful you recognized it and didn't say 'I don't know'," he said with a small grin.

"What's the ketchup for?"

"What? You don't eat ketchup with your grilled cheese? Don't talk such nonsense with me," he said with a short laugh. "If you're still hungry, I can whip up something else. I'm a simple guy. Maybe this isn't the right meal."

"I love it. Like I said, it smells divine."

"Well, to be honest, I thought it would make you feel better."

"Why?"

"It's silly now that I think about it. But when I was younger, I crashed my bike, pedal bike, really hard. So hard, I scraped the hell out of my knee. Blood gushing, gravel stuck in the skin. It was bad. I was a kid, no more than ten years old, but old enough to be considered big, you know. I cried like a baby. My mom cleaned me up, patched my boo-boo, as she called it then, and proceeded to make me a grilled cheese sandwich. It was my favorite meal as a kid. As soon as I saw it coming my way, the pain in my knee didn't feel as bad. I thought of that and wanted to take the pain away."

Wow. He continued to confirm what a sweetheart he was. Her smile grew even larger. "You accomplished your goal. Thank you, Logan."

"Good. You enjoy. I'm going to pick up the kitchen."

She nodded and grabbed a triangle, smiling again at the way he prepared her meal. Simple and cute. His mom probably always cut his sandwich into two triangles as well. She dipped a small piece into the ketchup and took a bite. Pure deliciousness hit her taste buds. It may be a simple meal, by what he considered a simple man, but as her first memory of tasting food, it was delightful.

She nibbled a few more bites when she heard him say, "I'm going to step outside and make a few calls. Will you be all right?"

She jerked her head toward him, dropping the triangle. "Calls? Who? What's going to—"

"Hey, hey, honey, calm down," he said in a rush as he took quick even steps back to the couch and knelt by her. "What's the matter? What brought the sudden panic?"

"I don't know."

He lifted a corner of his mouth in the delicious way she enjoyed. Every time she saw it, it made her insides burn with longing. Longing for his touch, his soft hands to cradle her cheek, or run down her arm, or clasp his hand firmly with hers. Longing for him to pull her into his arms, swaddling her body close to his. Longing for his sweet, calming words to run down her spine and settle in with reassurance. So much longing. She treasured that smile of his.

"You don't know. I swear, honey, you're gonna bring me to my knees every time you say that."

"You're already on your knees."

"The lady has jokes." He touched a soft hand to her cheek. "I need to call my deputies."

"But—"

He put a finger to her lips. "Let me finish. It doesn't take a genius to paint a picture here. You have bruises on your wrists, which tells me you were restrained. You have bruises all over your body, which tells me you were subject to beatings or something of the sort. Leaves and twigs were in your hair, on your clothes, as well as small scratches here and there. That tells me you were running in the forest, possibly even tumbled a bit. When I put all of that together, I would say you were hidden somewhere in these woods and managed to escape. I need to find where you were held and who did this to you. If I can find the *where*, it will lead me to the *who*. And when I find this person...well, I'm the sheriff."

"And you're gonna jack him up," she said softly.

"After seeing the extent of your injuries, I might do more

than that. We need to find some answers. Don't you want to know who you are?" he asked quietly.

"Yes, but I'm scared. Strangely, you make me feel safe. I hate when you talk about someone else walking through that door."

"Don't be. They're all good people. I promise."

"Please, Logan. Please, don't. I can't..." She looked down to her lap to hide the tears that wanted to escape. "Please..."

He placed a gentle hand on her face, lightly forcing her to look at him. "It goes against my better judgment to do that. That's a very difficult thing you're asking me. I should've called right away."

"Please, Logan...please. Not tonight," she whispered as a tear slid down.

He brought his hand up a little, wiping her tear away with ease. "Please, don't cry. If you stop crying, I won't call...until tomorrow. No arguments tomorrow. Are we clear?"

She shook her head lightly, steeling her features into bravery. "Thank you."

"Finish your sandwich. Is it good?"

"Just as divine as it smells," she whispered, leaning her head into his hand he had yet to move.

"You're going to be my undoing, darling." He rubbed his thumb over her cheek and then abruptly stood up. "It might get chilly tonight. October's already been rearing its ugly head into winter. I'll start a fire. Eat up."

She nodded as he walked away to the fireplace in front of them. She picked her triangle back up, took a small bite, and tried to get back into the delicious taste. It didn't take long as she watched him build a fire as efficiently as he made her food. He hadn't changed shirts yet, still wet from grabbing her out of the tub. The memory, cherishing it, as she didn't have many, made her suddenly wish to be cradled in his arms again. He made her feel safe. When he talked about bringing her problems to other people, she couldn't help but panic. She just wanted him to hold her and tell her it would be all right.

"I'm going to step outside—" he raised his hand quickly to finish, "to get more wood. I promise not to call anyone without your knowledge. Do you trust me? That look on your face says otherwise right now."

She wanted to trust him. Just like she wanted her memories back. "I trust you, Logan. Just...it's dark out."

"It is, but the wood is leaning against the cabin just around the corner. I'll be within shouting distance. If you need me, just holler."

She nodded, afraid to say anything. He nodded back and walked outside. The soft click of the door had her dropping her sandwich again. As delicious as it tasted, she couldn't eat another bite if she tried. Not with him outside in the dark. Oh, the darkness.

A shiver consumed her. Why did the darkness terrify her?

Only consuming half of a triangle, she felt horrible that she couldn't muster another bite. The pillow felt divine as she rested against it and strained her ears to listen, to wait for anything. She wasn't positive for what. He was taking too long. What if something happened to him? Was he hurt? Did he leave? Maybe he really did make a phone call.

Shaking from the multitude of scenarios running through her mind, to her relief the cabin door finally opened. An armload of wood dangled in his embrace and a sweet smile directed right at her. "Miss me?"

"If I said yes, would it go to your head?" she asked coyly.

Where did that come from? She wasn't sure, but his

gorgeous smile had it popping out of her mouth without thought.

"Depends. If it's because you were worried and scared, then no, I'd just feel bad. If it's because you were dying to see my handsome face again, then maybe, yes," he replied truthfully as he walked further into the living room. Why had he asked such a dumb question to begin with?

The wood rumbled in the tiny confines as he tossed it into the wood box and turned toward her with his lip-curling smile. "Well, honey, you didn't answer my question." Because now his curiosity needed to know.

"Maybe a little of both."

"Well, then I suppose I'll let it go to my head a little," he said, curling his lip up more.

A smile lit up her eyes, making him feel slightly better inside for being so callous with his words. He shouldn't tease her. Yet, when he thought about their tumultuous night, she had teased him on several occasions. Sometimes facing a mountain of terror, all you could do was find a modicum of humor.

He went back to building a fire and tried to get her fear, her bruised body, and her horrifying cries out of his mind. Instead, he tried thinking of her fierceness, her strength, and her gentle beauty.

She thought she wasn't beautiful. Probably because of the dirt, scratches, and everything else covering her body. But he hadn't lied.

Beauty wasn't just in the face or the perfect features, although he saw those features just fine after cleaning her up. Her hair was a bit knotted, and although he enjoyed the way the light hit it, giving it a golden glow, he thought he should find her a comb. It fell to her shoulders, maybe even longer once it was fully combed. She had a small nose, even covered with a long scratch, it appeared dainty and cute. Small, defined lips that every time punctured a smile made him want to press a tender kiss in thanks.

He knew once she completely healed, she would be a knockout beauty that turned heads with ease. Her real beauty he enjoyed was her undeniable strength. She fought him when he first staggered into her in the bathroom, and she pleaded with him to make no calls. Both strengths in his eyes. It wasn't easy reaching out to a person, telling a complete stranger you're scared. She had to be going out of her mind not remembering a damn thing about herself. Yeah, she was tough—and that was beautiful as hell.

Sighing, something he needed to stop doing, he stoked the fire a bit. What did he do now? He ached to get started on finding whoever did this to her, yet she wouldn't let him. Not that he could do much at the moment. It was too dark to start tracking where she came from.

She didn't need his help anymore tonight, she was clean, treated, and fed. He turned around, wondering what to say, then smiled in defeat. Well, there was his answer. She had fallen asleep.

He walked quietly over to her and pulled the blankets a little higher. She shifted slightly at the contact, but her eyes remained closed. Her plate of food sat on the floor, barely touched. That wasn't good at all. She needed to eat. She was skin and bones, giving him a clear idea she had been held a while. Her stomach probably couldn't handle much right now. Baby steps.

He had noticed the bloody footprints littered around the

front door toward the bathroom when he ran out of the bathroom to grab her some clothes. She definitely stumbled inside as the footprints crisscrossed in a jagged line. He threw away the rest of her food, cleaned the plate, and started to clean the floor.

After completing that task, he grabbed her ragged dress and threw it into a bag as evidence. What an idiot! He really should've called the doctor and Derek right away. Potential evidence probably washed away when he bathed her. No use worrying about it now.

When he finished picking up the cabin, he checked on his mysterious guest. She was still sleeping peacefully and looking painfully delicate. Damn, if he didn't want to wrap her up in his arms and take away the pain.

He hated to move her. The thought of her waking up at the jarring movement was a distressing notion. How would she react if he wasn't in the room when she woke up? He saw the fear in her eyes when he stepped outside and each time out of the bathroom. It had immediately melted away when he stepped back into her view. He didn't know what that meant and refused to dwell on the matter. Instead, he grabbed another pillow, some blankets, and made a small bed on the floor next to the couch. Before long, he fell asleep.

He had no idea of the time, but it was still dark out when a piercing scream pelted his ears. He jerked upright to see her thrashing on the couch, crying, "Please, stop! Let me go! No, no, no!"

Before he could crawl over to the couch and quiet her down, she tumbled onto the floor next to him. It should've woken her up, but it only increased her cries, "Don't hit me! Please, let me go!"

A fist came toward his face as he grabbed her by the

shoulders, managing to dodge the blow. "Hey, honey, shh. It's all right, it's Logan. Come back to me."

She continued to fight in his arms, screaming terrifying words and flailing everywhere. He finally had no choice but to roll on top of her and pin her down gently. "Sweetheart, hear my voice. It's Logan. I won't hurt you. Please, stop. Wake up."

Her screaming stopped, but she continued to lightly struggle beneath him. "That's right, honey. Don't fight me. It's Logan. You're safe. I won't hurt you."

Her struggling turned into jerky movements as she started to cry. Her arms wound around his neck and held him tightly. "Logan. Oh, God, Logan."

He pulled her closer and rolled to his back, bringing her with him. "Shh, it's okay. You're safe."

"Don't let him find me, Logan," she whispered in a strangled breath.

"Who, honey, tell me?" he whispered back, hugging her tighter.

"I don't know."

Before he could stop, a chuckle escaped.

"You find that humorous," she said softly, yet no anger lacing within the words.

"No, I don't. It's just you say it in this...voice that...I don't know why I laughed. What do you remember? The things you were screaming, well, they weren't pretty."

"I don't...it was dark—a very small room with no windows. I saw chains on my wrists, and he was hitting me. He kept saying something."

"What did he say?"

"I couldn't make it out. My mind only registered the pain."

"Can you describe what he looks like? His voice, even if you can't remember the words?"

"No. It wasn't a clear picture. I don't want that memory. Take it away, Logan," she cried as she buried her head into his chest.

He squeezed her tighter and heard her breathing become ragged. With a soothing hand, he rubbed her back. Her tears were like a stake to the heart. So damn painful to hear. "I'm sorry that you had that horrible nightmare. I'm sorry if I just hurt you. If I could take all the pain away, I would."

She continued to lightly cry into his chest as he rubbed her back softly, whispering encouraging words. Before long, her tears morphed into silence. Tiny breaths left her mouth as she finally fell into a peaceful sleep. He kissed the top of her head and tried to fall back asleep with the beautiful angel in his arms.

SHE AWOKE to the wonderful aroma of bacon. Her back was stiff, the ground hard as a rock. Wait, no. The cabin floor, not the ground or the—it was right there in the back of her mind. Why couldn't she remember? She remembered vividly falling into his arms from a horrible nightmare. More likely a memory. What did he think about her now? Panic spread. Could he hear she was awake?

A sweet humming sound filled the room. His calming tune relaxed her enough to turn toward the kitchen. The couch was in the way, making it impossible to see him. She suddenly wished she were lying on the couch so she could enjoy his fluid movements as he shifted around the kitchen in his charming, proficient way.

The humming stopped, making her sigh from the loss. She gently closed her eyes to hear it again in her mind.

"How bad are you hurting?"

Her eyes flew open to see him take a seat on the couch.

"I'm fine."

"Why'd you sigh? How can I help?"

"Such the helper, Sheriff. Do you ever stop wanting to help?"

"Do you always avoid a question?"

"I don't know," she replied, a slow grin creeping up as she said it.

"I just bet you don't," he said with a delightful grin. "And it's Logan, not Sheriff. And yes, I never stop wanting to help. Are you hungry? Breakfast is almost ready. Then I figure we should slather a bit more salve on those wounds."

"Okay."

"Just okay. To what specifically?"

"To it all. Breakfast smells divine, once again."

"Well, I certainly hope your belly can handle more than last night. You need food," he said, standing up.

"Are you calling me skinny?"

"You're below skinny. You need to eat. Don't make me worry any more than I am." He walked away without another word.

He already worried too much, that was very clear in his voice. She could only eat until her stomach protested.

"I'm bringing the food to you, so don't get up. If you need help sitting, just give me a minute here. I'll be there in a jiffy."

She decided she didn't need help, or at least wanted to see if she didn't, and tried to sit up. Aches and pains everywhere screamed in protest. Not one spot stayed silent. A small amount of joy filled some of those aching spots as she scooted back toward the couch all on her own. A heavy sigh escaped when her back hit resistance.

Logan walked into the living room with two plates. “Do you want to eat on the couch? Would that be more comfortable?”

“This is fine. You didn’t have to go through all this trouble.”

He carefully took a seat next to her, holding both plates. As soon as he positioned himself, he handed her a plate. “Sure I did. You need food. I need food. No big deal to make a little extra. How bad do you hurt?”

She picked up the fork and moved the eggs around a bit. “I managed to sit up by myself.”

He glanced at her. “Well, considering that didn’t answer my question, I’m going to say you’re avoiding the answer again.”

“I hurt. Everywhere. But I managed to sit up by myself. I feel good about that.”

“The best thing for you to do today is rest. Lots and lots of rest. I’ll stop talking now because I really want you to eat.”

She nodded and grabbed a small scoop of eggs. Pure deliciousness hit her taste buds again. The man could cook, that’s for sure. They ate breakfast in comfortable silence. He cleared his plate in record time. A quick glance at her plate showed only a quarter of the food missing.

“Don’t you like it?”

“You’re a wonderful cook, Logan. My stomach just protests after a few bites.”

“I hear what you’re saying, honey, but you have to eat. You don’t look like you’ve had a decent meal in a long time. You have to get back in the habit of it. Give me a few more bites. Please.”

"Only because you said please." She took another small bite.

He watched her in silence as she took five more tiny bites of food before she finally set the fork down.

"Thank you."

"No, thank you for the lovely breakfast."

He left her side for a few minutes, then came back with the jar of salve. "So you hurt everywhere. It hurts so bad you need my help, or you can manage today?"

There was no mistaking the concern and compassion in his eyes. "I managed to sit up by myself..."

"So you've said several times. Then I guess you don't need my help." He held out the container in front of her.

"I think I need to use the bathroom. Can you help me there?" she said, grabbing the container.

"Of course. I should've asked right away if you needed to use the bathroom." He scooped her into his arms with ease and carried her to the bathroom. He gently placed her on the toilet, the lid still down, and backed up. "Take your time. Holler for me when you're done, and I'll bring you back to the couch. You really should try to stay off your feet until they heal."

"Thanks."

She waited until he stepped out of the bathroom before she started the painful process of standing up and pulling her pants down. Taking care of business quickly, the pain in her feet as she walked to the sink to wash her hands almost had her dropping to the ground. It was like standing on a pit of hot coals. For the life of her, she couldn't manage to pull her face away from the mirror.

Who was she? Why couldn't she remember?

No recollection came to her as she traced the outline of

her face. Nothing. No memory. No strange feeling. No intuition of who she was. It made her want to cry.

She jumped in her spot and grimaced when a soft knock sounded on the door.

"You okay in there, honey? You haven't hollered yet, and I was getting worried."

Suddenly, the numb feeling in her feet almost made her fall down. How long had she been standing there? She grabbed the counter for support. "Fine. Just fine, Logan. I'll be done soon."

"Okay. Just holler."

She quickly lowered the toilet lid, sat down, and began the slow process of putting the salve on as many spots as she could reach. When she covered most areas, she set the container on her lap with a heavy sigh. If she didn't hurt before, she certainly did now with all the movements she made. She took a deep breath, hollered for Logan, and waited less than five seconds before he opened the door. It almost made her laugh, thinking he had been waiting right outside the door.

"How'd you do?" he asked as he held out his hand for the salve.

"Well, I got most of the spots. I can't do my back. It hurts to stretch like that. And it sort of hurts to bend toward my feet as well."

"I got you covered." He took the salve with a gentle smile mingled with concern and knelt in front of her. "Your feet concern me. I don't like how red they look."

"Maybe I stood too long," she said softly.

"Maybe..." He stood up. "Can you turn a little?"

She turned sideways on the toilet and shivered as he raised her shirt. Before he could ask, she grabbed her shirt that had bunched near her shoulders to hold for him while he applied the medicine on her back. A few minutes later, he grabbed the shirt from her hold and gently lowered it.

He put the salve back in the medicine cabinet and shut the door with an audible click. The sound made her jump as it interrupted her imagination of his soft hands on her body. Without any warning, he picked her up as if it was the most natural thing in the world for him to do.

"You're as light as a feather. Promise me you'll eat half of the meal for lunch."

She wanted to sigh with contentment as she leaned her head against his chest while he walked her back to the living room. "I'll try."

He set her down, grabbed the pillow and blanket from the floor, and helped her get comfortable on the couch. "Be right back."

He left the room, and not a minute later, came back with a pair of socks. "Let's cover those feet up. I want them to heal."

"I shouldn't have stood so long. It hurt so bad. I don't know what I was thinking," she said, as he carefully put the socks on her feet.

"Why were you standing so long?"

"Staring. Who am I? I don't even recognize myself in the mirror."

He saw the tears build up in the corners of her eyes. The torture and sadness he heard in her voice made him want to cry a little himself. He suddenly wanted to wrap her back up into his warm embrace. This just wasn't right.

"We'll figure it out. I promise."

"How can you sound so sure?"

"Because any other option is unacceptable. And since we're on this subject, I'm going to call my deputies now."

"Please, Logan..."

Her hands shook. That action ripped his heart apart as he knelt down and gently grabbed one of her hands. "We talked about this last night. I'm calling, and you can't stop me. I know you're scared, but you don't have to be. I'll even stay in the cabin while I make the calls. We need to find out who did this. *I* need to find out."

"Please..."

"No, honey. You can't beg your way out of it today. What are you afraid of?"

"I don't know."

"Are you sure? Don't be afraid to tell me. Are you afraid to tell me something?"

"No. I feel safe with you. I don't know, Logan. I just don't know," she said, hanging her head down.

With his other hand, he raised her head to meet his eyes. "Please don't cry. I'll take care of you. Until we figure this out, you have nothing to worry about. I won't let anyone hurt you, I swear. Do you trust me?"

She nodded. "I do."

"Good. Now I'm going to go make some calls. I won't leave the cabin. I promise."

Reluctantly, because the more he touched her, the more he never wanted to let go, he removed his hands and stood up. Reaching for his phone on his belt, he called Derek first as he walked to the kitchen. He picked up the mess from breakfast as he briefly informed Derek of what transpired last night.

He left out some details Derek didn't need to know. Like the fact he held her naked in his arms right before he settled her in the bath and proceeded to wash her body. Or that he soothed her back to sleep after the horrible nightmare and continued to hold her throughout the night as she slept—and enjoyed it.

Next, he called his sister, Kat. He explained just as much as he had to Derek, but added that he needed her to stay with his mystery woman while they did a little tracking. When he finished both calls, he glanced over to the couch to see her staring at him, the fear still registering in her eyes.

"Who's Kat?" she asked as he walked over to her to kneel by her side. "And what did you mean by tracking?"

"She's my sister. You'll like her. She's also a nurse. I would like it if you let her take a look at you. I'm no...you know...and I want to make sure there's no need to take you to...you know."

"But I'm fine. Just sore."

"Your feet worry me. Those bruises on your stomach worry me. And your memory loss worries me. Just let her take a look."

"What did tracking mean?"

"Dodging me again." He shook his head at her refusal to agree with him. "Kat's going to stay with you while Derek and I go tracking through the woods. I need to find where you were held. Do you remember what direction you came from when you spotted my cabin?"

"Don't leave me, Logan. Oh, please, don't do that," she exclaimed, grabbing his hand that had been resting lightly on the cushion.

The thought of him leaving filled her with so much terror, his hand actually hurt as she squeezed it hard. She had a very strong grip for a woman who looked so weak.

"Honey, it's okay. I promise. My sister—"

"No. Logan, please."

"Calm down. Listen to me," he said, reaching over to

cradle her cheek, rubbing a soft thumb where a tear ran down. "I have to for a little while. I need to find some answers. You'll like Kat. She's my sister. If you trust me, you can trust her. I promise. Let me help. You know the need I have to help. I have to do this. I'm the sheriff. It's my job."

She closed her eyes as if none of his words mattered.

"Sweetheart, please. Don't shut me out like this. I need you to agree with me and tell me what you remember."

Her eyes popped open. "You won't be gone long?"

"I'll try not to be."

She stared at him, the terror still lingering in the depths. "I don't remember what way I came from."

"Did you immediately walk right up to the steps, or did you have to circle the building first? Take your time. Close your eyes if you have to. But just try and think for me."

He started to lower his hand from her face when she grabbed it, pressing it back to her cheek, and closed her eyes. He couldn't understand why she slapped her hand over his. Did she like his touch, or need it? Because he felt the slow desire to require both.

This nameless woman was starting to get under his skin and make him feel things he hadn't felt in his life. For instance, failing to do his job properly last night as evidence probably floated down the drain. Or how he could feel himself wavering as she pleaded for him not to leave. He hated when he heard that fear, that terror enter her beautiful voice.

But he needed to do this. He had to find the bastard who laid a hurtful hand on her.

After a few minutes, she finally opened her eyes. "I think I walked around the cabin and felt the railing until the steps appeared. I remember a hill and a big tree lying on its side. I don't know where I saw these things, but they're jumbled in my small amount of memories I do have."

"That's good. Now that wasn't so hard, was it, honey?" he said with a tender smile.

"Not when you touch me. Your touch calms me. Your presence calms me. I don't want you to leave this cabin. Please, Logan, please. I feel safer with you here."

He leaned in closer, a few inches from her lips, as he stared into her eyes. "I'll try to be quick, but I have to go. You'll be in good hands with Kat."

She responded by lowering her eyes to his lips. Any other response would've had him moving away from her, but instead she glanced down. That was his first complete undoing as he closed the distance and pressed his lips lightly to hers. Before he had a chance to deepen it, a car door slammed.

4

"Got another smear of blood over here." Derek pointed to the ground where a few leaves held a trace of her blood from her grueling escape.

"Okay, back to the right. Damn, she was really weaving through these woods. I don't even know how she made it to my cabin with the way her feet looked. We're what...about a half mile away?" Logan said, looking behind his shoulder in the direction his cabin sat.

They had easily found a trail of blood behind his cabin, he assumed from her damaged feet, and immediately started to track. About 500 feet into the woods, he saw a large tree lying on its side and guessed that was the tree she was talking about. Now he wanted to find the hill she mentioned. So far, nothing but stretches of trees and bushes stared back at them.

Derek nodded, his eyes still on the ground. "Yeah, I'd say that's a decent guess. Why didn't you call last night? That's not like you, Logan."

Logan ran a hand over his face, sighing heavily. "I don't know, Derek. You should've seen her. When I first stumbled upon her, she fought me like I was attacking her. Once she calmed down, every time I mentioned a doctor or calling anyone, she freaked out. I figured it wouldn't hurt to wait until morning. She couldn't recall anything anyway, and it was dark out. She was scared. I didn't want to increase the panic."

"Yeah, I know what you mean. She didn't look too happy about you leaving. She looked scared, petrified even. I think she's a little attached to you already."

Logan kept his eyes on the ground as they walked forward, dragging another hand over his face. "She's just scared, Derek. She has no memory."

Derek stopped walking and pointed to the ground. "Got more blood over here. You didn't look too happy leaving her either."

Logan glanced at him. "Are you going somewhere with this conversation? Spit it out already."

Derek shrugged and continued onward. "Just pointing out some facts. I think you might be a little soft on her. She's sorta pretty even with all the scratches covering her face. You soft on her?"

"I'm just doing my job. Don't worry about me. I'm soft on everybody. You've never heard Charlotte call me a damn softie?"

"That's true. She does call you that. Where's she gonna stay, you know, until we figure out who she is?"

"She can stay at the cabin. Do you honestly think she's going to go anywhere else right now? Like you pointed out, she didn't even want me to walk out."

"She could always stay with Kat. You know, maybe spending some time with a woman will make her feel better."

"Yeah, maybe." Logan ran another stressful hand over

his face at the prospect of his mystery woman leaving. He suddenly didn't like that idea.

"Well, hopefully we can figure out who she is by her fingerprints. If not by that, then maybe Charlotte can match her picture with missing persons. Someone had to have filed a report that she's missing. She did seem hesitant to let you take a picture and her fingerprints before we left."

"Derek, she's scared. Imagine losing your memory and having no clue who the hell you are. You'd be scared. And I hope something pops up as well. Her family has to be worried. Maybe she's even married." Why hadn't that crossed his mind before he kissed her? Such a dumb move earlier. No more kissing or even touching.

"Yeah, maybe."

"I need you to talk to Dr. Matthews for me. I don't want to leave her. You're right. She didn't like it when I left. I don't want to stress her out any more than she already is. She can't even stand to hear the word doctor. I need to know why."

Derek stopped in his tracks. "You think Dr. Matthews had something to do with this?"

Logan shrugged. "Not really. Although, I didn't think Baxter would kill his daughter. Just talk to him, feel him out. Let me know what you think."

"Gotcha. I'll talk to him today after we're done here."

They kept walking another twenty minutes in silence, to Logan's great relief. He didn't want to think about her being married, her leaving his cabin, or her beautiful face in general. He needed his focus. Her prints coming back would be the best thing all around. It'd be the easiest way to identify her and send her back to her family, far, far away from his troubled thoughts. If nothing showed in the system, Charlotte would have a heap of work combing through missing person reports to match her picture. Definitely the easiest solution for everyone involved was if her prints came back right away.

"Looks like a hill to me," Derek said as he pointed in front of them.

"Geez, when she said a hill, I was thinking something small. That's a pretty steep hill, and long." Logan shook his head as his eyes caught a glimpse of gray. With quick strides, he picked up a small patch of her dress she had been wearing near the bottom of the hill. "Damn. I think she might've rolled down this hill. This is from her dress. Probably why she was covered with leaves and scratches everywhere." Logan glanced up the steep hill.

"Could explain how she lost her memory. Knocked her head while rolling. It's amazing she didn't kill herself rolling down this. What do you think...fifty feet high?"

"High enough to cause damage like it did. Let's climb." Logan grabbed a bag from his jacket pocket and tossed the rag into it before placing the bag back into his pocket. With the torturous thoughts of her rolling down this monstrosity, he started to climb.

"WELL, I have to admit, my brother did a decent job of patching you up," Kat said, taking a seat on the small chaise lounge that sat to the couch's left.

"Yes, he was very gentle," she replied, as her fingers played with the blanket.

Kat's hands had been as soft and gentle as Logan's, but they hadn't made her tingle like his touch. Kat had looked at her stomach, tenderly checking to make sure her ribs weren't broken by the bruising she had, and determined they weren't. Although she had an intense feeling, she needed x-rays to confirm, but that would never happen. Just the mere thought of stepping into a hospital made her break out in a sweat. Kat also took off the socks, washed her feet, reapplied the salve, and wrapped them with gauze instead.

"Your vitals look good. Your reflexes are good. You remember normal every day stuff, like what's in this cabin and what its function is, but when it comes to personal questions about you and your life, that's where you're drawing a blank. No memories whatsoever?"

"I had a nightmare last night," she whispered.

"It could've been a memory. What happened?"

"I was chained to a wall. He was hitting me. It was dark, no windows. That's it."

"You don't remember anything important about this man?"

She shook her head no, quickly wiping a tear away.

"That's okay. We'll figure this out. You're safe now. I don't think you have a serious head injury. Otherwise, even normal mundane stuff would be a blank for you. Obviously, you were held captive somewhere, and your mind can't handle that. I think the stress of this whole situation is blocking your memories of who you are."

She suddenly glanced at Kat. "Really? What happens if I can never remember? What happens if it was something so horrible that I just never let go?"

"You'll remember. You're safe here in Lucky."

"You sound as sure as Logan. Do you know that?" she said with the tip of her lip curling up slightly.

"Well, he is my big brother. I learned a lot from him growing up. He's always so confident. I always admire his determination, his forte in making decisions. That's why he makes such a great sheriff."

"He does. I kicked him...when he first found me. I hurt him. I didn't mean to. I'm so sorry," she said suddenly, wiping another tear from her face.

"Don't be. He's a tough guy. I would've fought back, too, if I was in your situation. You were just scared. Still are, a little. But hey, consider us friends now."

At that, she gave Kat a wider smile. She was a lot like her brother. Even with her words. "Thank you, Kat."

"I thought I heard my brother call you honey. Is that what you want people to call you until you remember your name?" Kat said with a sly grin.

"I'm still thinking of a name until we know my real one. Any ideas?" She looked down at her blanket again, fiddling harder with the edge of it.

"Hmm...no. Let me think about it. Do you like tea?" Kat said, standing up.

"I don't know."

"Well, let's find out." Kat winked and walked to the kitchen.

As Kat prepared the tea, she sat on the couch looking around the room. The chaise lounge, a cream color, looked soft and comfortable like the couch. Behind the chaise, the fireplace lingered with a small charred pile of wood and ashes. The simple look reminded her swiftly of Logan. When would he return? She really needed him to return.

Bookshelves, one on each side of the fireplace adorned the walls. On the shelves sat picture frames of Logan and she assumed his family. Mixed in with the frames were books, magazines, and other various knickknacks that she figured held a special spot in Logan's heart.

She glanced down at the floor, eyeing the blankets and the lone pillow Logan had used to sleep. Then she eyed the wooden floor, a beautiful auburn color that added a sweet essence to the cabin. Auburn?

"Hey. A...honey...are you okay?" Kat said, kneeling in front of her, holding a cup of tea.

Jolted out of her thoughts, she glanced at Kat. "I'm fine."

"Did you remember something?"

"No."

Kat nodded and held her hand out. "Here you go. I hope you like tea."

She grabbed the cup and took a small sip as Kat resumed her spot back on the lounge.

"It's different."

"Yeah, not everyone likes tea. I find it soothing myself. I'm more of a tea drinker than a coffee drinker."

"Coffee? Now that sounds good."

"Well, when we're done with tea, I'll make some coffee. Maybe you like coffee. See, you'll remember in no time. Let's think of a name, though. I felt weird calling you honey, but you weren't answering me."

"Okay. Fire away."

"Me? Oh, geez. I have a twisted mind sometimes. You might not like my suggestions. Do you have any?" Kat asked with a laugh.

"I don't know."

"You say that a lot. Maybe I'll make an anagram out of it," Kat said, laughing harder.

"Well, when you don't know, you don't know," she said, laughing a little as well. "But I like that idea."

Kat snapped her fingers. "I got it. It's not a lot of letters out of I don't know, but it's using three." Kat pointed at herself. "Kat." Then pointed at her. "Kit."

She laughed even harder. "That is twisted."

"I told you. But hey, we're friends now," Kat said as she chuckled. "Damn, I'm good."

"Thanks for making me laugh."

"You're welcome. Let's think of more. Let's see. Wondo...Doni...Wind...Woki...Kid..."

She held up her hand. "I'm good with Kit. Although, I sort of like Doni."

"Yeah, we can go with Doni. Maybe your real name is close to that. Does it feel familiar?"

"I don't know."

Before she knew it, they were both giggling like crazy.

"Can we try something?" Kat asked, taking another sip of her tea.

"Sure."

"I want to spit a round of questions at you. The first thing that comes to mind, I just want you to say it."

"Is this like a memory game or something?" Doni asked, playing with the cup in her hand.

"Yeah, sort of. I'm going to go fast, so keep up with me and don't think, just say," Kat said, leaning forward a bit.

"Okay."

Kat nodded and set her cup of tea on the floor. "All right. Take a deep breath, Doni. You're in for it."

Doni laughed as she took a deep breath and nodded that she was ready.

"What's your favorite color?"

"I don't know."

"Scones or muffins?"

"Muffins."

"Sweet or sour?"

"Sour."

"Short or tall?"

Doni laughed. "Huh?"

"Don't think, just say, remember?" Kat laughed back.

"Tall."

"Brown or blue?"

"Brown."

"Soup or salad?"

"Soup."

"Married or single?"

"Single."

Kat raised her brows at that but kept on firing her questions. "Brother or sister?"

"Brother...brother...I think I have a brother," Doni said, sitting up straighter. "It's right there, on the tip of my mind, his name."

"Good, Doni. This is good. I don't think you're married either."

"You really think so?"

"Well, I can't say for sure, but yeah. The subconscious is a powerful thing."

"That was a good exercise. Thanks, Kat."

"Are you okay? You look sad now. I have to say, not an expression I'm fond of. So, knock it off," Kat said with a gentle smirk.

Doni laughed lightly. "I can't help it. A brother. I feel it. It's right there. Do you think he's worried about me?"

"Of course. Why wouldn't he be? You're awesome. I pretty much know everything so no point in arguing with me."

"I like you, Kat."

"I like you, Doni."

"Would you mind if I rested my eyes?"

"Nope. Rest is good for you. You should, actually," Kat said, grabbing her cup of tea from the floor and stood up.

"You'll wake me when Logan gets back. Like, right away?"

"Of course. Right away." Kat reached for her cup of tea. "Are you done with that? I can take it."

Doni nodded appreciatively, handing it to Kat. She scooted lower onto the couch and closed her eyes as Kat walked to the kitchen.

KAT POURED herself some more tea, leaned against the counter, and glanced over at the couch. She smiled wide as she raised the cup to her lips.

A few hours later, Kat finally heard voices coming up to the door. She stood up quickly from the table just as Logan entered. A finger to her lips and a shooing motion with her hands had Logan quietly retreating his steps back outside.

"How long has she been sleeping?" Logan asked, the concern clear in his eyes.

"A couple of hours. Did she get any sleep last night?"

"Besides the moment she woke up in complete terror, yes, she did," Logan said, rubbing a hand down his face.

"She mentioned that to me. Did you find something?" Kat asked, placing her hands on her hips.

"No. We were able to track her to the hill she mentioned. We think she took a tumble down it. Very surprised she doesn't have more injuries. Tracked her blood trail another half a mile from the hill's top where it slowly started to die. Nothing around the area but trees and more trees," Derek said.

"She made a mention of no windows in the room. Maybe it's somewhere underground," Kat said.

"Could be. We didn't see anything unusual. We'll have to

take another look. Spread out further, maybe with some four-wheelers so we can cover more ground a little faster. It's getting too late for that now," Logan replied, running a hand through his hair. "Is she okay? Did you check her out a little more? Does she need to go to the hospital?"

"No, she's fine. No cracked ribs, but very bruised. I took the socks off and wrapped her feet in gauze, though. Make sure to check and re-wrap her feet daily. I don't believe she has a serious head injury. Her memory loss is, I think, repressed by her."

"Too much trauma?" Derek asked.

"Yeah. Something bad happened to her. I don't think I even want to know." Kat shivered just picturing the horrifying things Doni probably endured. "Oh, she has a brother."

Logan looked confused. "How do you know that?"

"I played a little game with her, throwing out questions really quickly. She likes muffins, soup, the color brown," Kat said, pausing for a moment as she raised a brow at Logan. "Tall..."

"And you keep looking at me like that, why?" Logan asked.

"I think she's becoming too attached to you, Logan. She was very panicky for a long while after you left. I eventually got her to calm down, and now I'd say we're friends. She insisted I wake her up immediately when you got back. Your eyes are brown. You're tall."

"You like muffins and soup, too," Derek added in with a grin.

Logan pinched the bridge of his nose. "Are you two done? I helped her last night. I was the first person she laid eyes on. Maybe she's a little attached because of that. Don't read anything into it. Back to the brother part, please."

Kat gave him a sassy grin, puckering her lips as she thought of digging deeper. “I said brother or sister, and she popped out brother, then hesitated and sounded very sure she had one. She’s also not married. Unattached. Free to date. Single.”

Logan gave Kat one of his special glares just for her. “And you know the marriage part, how?”

“Same game. I said married or single. She said single,” Kat said.

“You drive me nuts sometimes,” Logan said.

“Good kind of nuts, though. I did good. Admit it.”

“Were you always this annoying growing up?” Derek asked as he chuckled.

“Of course, Grahamikins,” Kat said, blowing him a kiss.

“I hate it when you call me that. Don’t call me that, Kitty Kat.”

Kat raised a brow with a pointed glower at him when Logan said, “Did she remember her brother’s name?”

Kat slowly moved her annoyed face from Derek to Logan. “No. Thought of a name for her as well. I called her honey, and it was just weird.”

“Why would you even call her that?” Derek asked.

“She wasn’t answering me and had this, like, glazed look on her face. She snapped out of it when I called her that. I asked if she remembered something, but she said no. I think she sort of was, though.”

“What name?” Logan asked.

“Doni.”

Derek laughed. “That sounds like a guy.”

“Yeah, well, she liked it. I made it up out of the words ‘I don’t know’ since she kept saying that a lot. I first said Kit, but she liked Doni better,” Kat said.

Logan smiled at that.

"I like Doni much better than Kit. Really, Kat?" Derek said with a grin.

"We were having fun," Kat said with a smile.

"Maybe she should stay with you. I mentioned that to Logan already." Derek gave Logan a hesitant look, who made no response.

Kat glanced at him as well. "As much as I'd like that, and I would gladly take her in, I don't think she will. Like I said, she seems very attached to Logan. We can suggest it to her. What do you think, Logan?"

"Whatever she wants. I just want to help her in any way I can and find the bastard who hurt her. If she agrees, I want you to keep your gun handy."

"You don't trust her?" Derek asked, surprised, jumping in before Kat could respond.

"Of course I do, but we don't know who took her. And before the incident with Baxter, I would've never thought anyone I know in this town capable of that sort of violence. I know better now. Someone in this town is the most likely culprit at kidnapping her and holding her against her will. I want Kat armed in case that person tries coming back for her. It just occurred to me when Kat asked me what I thought. She escaped. With the extent of her injuries, do you honestly think someone just let her go? She had to have escaped." Logan ran another hand through his hair.

"Well, on second thought, maybe she should stay with you. I have to work. We shouldn't leave her alone if that's the case. You have off for the next week," Kat pointed out.

"Damn, I guess you're right, Kitty Kat," Derek said.

Kat glared at him, then eyed Logan when he said, "Okay, she stays here for the week. Let's keep the possibility of this person coming back for her between us. I don't want to scare her any more than she already is."

"Who do you think could do something like this?" Derek asked, mimicking Logan's frustrated hand combing through his hair.

"I have no idea. I never thought Baxter would kill his ten-year-old daughter," Logan said with a heavy sigh.

"Well, on that note, I'm going to wake her up," Kat said, turning around.

"Don't wake her up. She needs her rest," Logan said, annoyed, getting Kat to stop in her tracks and glance at him.

"I told her I'd wake her up right away when you got back. I've already gone against my word. She needs to trust us, Logan, and if I don't keep my word, she won't," Kat replied with a firm tone. "Keep playing the word games with her. Her memory may come back soon. And don't ask her questions. Give her two words to pick from, like small or large." Kat smiled, turned around, and walked back inside.

"WHY WOULD she use the words small or large as an example?" Derek asked, amused.

Logan pierced a pointed glare at him. "First words to pop into her head, I guess.

"Right. I'll check in with Charlotte and call you with the progress. But I'll head over to Dr. Matthews first," Derek said, heading to his car.

"Thanks for the help today," Logan said, waving a hand good-bye. "And we'll get the four-wheelers out tomorrow."

"Yep. Sounds like a plan." Derek slid into his car and slammed the door shut.

Logan opened the cabin door and stopped in his tracks as he reveled in the most beautiful smile he had ever laid eyes on.

"You're back. It's almost dark. What took you so long?" Doni asked, still a little groggy from her nap.

Logan closed the door and made a few quick steps until he was kneeling right by her side. "We were tracking. We found the tree you mentioned and the hill. I'm pretty sure all these scrapes and scratches are from the hill."

"You think I fell down the hill?"

"I know. Your feet, albeit very sore and damaged right now, provided an easy trail for us. We followed a small blood trail to the hill's top, then for roughly another half mile until it disappeared. We didn't see anything else. I'll figure this out. Don't worry." Logan almost reached for her cheek until he saw his sister standing in the kitchen.

"Such confidence. Your sister's just like you, you know," she whispered.

"I'll take that as a compliment," he said with a bit of hesitation.

"Yes."

Logan smiled and stood up as Kat walked over to them. "He's a lug nut sometimes. Don't fill his head with too many compliments, he might blow up."

Doni laughed as Logan raised an eyebrow at her mockery, but refrained from responding. He liked hearing her laugh. Not like her tears that brought a strange pain to his heart.

Suddenly Kat said, "Chicken or steak?"

"Steak."

"Ranch or Italian?"

"Ranch."

"Breadsticks or rolls?"

"Rolls."

"Minnesota or no?"

"No."

"You might want to expand the missing persons search out-of-state," Kat said, walking back to the kitchen. "I'll get the steaks a-cooking. You do have steaks, right, Logan?"

"Yeah, in the freezer. No rolls, though," Logan said with a grin.

Kat looked at him. "I'll be sure to bring some next time I come."

Logan knelt back down by Doni. "I guess that game works well. I'll have Charlotte expand the search outside of Minnesota. Anything else ring a bell?"

"No, but she said to pick the first word that comes to mind. I...I could be wrong," Doni said with a tremor.

Logan almost reached for her hand, but his sister slammed a cupboard, and he managed to stop himself. "I don't think so. I think that's your memory trying to break through. We'll check all of Minnesota, just to be safe, but it sounds like maybe you're not from here. You have a brother, and you're not married."

"When did she tell you that?"

"Right before she woke you up. I really didn't want her to wake you. You need the rest."

"I wanted to see you. I was worried."

"Well, I'm here now. I'm all yours for the rest of the night," he said with a wink.

5

DEREK PULLED on the clinic doors, the locks firmly in place. He saw Dr. Matthews walking down the hallway toward the back. He knocked on the door, waving at Dr. Matthews as he turned around.

Waiting patiently for Dr. Matthews to open the door, words tumbled around his mind as he tried to figure out what he would say.

"Deputy Graham, are you okay? I was just closing for the night," Dr. Matthews said as he pulled the door open and gestured for him to step inside.

"Just fine, Doc. Just need a moment of your time, if you don't mind."

"No, no, that's fine. Come on back to my office. Can we talk while I put some files away?" Dr. Matthews locked the door again.

"Of course."

Derek followed him to his office situated on the opposite end of the clinic. He glanced around as Dr. Matthews went to his desk and started to collect all the files that were in disarray on the surface.

"It gets so busy in here sometimes that I don't have time to put one file away before another one lands in my hand. It was extra busy today when Kat had to leave me early."

Derek cleared his throat. "Yeah, Doc, that's why I wanted to talk to you. The sheriff found a woman last night in his cabin. No memory, bruised, but overall, she seemed fine where she didn't need to go to the hospital."

Dr. Matthews frowned with surprise. "Are you sure? Memory loss can be a tricky thing. How come I wasn't informed? Why didn't the sheriff want me to look at her? Not that I mind Kat did, she knows what she's doing. She's a wonderful nurse."

"She's scared, Doc. The sheriff thought it was better if a woman looked her over, you know."

"Of course. Do you know what happened to her?"

"No, we're still in the preliminary stages. She just showed up out of nowhere. No identification on her, no memory of anything or who she is. We're searching the woods for any signs of where she came from. Charlotte's running her prints, so we hope to get something back from that."

Dr. Matthews sat down, his frown deepening. "That is just terrible to hear. First Mr. Baxter. Now this. What's happening to our town, Derek?"

Derek took a seat across from him. He knew the doctor was in shock as he always kept it professional, even though Derek didn't mind if he addressed him by his first name. He rarely displayed this sort of emotion. He knew how to keep it together and not lose his cool. Derek had been here to help Logan with Brittany's body. He could barely function, his emotions exposed to the world. Dr. Matthews, though, reacted with detachment, calling out orders with a calmness that indicated he dealt with this sort of cruelness on a daily basis.

But he didn't. They rarely saw this kind of terror in their small county.

Dr. Matthews was just that kind of person. He always liked to keep it professional. He knew, in that moment, Dr. Matthews had nothing to do with this woman. His gut told him so, and his gut had never been wrong. Logan told him to get a feeling from the doctor, and he felt secure enough to share their concerns with him.

"I don't know what's happening in this town anymore, Doc. I wish I did. The sheriff tried to get her to come in, but she refused. She's terrified just to hear the word doctor. Why do you think that is?"

Dr. Matthews looked up, reflecting. "Oh, a multitude of reasons. Maybe she's always had a fear of doctors. Maybe she's just scared in general. Or...maybe because a doctor is the one who hurt her. What do you think, Deputy Graham?"

"I think those are all good reasons." Derek leaned forward. "Not that I think you hurt her. That wasn't what I was suggesting at all."

Dr. Matthews smiled. "You're doing your job. Never leave anyone out of the equation, including me. I am the doctor of this town. It makes sense to question me first. My life's an open book, like most people in this town, or, at least I thought so."

"I guess we're all capable of hiding things. Here's a picture of her. It's not pretty." Derek handed his phone to Dr. Matthews.

He puckered his lips as he stared long and hard at the picture. "I don't recognize her."

"We think she rolled down a hill. Most of those scratches are fresh, most likely from that."

"I'll help in any way I can. I trust Kat's judgment, I really do, but I'd like to see her myself."

Derek hesitated to answer, reached for his phone, and clipped it back to his belt. "I'll have to talk to the sheriff, Doc. He's slightly protective of her right now. If she's scared to hear the word doctor, I'm not sure she'll want to actually see one."

"Well, for my peace of mind, I would appreciate it. For yours, and Sheriff Caldwell's, perhaps it will give you peace of mind that I didn't do anything. The mind is a powerful thing, Deputy. She could be repressing her memories because of something terrible that happened to her. Even if she doesn't remember me, hypothetically saying I was the culprit, from deep in her subconscious, her reaction would shine through. Trust me on that."

Derek laughed a little at the lunacy of this conversation. "So what you're saying, Doc, is that you had nothing to do with harming her. To prove that, you want to see her. She won't react to you because you didn't do anything. But if for some strange reason she does, does that mean I can arrest you and consider you guilty?"

Dr. Matthews laughed with him. "Yes." He started to gather his files again. "I would also like to make sure she is all right. Head injuries can be dangerous. She really should go to a hospital."

"Well, unless we drug her or tie her up or force her in some sort of way, she's not going to step inside a hospital. Trust me, Doc, the terror I saw in her eyes when Kat suggested it was immense. She refused left and right. I don't think that's going to happen."

"Talk to the sheriff. I want to see her myself."

LOGAN TOOK his time picking up the cabin, doing the dishes, and anything else he could think of before his eyes told him they were ready for bed. Then he saw their cups and plates near the couch from their bedtime snack and decided he needed to wash them, too. Anything to keep his mind off the beautiful woman lying on his couch, waiting for him.

He could feel her eyes watching him as he moved around, yet she didn't say anything. He hated to admit that he liked her looking at him. Just as much as he would've liked to watch her. She was slowly getting under his skin, and he wasn't sure if he liked it. It wouldn't do well to get too attached, or act on the emotions swimming through his veins every time he thought about her.

His sister had stayed for supper but bowed out after they ate. Only one night. Yet, he found himself wanting to reach out to Doni, as she liked to be called now, as he had the first night. But he couldn't. Because his damn sister wouldn't leave right away, she just had to stay for supper. He didn't need her reading into anything. He didn't even know how to react to his own emotions. One thing he knew for sure, he enjoyed touching her. It played hell on his body that he couldn't when he wanted to.

He thought back to the conversation he had with Derek. He trusted his instincts when Derek told him Dr. Matthews had nothing to do with hurting Doni. That's the same thought he had. He'd known the man since he was a child, seeing him for every illness and check-up for as long as he could remember. Dr. Matthews was a good man. He just wasn't sure he wanted him around Doni.

"Logan?"

He turned his head toward the couch as he put the last plate away. "Yeah, honey."

"Can you...can you come here?"

Still the slight fear in her voice. Why? Bending down on his knee had become a fast habit he created since finding her. "What's up, sweetheart? Do you need to use the bathroom again?"

She shook her head. "No. I...you know...umm..."

He hadn't grabbed her hand since before he left in the morning to track her bloody footprints. He suddenly couldn't stand not holding her hand as she struggled to speak. "Take your time. What's wrong?"

"You mentioned letting me sleep in the bedroom tonight. The only bedroom."

"Yeah, you need your rest. It's a comfortable bed. I'll sleep out here, no problem."

"But I don't want to."

Well, that was a surprise. "Why not?"

"I feel better out here. It...it doesn't feel as confined."

Flashes of her nightmare swarmed him.

A small, dark room with no windows.

Confined.

"Of course. It's no problem, sweetheart. I understand."

She looked away from him, her body shivering.

"I'm sorry, Doni," he said, loosening his grip on her hand.

She squeezed his hand tightly before he could fully let go and whipped her eyes to his. "Why are you sorry?"

"For not using the name Doni. I know you like to be called that now. I'll try really hard not to call you anything else."

"I don't mind that. Don't be sorry."

"Then why are you shaking? I can feel it. What else is bothering you? I won't hurt you."

"I know that. I just...can you sleep on the floor out here?

I'd feel better with you close by," she said, biting her bottom lip.

"I can do that. I don't want you scared of me. You'll let me know if you ever are."

"I will."

"Well, I can feel the chill coming in from outside. Let me get a fire going for tonight, and then we can hit the sack. I'm tired. How about you?"

She shook her head. "I feel like I slept most of the day, but I am tired."

"That's because your body is healing. It needs the rest. You'll be up and at 'em in no time. Let me get that fire going." Logan pulled his hand away.

He stood up, turning around with quick feet as he let loose a silent sigh and walked over to the fireplace. The sudden urge to kiss her again had consumed his senses.

Two choices grappled his sanity—either jump in for the dive or walk away. Walking away seemed like the better choice. Neither had brought up the short kiss from earlier, and quite frankly, he didn't know how to bring it up. He didn't know why he had done it in the first place.

He was the sheriff, and he needed to remember that. His job was to help her, not seduce her. If not for the potential danger plaguing her, he might've convinced her himself to stay with Kat. But he was concerned for her safety. He felt better knowing she was within his eyesight.

What did that tell him?

So many things he probably shouldn't dwell on except one. He was trying to protect her. That's it.

He quickly made a fire, changed into a new shirt and sweats, even though he normally only slept in boxers, and settled into his makeshift bed on the floor.

"Do you need to use the bathroom? I should've asked before I laid down," Logan said, turning toward her.

She was looking down at him with a tender look. "I'm ready for bed. Thank you, Logan. I know the floor isn't that comfortable."

"It's just fine, honey. I've fallen asleep on that couch. It's not that comfortable either."

"It's fine. Goodnight, Logan."

He gave her a wink and watched as she closed her eyes first. He lay there for a while watching her sleep, vowing to himself he would never stop looking for the answers to her mystery. She needed to know. So did he.

His sister's game may have unlocked a few answers. Could they trust those answers? Was she really single, not married, like Kat's little experiment suggested? The risk involved was too high. He rolled over to the other side, knowing sleep would never come if he stayed that way.

The night was still pitch black when a chilling scream pierced his ears. Like the night before, the same terrifying words spilled from her lips. This time he was a little more prepared, having scooted closer to the couch in case she rolled off. He had an intuition that another nightmare would occur. Before he could sit up and grab her, she fell off the couch right into his arms.

He wrapped his arms around her as she struggled. "Shh, honey. Don't fight me. You're safe. I got you."

Unlike last night, she calmed down instantly when she heard his voice. The tears came easily as he rubbed her back soothingly, whispering encouragingly into her ear that everything would be all right. That she was safe. Nobody could hurt her anymore.

"I'm sorry, Logan," she whispered into his chest.

"You have nothing to be sorry about."

"I fell on you. I'm still lying on top of you."

"And I'm okay with that. I don't want you to be scared or having such horrible nightmares. You know you're safe now, right?" he whispered, kissing the top of her head in reassurance.

"Yes. I feel safe with you."

"Good. I won't hurt you or let anyone else hurt you ever again. I promise," he said, rubbing her back in slow, small circles. "What was it about?" She shivered in his arms. "It's okay, honey. We need to talk about it. You can't bottle it up. Talk to me. You're safe. You're in my arms, and nothing can hurt you."

"Don't let him get me, please, Logan," she cried softly as she pressed her face further into his chest.

"No one will get you. I swear on my life. You're safe," Logan said firmly, pressing another soft kiss to her head. "Do you remember anything new?"

"No. Just hold me, Logan. Please. I can't...let me stay right here."

"I'm not letting you go anywhere." He tightened his hold.

He tried breathing easy as she lay in his arms, cradled just perfectly into his body. She felt so good pressed against him like this. It was hard to control his body's reaction. Hearing her whispering words of terror helped to dispel that control. The minute he felt her even breathing, knowing she was asleep, he couldn't help but let his body react to her softness. Damn. He wished she didn't feel so good pressed against him.

Before it came too prominent and obvious to her even in sleep that he was hard as a rock, he slowly rolled her to his side and let her head rest lightly on his chest. He missed her sweet body melting into his flawlessly, but too much temptation swamped him lying that way. Yet, to his chagrin, the temptation still swirled in his veins with her this way.

What was he doing? He was the sheriff. He shouldn't be having these lustrous thoughts. As he continued to lie there, enjoying her warm body next to his, he didn't care about any of that. He'd help solve this mystery, and when he was done, he'd make her his. He suddenly didn't want to lose her from his life.

"Hey, Doc. Thanks for coming," Logan said, reaching out to shake his hand.

Dr. Matthews gripped his hand tightly, as he normally did. "Are you sure? You sounded hesitant on the phone."

"I tried to bring up the hospital again this morning, and it didn't go so well. I'm not sure we should introduce you as a doctor right away. She's fragile. I want to tread lightly." Logan didn't know any other way to put it. He didn't want to lie to her, but the thought of calming her down in front of Dr. Matthews, Derek, and Kat didn't sit well with him. He'd be too tempted to pull her into his arms. And he certainly didn't want to do that in front of them.

"Whatever you think, Sheriff. How is she feeling today?"

"Good. She said her head didn't hurt as bad today. She had a headache yesterday. Her body is achy and sore, but otherwise healing just fine."

"That's good to hear. Lead the way." Dr. Matthews gestured toward the cabin door.

Logan nodded and opened the door, trying to hide his nerves that tingled in every vein. He didn't want her upset. He smiled reassuringly at Doni as Dr. Matthews walked in after him. Her face showed signs of fear and confusion. She didn't like it anytime someone else stepped into the cabin. He normally gave her advanced warning when someone new would be coming, but he didn't mention the possible visit by Dr. Matthews. Words had failed him. So he didn't say anything. It was completely his fault that she looked scared and confused.

The fear was normal. The confusion not so much. But it was a good sign. That confirmed everything he believed. She had never met Dr. Matthews in her life, that was if Dr. Matthews's theory was correct.

"I want you to meet someone. This is Do—ve Matthews." Logan could've kicked himself in the ass for almost calling him doctor.

A smile tinged her lips. "Dove?"

Dr. Matthews coughed, most likely to cover up a laugh. "A nickname, rarely used, but there it is. A little silly, isn't it," Dr. Matthews said with a gentle smile and took a seat on the lounge near the couch.

"You can call me Doni." She smiled back, but the fear was prominent in her voice.

"Thank you. I was in the area and thought I'd visit. How are you feeling?" Dr. Matthews said softly as his eyes trailed her body from top to bottom.

Logan sat next to Doni by her feet and noticed her suspicious look directed at Dr. Matthews. He laid a tender hand on her leg. "He's a good friend. You can trust him."

"I'm feeling okay. Sore, but okay," she answered hesitantly.

"I'd like to make sure. Just a quick exam. Nothing over the top. Head injuries and memory loss are very concerning."

Doni's eyes bulged with shock. "Who are you? Are you a do—who are you?"

"I—" Dr. Matthews stopped speaking when he saw the nasty glare from him.

Logan's lips pulled into a thin line, his fists clenched at his side that Dr. Matthews had the audacity to say anything like that. He should've figured. When had Dr. Matthews ever held back? He was a straightforward, to the point, in your face, get right down to business sort of man. But he had trusted Dr. Matthews to listen to him outside.

Instead of shouting at him in anger, he loosened his hands and knelt in front of Doni. "I'm sorry. His name is Dr. Matthews. Kat's boss. He was very persuasive in wanting to make sure you were okay. I'll kick him out if you really want me to, but it would make me feel better if you let him check you out."

"Kat already did," she whispered, the terror slicing in her words.

"I know, but why do you think you're scared whenever I suggest seeing a doctor?"

She glanced at Dr. Matthews. "I have no idea. I just feel this intense fear when you suggest it. It consumes my body."

"Is it consuming you right now?" Logan had to ask. He was almost afraid to hear the answer.

She stole another glance at Dr. Matthews. "Is he really a doctor?"

"Yes. I've known him since I was a kid."

She paused. "No, it's not consuming me. He looks nice. I can't explain why I'm scared. He doesn't look that scary."

Logan wanted to breathe a sigh of relief. "He's not. He's very nice. Let him look you over. Please, honey."

"Okay, Logan. For you."

Logan backed away, giving Dr. Matthews another glare but permission to examine her.

He waited with Doni while Dr. Matthews grabbed his

medical bag from his car. When he stepped back inside the cabin, he came alone. Kat and Derek obviously intended to continue to wait outside. He had asked them to hang out on the porch when Dr. Matthews arrived. He wished he had let his sister in the cabin now. Doni looked uncomfortable while Dr. Matthews examined her. Not scared, though. That was a plus. He sat on the lounge's edge as his nerves danced every time he saw her cringe in pain.

He stood up the minute Dr. Matthews finished.

"Everything looks good. Ribs are sore. I don't think they're fractured or anything, but an x-ray would confirm. I would like to do one, just to be safe."

"I'm fine. You just said I was fine. I don't need one." Doni curled into a ball away from him.

"It's okay, Doni," Logan reassured her, then looked at Dr. Matthews. "Is it a must? Do you really think they're broken, fractured, or anything like that?"

"No, I don't. I'm a cautious man, you know this, Sheriff."

"I know. Doni's been through a lot. If she doesn't want to go, then I don't want to make her."

"Fair enough, but I want to see you in my office next week to see how you're healing." He smiled warmly at her.

"I...I'm fine."

"We'll talk next week, Doc. How's that?" Logan wouldn't push her or let anyone else, for that matter.

"I suppose that's fine. I know you're scared, Doni. I understand. We'll do this at your pace. If anything, I can make another house call. How about that?" Dr. Matthews suggested.

"I guess, Do—ve."

Dr. Matthews grinned. "We'll figure out why you don't like doctors or even saying the word. You are more than welcome to call me Dove. Makes me feel young."

"Dove isn't a nickname, is it?" she asked, glancing between the two, a small smile hiding.

"I said I was sorry," Logan murmured. "I didn't want to frighten you, knowing he was a doctor. Do you forgive me?"

"Yes. Because you were looking out for me, I appreciate that, Logan." She turned her attention to Dr. Matthews. "Thank you, Dove."

"You're welcome, my dear. Get plenty of rest. I'll see you next week."

"I'll be right back, honey. I'm just going to walk Dr. Matthews out."

Logan walked outside with Dr. Matthews and let his anger spew the minute the door clicked shut. "If I didn't respect you, I would be sorely tempted to hit you."

"What happened? Shit! Do I have to get my handcuffs out?" Derek asked, standing up from the rocking chair where he and Kat had been waiting patiently.

"No." Logan held up a hand to let Derek and Kat know to keep quiet. "What were you thinking, Doc? We had an agreement."

"I was thinking that I assessed a situation and decided she could handle it. She's been through an ordeal, a very traumatic one. She's scared, I know. But she's also tough. I could tell. She took it just fine."

"I wouldn't call that fine. I would call that lucky. And it pisses me off what you did."

"I can see that. My apologies, Sheriff. It's done, though. Does it ease your conscience I'm not the culprit? It eases mine," Dr. Matthews said.

"I never honestly thought you hurt her. Why does she fear doctors?" Logan wanted to apologize for his behavior but couldn't find it in himself to do it.

"I don't know. I'm sure that answer is buried within her

memories. Give it time. She'll gain them back. She's repressing them for a reason. Call me next week. I want to see her again." Dr. Matthews stepped off the porch and made his way to his car.

"Thanks, Doc," Logan shouted before Dr. Matthews could close his car door. That was the closest he would get to apologizing, or at least expressing that his anger was mellowing down.

"You're welcome, Sheriff."

"What the hell happened in there?" Kat demanded as soon as Dr. Matthews drove away.

"Nothing brutal, I suppose, but enough to piss me off." Logan turned around, running a hand down his face.

Now to see if Doni was really upset with him. God, he hoped not.

6

"Do you have to go again?" she whispered close to his lips.

His self-control was slowly weaning down to nothing. But the sound of his sister closing the bathroom door had him backing away a little. "I told you we were checking out the woods again today. We're going to take some four-wheelers out to cover more ground. You didn't mind Kat yesterday, right? And I apologized about Dr. Matthews. I really hope you're not mad at me."

"I'm not. I didn't like it, but I guess I understand. I like your sister. I just...I feel better with you around. Don't leave me, Logan."

"I know. I enjoy spending time with you as well. I shouldn't, but—"

"Why shouldn't you?"

Logan took a deep breath as he ran a ragged hand over his face. "Honey, I'm the sheriff. I...I'll be back later this afternoon. You're in good hands with Kat."

"Be back before it's dark?"

"I promise. And Kat brought rolls. We'll have rolls

tonight." He curled his lip up in delight. "Hamburgers or hot dogs?"

"Hamburgers."

"Ketchup or mustard?"

"Mustard."

"Hot or cold?"

"Hot."

"I think you're pretty hot, too," Logan said with a wink and stood up before he gave in to the urge to kiss her.

She started to giggle. "Is that what you meant?"

"No, but I like hearing you laugh."

"Whatchya laughing about?" Kat asked, walking back from the bathroom.

"Rolls," Logan said as he winked again at Doni and made his way to the door.

"Promise you'll be back before dark?" she asked again, the fear touching her voice.

His hand tightened on the handle. "I promise. Now give me a sweet smile to get me through the day."

She slowly raised her lips in a delightful smile. Logan opened his mouth, wanting to say more, but turned his mouth into a smile instead. Before he could change his mind about staying with her, he stepped outside and closed the door with a quiet thud.

DONI GLANCED AT KAT, who had taken a seat on the lounge, a smile on her face that had Doni wanting to squirm. She could feel her cheeks flaming with heat and had to avert her gaze.

"If I'm not mistaken, I'd say you guys weren't laughing about rolls," Kat said with a mischievous gleam in her eyes.

"Why do you say that?" Doni asked, suddenly fiddling with the blanket.

"Just a hunch," Kat replied with a sly smile. "Everything okay? I hope you were okay in here with Dr. Matthews. He's a great boss and a very kind man. He can be point blank with his words, but he means the best."

"I survived. He didn't scare me. I don't know why the thought does. He was very nice. I wish I could remember. I hate not remembering."

"Don't push it. It'll come back to you. Just let it come naturally." Kat smiled. "Well, not much to do but let you rest. Wanna play a game?"

"Can we forgo the memory game awhile? Logan and I did a bit of that this morning over breakfast."

"How about a card game? Have you ever played the game War?"

"I don't know."

Kat stood up with a wry smirk. "Girl, come up with a new way to say that."

"Why? I enjoy the smiles I get when I say it."

"Oh, so it's not just Logan's smile you enjoy. Good to know," Kat said, walking by her as she ventured into the kitchen.

Doni blushed but feigned innocence. "I have no idea what you're talking about."

"Hmm, mmm, sure you don't." Kat cocked her head to the side with a hand on her hip. "Coffee?"

"Sounds good. I enjoy that much better than tea. And then I'd like to try this game out," Doni said, the redness still smothering her neck to her cheeks.

"Let me brew a pot, and then I'll grab a deck of cards. Do you like the clothes I brought? Do they fit okay?"

Doni fixed an appreciative smile at Kat. "They're wonderful. Thank you for lending them to me. You shouldn't have brought so many. A whole suitcase, Kat?"

Kat shrugged. "I have a lot of clothes. I won't miss them. The underwear I bought, though. Not sure even I would wanna wear someone else's undies."

Doni laughed as Kat gave her a mock grimace. "I think I agree."

Kat went to work getting the coffee ready. As the coffeepot filled up, she dragged a small corner table that was near the wall until she had it positioned directly in front of Doni. Next, she grabbed the lounge, giving it a few heavy tugs until she had it set up on the other side of the table. She went to the left side of the bookshelf, pulled open the cupboard on the bottom, and grabbed a deck of cards. Once finished with that task, she checked on the coffee. She poured two cups and took a comfortable seat across from Doni.

"Okay, the name of the game, win all the cards and try not to lose. I'm a shark and I hate losing. That's the only warning you'll get," Kat said, raising a brow.

"Well, I have this strong feeling that I hate losing as well," Doni said, raising a brow right back. "How exactly do I win all the cards?"

"Easy. I'll deal the entire deck out between us. We'll each lay a card face up. The person with the highest card wins. Now if we both lay the same card, war is declared," Kat said with flair, fanning her hands in the air. "If that happens, we both lay three cards face down, and then we flip another card face up. The highest card laid wins the entire stack. We play until someone wins every single card. Everything make sense?"

"I think so. Sounds easy enough."

"Great. Nobody else will ever play this with me. You're in for it."

"I can't wait. Bring your game, Kat."

Kat's smile widened as she shuffled the cards. Five hours later, when Logan and Derek walked into the cabin, they were still playing.

"Ha! That's what I'm talking about. I won that battle. And I'm getting close to winning the entire war," Doni said as she scooped up the pile of cards from the recent battle where they each flipped over a five.

Kat moaned in defeat.

"Logan. You're back," Doni said with a bright smile when she finally noticed him.

"I should've warned you about this, honey. Kat's very ruthless when it comes to playing cards." He sat down on the couch near her legs.

"She's just as ruthless. She's been beating me a lot," Kat said with irritation.

"Oh, yes. I enjoy this game a lot. We're having so much fun. You weren't gone very long. I'm glad you're back." Doni adjusted the cards in her hands.

Logan tipped the corner of his mouth up as he glimpsed at Kat, then brought his eyes back to Doni. "Honey, we've been gone for five hours. Are you telling me you ladies have been playing this game since we left?"

Doni's eyes bulged as she glanced at the window. The sun still shined with happiness.

"I promised I'd be back before dark. It's not dark yet, but it is getting close to supper time," Logan said.

"I hadn't realized the day went so fast. I feel like we just started playing," Doni said, calming down a bit, his mere presence by her legs enough.

"We aren't done. Go make supper. We have gaming to do here. Just so you know, we played other card games besides War, but this seems to be our favorite. Now go." Kat shooed Logan away with her hands.

"She's right. I'm getting there. I almost have the entire deck in my hands," Doni said with a triumphant smile.

"I never lose this much. I'm not starting today." Kat laid down a card face up.

"Oh, boy, I think this is bad. You're both crazy when it comes to playing cards," Logan said with a chuckle.

"Crazy can be good. Right?" Doni asked.

Logan's face softened, his eyes crinkling into thought as he held her gaze. "I guess I can handle a little crazy."

"Go away. You have supper to make," Kat said.

Logan looked at Kat and changed his look to feigned annoyance. "And this is why I won't play cards with you. I'll go and make supper."

"Will you play with me? I like this game," Doni said with a gentleness that would've brought him to his knees if he had been standing.

He placed a soft hand on her leg. "I would love to play with you. Like I said, I can handle a little crazy."

"You're in for it. She's more than a little crazy. Trust me," Kat said with a laugh as she held her hand out to Doni. "It's your turn. Lay a card down and quit making eyes with my brother. He has supper to make, and I have a game to win."

As if she didn't hear the last part about Logan, she placed a card face up, smiling triumphantly at Kat when she won the round. "Don't forget the rolls, Logan. I have to beat your sister now in this game. Is that okay?"

"Honey, you can beat her anytime you please. She needs to lose for once." Logan lightly squeezed her leg before standing up from the couch. "Don't mind me, ladies. I'll holler when I'm done. Are you staying for supper, Derek?"

"Uh, yeah. I ain't missing this for the world. I swear the last time I played with Kat, she was gonna slit my throat," Derek said with a mangled laugh.

"Playing cards is serious business, Grahamikins. Don't mess with me," Kat said, as she kept her eye on the cards and scooped up the cards this time as she beat Doni's three with an eight.

"I'd never mess with you, Kitty Kat," Derek said, heading further into the kitchen to help Logan.

Logan was by the fridge, pulling out ingredients for hamburgers, when Derek whispered, "Well, good thing she was occupied. I guess she didn't worry as much as you thought she would. Kat does a good job of distracting her."

"I'm glad. I was really worried about leaving her again. You should see the fear every time I step out of her view. She kept asking if I'd be back before dark. She really hated the thought I'd be out in the dark."

"I don't think it's so much you being out in the dark. I think it's her fearing the dark without you around. You were sorta flirting, sorta a bit. You sorta, kinda like her, Sheriff?"

"You sorta, kinda have a way of asking that, Derek," Logan snapped quietly. "You sorta, kinda have a thing for my sister?"

Derek's smile dipped. "Just making sure you know what you're doing. Another day with no answers, no clue where she popped out of the woods from. What happens if we never find the answers?"

"I will find the answers, Derek. I know what I'm doing.

Don't worry about it. And keep your opinions to yourself. I don't want rumors running around town."

"I'd never do that."

"Good. I'd hate for everyone to know you're soft on Kat," Logan said as he went back to preparing supper.

"Low blow, Sheriff, low blow. But well played," Derek said with a laugh. "Need help?"

"No. Go monitor the game. I have this strong feeling Doni's gonna be just as ruthless as Kat," Logan said just as Doni whooped with laughter. "Yeah, definitely gonna be just as ruthless. Admit it, you like that about Kat."

Derek gave him a wary eye, weighing his words. "I suppose I like it just as much as you like it about Doni."

"Fair enough, Derek," Logan said with a smirk. There were suddenly so many things he liked about her. He was glad to be back; just as happy as the smile on her face indicated she was glad he came back. He was sinking fast into her clutches.

The night flew by. Doni beamed with happiness that she won the game. Kat tried not to grumble too much because it was nice to see Doni so happy.

Logan had already brought Doni to the bathroom for the last time where she managed a bath on her own and applied the salve as well. Although, he did help her with her feet.

He deposited her on the couch, flipped the light off, and plopped down onto his bed on the floor. The fireplace provided a nice glow around them.

"Logan?"

He looked up at Doni, her face illuminated softly by the fire. "Yeah, honey."

"Um...you know...I would..." She took a deep breath and closed her eyes.

He scooted closer to the couch and grabbed her hand that hung loosely over the side. "Don't ever be afraid to tell me something. I'll always understand."

"Thank you for sleeping out here with me," she finally said, opening her eyes as the last word left her soft mouth that always invited him in.

"Of course. I understand why. I don't want you to worry or be scared about anything. I'm sorry we didn't find anything today and that your prints weren't in the system. You could've had answers by now."

"I'm not that sorry."

"Why? Don't you want to know who you are?"

"Yes. But not if I'm a criminal," she whispered with a strained breath. "You wouldn't like me if I was a criminal."

Logan sat up, scooting even closer to the couch until he was mere inches from her face, his hand still holding hers near the floor. "It wouldn't matter. I'd like you no matter what. Your prints could be in the system for a multitude of reasons. Sure, being a criminal is one of them. Applying for a job is another. It doesn't mean you did something bad if your prints are in the system. But like I said, it wouldn't have mattered."

"Are you sure?"

"I'm positive. I'll figure this all out. It's not going as fast as I would like. I sent your dress down to the lab in the Cities for analysis. My department is too small. We don't have the capabilities to process the evidence ourselves. I wish we did. They told me it could take a couple of weeks to hear anything back. I don't seem to be helping as much as I want to."

Her eyes shined with amazement. "You've helped, trust me. I don't think I would be sitting calmly on this couch if you hadn't."

He brushed a lock of hair away from her cheek. "There's something about you, honey, that tears me up inside. I don't just mean in the sense of helping."

"What do you mean?"

"I mean, when you look at me like that, I have a hard time looking away." Logan brushed another tender caress across her cheek. "I shouldn't do anything about it because I'm the sheriff. We don't know who hurt you or why. It's an open case and I just shouldn't do anything."

"Do what? What shouldn't you do?"

"Are you trying to drive me insane with your sweet, innocent questions?" Logan asked, running a hand over his face.

"You do that a lot. It's adorable," she said with a tender smile.

"Do what?"

"Run your hand over your face when you're frustrated, nervous, agitated. Am I making you feel that way? I didn't mean to."

"I never noticed. Maybe I am a bit. When you have a beautiful, sweet woman on your couch in your cabin, it's difficult not to be a little frustrated, nervous, and slightly agitated. Nothing you did, sweetheart. I promise."

"Do you really think I'm beautiful?" she asked shyly, glancing away from him.

Logan gently touched her face, tipping her chin back to his eyes. "Yes. I told you before. Beauty isn't just the outside of a person, even though you are. You're so beautiful inside. Sometimes it hurts thinking about it. You're lost in this world, no idea who you are, and yet, so brave. That is beautiful as hell."

"I freak out anytime you want to leave. How is that brave? I'm pathetic, if anything," she said in a tiny voice, wanting to lower her eyes, but he refused to let her as his hand cupped her chin firmly, yet gently.

"Brave. Trust me, darling. Nothing but brave. Maybe you freak out verbally. I just freak out internally when I leave you. Same thing. Guess that makes me pathetic, too," he replied, the truth of those words pouring out in waves from the tender look in his eyes.

"Really?"

"Really. Even when I find the answers, and I will, I'd like to be a part of your life."

"As a friend?"

"Yep, you're driving me insane with your sweet, innocent questions." Logan lightly laughed. "Do you want more than friends? I'm the sheriff."

"You keep saying that. Are you reminding me, or yourself?"

"A bit of both." Dropping his hand, he sighed heavily. "Honey, you're weaving your way into my heart. And not just as me helping you on this case. I mean, as a man wanting a beautiful woman. I keep saying I'm the sheriff because I am. I shouldn't have these kinds of feelings. I certainly shouldn't act on these feelings. I need to solve this case and that's all I should be focusing on."

"Maybe you will when we find the answers?" she asked so softly he almost didn't hear her.

He leaned closer, against his better judgment. "Do you want me to?"

"Yes. Just like how I want to sleep next to you tonight instead of on the couch. I keep falling off anyway. I feel better wrapped in your arms. That's what I was originally trying to ask. Can I sleep on the floor with you, Logan?" she whispered.

"When you ask me like that, how in the hell can I refuse?" he said, closing the distance between their lips.

Her soft moan filtered through his body, zapping him into a hardness he never felt in his life. He wanted her to the point of madness, yet knew he wouldn't cross that line, even as he pulled her into his arms and gently rolled her to the floor. Her moan had given him access, his tongue swirling with hers. The kiss was the sweetest, tenderest kiss he had ever experienced. As he held her in his arms, feeling her soft, delicate body against his, he knew he needed to stop.

Logan pulled his mouth away yet held her firmly to his body. "Honey, you make me forget when I shouldn't. I don't want to take advantage of you."

"You're not taking advantage. I know what I'm doing. I may not know who I am, but I'm certainly not dumb."

"What if you're married? Or dating someone? How are you going to feel when you remember? Where does that leave us...me?"

"But I'm not."

"You remember that? Or are you basing it on Kat's game that could or could not be reliable?" He released a heavy breath.

She puckered her lips in contemplation as her eyes became worried. "I suppose Kat's game, but it feels right. And if I never remember, are you going to keep me at arm's length forever?"

"You'll remember."

"You're always so sure."

"I have to be. I'm—"

"The sheriff. I know. Sheriff, you make me feel things I imagine I've never felt before. Sure, no memories. Right now, I don't care. I like being in your arms, and that's where I want to stay. So don't push me away, please," she said with a soft cry as she buried her head in his chest.

Logan blew out a silent breath as he squeezed her tighter and rubbed her back soothingly. "I'd never push you away, honey. My heart can't handle it. I'm all yours until you tell me otherwise. Just keep in mind what could happen when your memory returns. Keep in mind, I may not be able to give you back to another man. Especially having you in my arms now. Once something's mine, I don't like to share. You're in my arms now and that's where you'll stay."

7

DONI SAT on the wooden rocking chair outside on the cabin porch, the afternoon breeze blowing lovingly on her face. She had gotten used to feeling the wonderful breeze the last few days. Logan had made it a habit of bringing her outside to the porch to sit and enjoy some fresh air. Slightly chilly, but so fresh she didn't mind.

Sometimes silence would reign, and sometimes they talked. Mostly Logan. She enjoyed every minute of his stories. Stories of growing up, making mistakes, moving away, coming back, and his favorite part of life, this cabin. She could see why he loved it. The peace that surrounded his little haven helped her find a bit of peace from the current mess she was in. She didn't want to leave.

But his vacation was over. Tomorrow he had to report to work. His determination to find the answers on her case still hadn't weaned down, if anything, his determination increased daily. She still couldn't remember anything. Kat tried to visit every day, and between her and Logan, they played the memory game. The things she answered with felt right, but no memories ever surfaced. She had no idea if they were right or not. That made her feel even more lost.

Logan searched the woods when Kat visited, coming up empty each time. No trace of where she emerged ever smacked him in the face. She saw the frustration, the helplessness vibrate through his body every time he stepped back inside the cabin. He tried to hide it, but she had, quite easily, tuned into his moods without effort. It made it especially easy when he ran a rough hand over his face. She always hid a smile when he did. She couldn't help how adorable it made him appear.

Every time he got off the phone with Charlotte, his smile she loved disappeared.

Nothing new.

Charlotte still couldn't match her picture to anything on file in the missing persons' database. The number of missing persons in the country made her job difficult. Charlotte was taking her time so she didn't miss a thing.

Doni wanted to know who she was, but then, at times, she didn't. What happened if her life was horrible? Was she a horrible person? Did no one report her missing? Maybe nobody cared about her. Did she have a boyfriend or husband? Could she leave Logan and go back to this person she had no recollection of? The answer that always surfaced —no, she couldn't leave Logan.

At night he held her gently, always so careful not to hurt or increase the pain with any of her injuries. Although, as each day passed, she continued to heal, her injuries clearing up or becoming fainter. She could even walk without help, delicately, and very slowly, but on her own.

Each night, right before they closed their eyes, he would kiss her. A sweet, tender kiss that sent tingles of anticipation throughout her body. She wanted him to do so much more, but he never did.

And she knew why.

He was still hesitant to take that leap. He was the sheriff, something he said frequently. She figured it was his way to remind himself because she didn't care. His caution was making her think she would have to take the first leap because another night in his arms without taking more than just a kiss seemed like torture.

When her nightmares, or memories most likely, shot through her in the dead of night, he was always by her side to calm her. One simple touch, gentle squeeze, and tender words normally did the trick. She'd turn her face into his chest and cry softly until she fell back into a peaceful sleep.

The nightmares never deviated either. Always the same terrifying scene. Small, damp room with no windows. Chained to the wall and a nasty man hitting her, yelling. She could never make out the words or his face.

Just nothing.

She figured she was nothing until her memories came back.

"I don't like this look on your face, sweetheart. What's the matter?" Logan knelt in front of her, almost to the point of scooting between her legs as he rested his hands on her thighs.

"Nothing."

"No, it's something. You don't look happy, and I want to know why." Logan smoothed his hands further up her thighs.

"I'm nothing, Logan, just nothing. What am I going to do?"

"You're a beautiful, brave, funny, kind, aggressive... I could keep describing what kind of wonderful woman you are. But you are *not* nothing. What you're going to do is come home with me. Unless you want to stay with Kat. Just because my vacation is over and we're heading back to town, it doesn't mean I'm dumping you to the side of the curb. You didn't think that I hope?"

"Aggressive? I'm aggressive. Is it because I kicked you that one time?" she asked, tipping the corner of her lip up.

"No, not because of that. That falls under the brave category. Aggressive is for the playing cards category. You're ruthless, just like Kat. It's just a game," he said as his lips moved into a slow, sexy grin that she loved.

"It's a very fun game. You said you'd play with me and you haven't yet. I've only played with Kat so far."

"Yeah, I refuse to play with her because of her tendencies to overreact about things. I did say I would play with you. Can we at least make it a little more interesting?" Logan asked with a devious grin.

"I like interesting," she said, lifting her eyebrows as she hoped that comment meant what she thought it did.

"Then that's settled. Back to the issue at hand, you aren't nothing."

"What am I supposed to do? I can't keep sitting around. I'm feeling better. My feet are better. Every day it gets better to walk."

Logan lifted a hand and ran it over his face as he let out a sigh. He put his hand back onto her thigh just a little higher, getting closer to the spot she had been craving for him to touch. Every time he reached higher, he drove her a little more insane. "But your feet aren't fully healed, and I would feel better if you didn't do too much too soon. Let's start with one thing at a time. Where do you want to stay?"

"That's a dumb question, Logan. I want to stay with

you," she said firmly, her forehead bowing in wrinkles as she frowned.

"Well, I didn't want to assume. I want you with me as well," he said with a smile. "Don't look at me like that, please?"

She curled her lips back into a small grin just for his benefit. "And the next thing?"

"I was thinking if you want to come to the sheriff's office with me, you could help Charlotte at the front desk. I...I don't know if it'll be difficult for you to look through missing persons or not, but I thought maybe you could do that. It's been on my mind to ask, but I didn't want...I understand the feeling of restlessness. I figured you'd hit that sooner or later. What do you want to do? Whatever you want to do, I'll make it happen."

She lifted her hand that had been resting on the armrest and cupped his cheek. "You're such a kind, gentle man. Always worrying about me, my feelings, how I will react. Why do you put up with me and my hysterical ways?"

"Because it's easy. You make it easy with one simple smile directed my way. You're not hysterical either."

Before she knew what he was going to do, he grabbed her around the waist and pulled her closer. She dropped her hand from his cheek at the sudden movement and rested it on his shoulder, her other hand joining the opposite shoulder.

"Honey, your feelings are of the utmost importance to me. You may have no memory, but that doesn't make you nothing. Now answer my question. What do you want to do?"

"I would like to help Charlotte."

"Are you sure? I don't want you to do anything that may be difficult for you. If it does become difficult, I need you to tell me. No hiding anything from me, including your feelings. Are we clear?"

"Yes. I like it when you hold me like this. You should do this more often." She reached up to comb her fingers through his hair.

Logan closed his eyes for a brief moment, savoring her soft touch. "You tempt me too much, sweetheart." He opened his eyes to see her staring at him. "You shouldn't look at me like that."

"Like what?"

"Like you want me to devour you right here on this chair. Because I just might."

She puckered her lips in anticipation and leaned closer. "I want you to devour me, Logan."

He groaned right before he closed the distance and consumed her mouth. She fingered through his hair again, grabbing him tighter as her fingers slowly made their way to his back. His tongue dug in right away, tangling with hers as she pushed further into his lap. His knees ached from leaning on the porch, but with this beautiful woman in his arms, he didn't care.

He knew she could feel his hard bulge pressing nicely into her hot center because she lifted her body to press even closer. The movement made him deepen the kiss, deeper than he had ever taken it with her. He always tried to keep it light, with just enough desire to pull away. The way she moved in his arms made it difficult to remember why he should be gentle.

The next thing he knew, he was pushing back, the chair rocking to their movements. As he kissed her, she tangled her fingers everywhere on his back to his hair, and he relished in the small, soft touches. She pushed into him again, the chair rocking toward him as she did, his hardness growing to the point of pain. He needed her so badly.

Before he could do anything crazy, like stand up and carry her back inside the cabin, his knees finally gave out as she pushed into him again. He fell backward and to the side as she crashed with him. Sprawled across his body, she shook, her head pressed into his chest. Shit! She was crying. A nasty curse wanted to escape for making her cry when he heard a soft chuckle.

"Are you laughing at me?" he whispered.

She lifted her head, a bright smile illuminating her face. "No. I'm laughing because we fell over in such passion. You make me feel so alive, Logan."

"Oh, damn, honey. Me, too. We shouldn't do this. Not yet, at least," Logan added when her smile dipped.

"When? Because I like how you make me feel. Am I doing it wrong?"

"Hell, no. You aren't doing anything wrong. I just think we should take it a bit slow. It's only been a week. I like you in my arms. I really do. Now I'll never look at my cabin porch the same. I'll picture us lying here wrapped up in a silly embrace. What a beautiful memory," Logan said as he grabbed a quick kiss.

"It is a beautiful memory. It may only have been a week, but I feel like I've known you forever. You make it that easy."

"Remember what I said. You're in my arms, and it's staying that way. But we should take it slow."

"Should and want are two different things. Maybe we should, but that doesn't mean I want to," she said as she finally lifted herself off him.

"Trust me, honey. I know the difference. I feel the same,"

Logan replied as he stood up. "But we...let's move on, for now. I'm going to make one more sweep through the cabin to make sure I didn't miss anything. Go ahead and hop in the truck."

"Okay, Logan. For now," she said and slowly made her way down the steps.

Logan watched her for a brief moment, then abruptly turned toward the door and stalked inside. She was pulling at his heart and making it difficult to resist her. He was still wondering why he did. Then the thought of another man waiting for her somewhere made it easy to stomp down his urges. Could he trust Kat's little memory game? Was she really free and unattached? Did it really matter when she felt so delicious in his arms?

As he quickly walked around the cabin seeing everything in its place, he decided, no, it didn't really matter. He'd fight to keep her if he had to.

So why was he fighting the urge to make her completely his? Her body was healing nicely, the bruises barely making her wince as they tenderly kissed at night. She might be ready. He just didn't want to hurt her. He didn't want her to feel any pain, especially from him.

As he flipped the light switch off, he winced.

Only a week.

One week and he wanted that beautiful woman with a pain so real it could drop him to his knees just thinking about it. How in the hell had he fallen so fast?

He opened the door, shut it with ease, and glanced at her. A bright smile shined back as he made his way to the truck.

Oh, yeah. That's how he fell so fast. She made it so damn easy.

He opened the driver's side door, hopped in without

effort, and turned the key. "Everything's good. Ready to see the town? We'll drive through tonight and head home right away, but it's small so you'll see it all with just one drive."

"Don't you lock your door?" she asked as a frown appeared when she glanced at the cabin.

"No. Never have up here, and I'm not going to start."

"But anyone could just walk in. They could steal from you." Her frown deepened.

He cupped her cheek, pulling her face toward him. When her eyes landed on his, he gave her a sweet grin. "A beautiful someone did just walk in, and she wouldn't have been able to if I had locked my door. Before you came, I've never had a problem. I'm not going to worry about it. It's just not something I do. I don't want you to worry about it either. You have enough to worry about."

"When you put it that way, for a kiss, I won't worry about it."

"Are you bribing me with a kiss?"

"I am." She raised an eyebrow as she leaned her head into his hand with a devilish smile playing on her lips.

"Well, I can't refuse that sort of bribe." He leaned over the seat, cupped the other side of her face, and dove in for a kiss. If she thought he would make it light, he had no intention of doing so.

She immediately opened for him, tugging on his tongue, moaning in delight as she tried to scoot closer, but the seatbelt impeded her movement, making her groan in dismay. He felt the frustration in her kiss and clutched her face a little tighter. He pulled on her tongue with his own, then slipped it away, nibbling gently on her bottom lip.

He sat back, resting his hands in his lap to prevent himself from releasing her seatbelt and taking her right there in the truck. Or worse, hauling her back in the cabin and never leaving for the night as he ravished her to the point of sin.

"Did that suffice?" he asked a bit hoarsely.

"Yes, it did, Logan. Thank you. I'm ready to see the town," she said as she settled back into her seat.

He nodded, adjusted himself, and buckled up. Damn, how soon could they get home? What the hell would happen when they did? Keeping his hands to himself was getting harder and harder.

INSTEAD OF SLIGHT apprehension running through her veins of leaving her safe haven, she thought of getting to Logan's home and having her way with him. Hearing the slight roughness in his voice, she knew he was wavering in his desire. He was leery, but she heard him wavering.

She would break him before the night ended because she refused to wait any longer. She needed this. The exact reason why was a mystery, but she didn't think it was just lust running through her body.

"Long thoughts over there again. What are you thinking about? Are you nervous about leaving the cabin?" Logan asked as he glanced at her again for the umpteenth time.

"I was nervous. You always know how I feel, very attuned to my emotions, very considerate. I'm not nervous anymore. I was thinking of how I'm going to seduce you tonight."

His hands slightly jerked on the wheel, straightening the truck before he veered off the road. "Are you trying to make me run the vehicle off the road, honey? You can't just say things like that to a man."

"Why not? You asked what I was thinking, and I was

being honest. Honesty is important." She smiled as he twitched in his seat and gripped the wheel tighter.

"Honesty is important, you're right. But still. Just throwing things out there like that...give me a little warning next time." A hand ran down his face, a little shaky in her estimation.

"Are you nervous for some reason, Logan?"

He glanced at her, his expression a strangled one. "You're trying to drive me insane. I just know it. You need to stop smiling at me like that. We talked about this, honey, and I...you're still healing."

"I'm feeling fine. I won't pressure you if you're really uncomfortable. I want you, Logan. And when you kiss me like you do, it just makes me want you more."

He wiggled in his seat a bit more.

"Uncomfortable?"

"You damn well know I am. Saying things like that." He flickered another glance at her. "You know this is a small town."

"You're changing the subject." The surprise was evident on her face, her brow lifted in amusement as well.

"No. I'm going to point something out to you. This is a small town. Tongues flap quite easily and quite frequently. I haven't said anything, but you know they're already flapping a bit about a mysterious woman being found and staying at the sheriff's cabin. They're gonna talk even more when you stay at my house. Are you sure you don't want to stay at Kat's?"

"Does it bother you people saying things about us like that? Do you want me to stay at Kat's?" Maybe throwing herself at him was wrong. This didn't sound like a man who wanted her in his home.

Without hesitating, he grabbed her hand and brought it

to his lap. “I don’t give a shit what people say about me. Never have and never will. Although, I am the sheriff and I should. Being the sheriff also makes it easier to tell them nicely to shut their mouths. I worry about what that’ll do to you. I want you with me, nowhere else.”

“Still worrying about my feelings. That’s why you make it so easy to like you, Logan. How can I resist that?”

“I never said you should. Just that we should take it slow.” He squeezed her hand lightly. “Don’t let anyone make you feel uncomfortable. If they do, you tell me who it is right away.”

“Logan—”

“No, honey, let me finish. If we’re being honest, then I should say something. I just don’t want to scare you.”

HE SUDDENLY WANTED to run a hand over his face.

But he couldn’t.

One hand held the wheel, and the other, her soft, luscious hand. He refused to release either of them. One for safety reasons, the other because the thought of letting her go tore his heart up.

“You escaped wherever you were being held. I don’t think this monster let you go. I never imagined monsters living in my town, but they do. The night I found you, I dealt with a monster that killed his own ten-year-old daughter that morning. I don’t want this person...this monster...to get you again. But if it’s someone from town, it’s a possibility. I want you to be aware of your surroundings and be with me at all times. If not me, then one of my deputies, my sister or brother, or Charlotte. No exceptions. I trust those people with my life. Anyone else in town, not so much. You mean too much to me to lose you. Do you understand what I'm saying?"

He slowed to a stop at the fork in the road. No other traffic graced the road. Not that he would've cared anyway. "I scared you, didn't I?"

"Maybe a little. Maybe a lot. I needed to hear that. How long have you considered this?"

"From almost the beginning. At the cabin, I wasn't too worried. Now we're venturing into town, and I have to go back to work. It'll get a little dicey. I want you safe. I honestly can't bear to think of anything happening to you, honey. You may think me resisting you is a sign I don't care as much, but no, that's not it. I can't lose you. To anyone."

"You should've told me right away."

"I didn't think you could handle it before. You're brave, but I still see the slight fear. Not so much as the days go by. Probably everything sinking in a little better, but...hell, who am I kidding? I didn't even want to tell you now. I need you to be aware."

He unbuckled his belt and scooted over to her side, leaning as best as he could as his foot still held the brake pedal. She looked so damn scared. Wiping that away would take a miracle, but he'd settle with a kiss. "I can't lose you. I'll figure out what happened. I promise."

"I know you will. I'm glad you told me. I'll be cautious."

"Good. Let's get home now." He kissed her one more time and shifted back over to his side. "I'm dying to see how you're going to seduce me. Any hints?"

"Nope. You'll just have to wait and see," she replied, a sly smile pasted on her lips.

He smiled back, liking the look a lot better than the grim terror that had settled when he uttered what he had. Turning right, he headed home. They couldn't get there fast enough. As soon as he pulled into his driveway, he wanted to sigh in relief.

"You okay? Been a little quiet." Logan unbuckled his belt.

She offered him a sweet smile. "Yep. I was enjoying the scenery and the town. It's very small. Is it really just a few shops lining the main road we drove through?"

"It is. Very, very small town. But a great place to live."

"Trying to sell the town to me, Sheriff?"

"Do you want me to?"

"No. You already sold me," she said so tenderly.

If he hadn't already given his heart to her, he definitely would've in that moment. "Well, then it was just a statement of the obvious. I see Kat's car. Hopefully she's started supper. Are you hungry, honey?"

"Yes, Logan, I'm very hungry." She gave him a look that said it wasn't food she was hungry for. She opened her door and hopped out of the truck carefully.

Groaning, he ran a ragged hand over his face. *You are the sheriff!*

Repeating those words daily, hourly, hell, every minute to stop himself from taking more than what he should from her, still made no difference. It just didn't matter. He was ready for her to seduce him and take it wherever this situation would lead. How could he resist her when she spoke to him like that? Or gave him those smoldering looks? No woman had ever spoken to his heart the way she did. And so innocently, too. Even as she sounded brave and confident, he saw the hesitation, the slight uncertainty in her eyes.

"What are you doing, Logan? Are you going to introduce me to the sweet-looking lady walking up to the house or what?" Seth said, knocking on the truck's window.

Logan jumped. So lost in his thoughts, he hadn't realized

he was still sitting in the vehicle. Way to look like an idiot. He opened the door and stepped out with more confidence than he felt.

"Watch it, Seth," Logan muttered as a veiled threat.

"Watch it, as in keep my paws off because she's going through something terrible? Or watch it, as in keep my paws off because you're already staking your claim?" Seth asked with a chuckle.

"Does it matter which one applies? The important thing is not to go there," Logan said, pointing a finger at him. "What happened to Stacy?"

"Stacy who?" Seth started around the truck with an extra quickness that Logan didn't let go unnoticed.

"So you two are fighting again?"

"I'm done with her. There is no Stacy. There is a beautiful woman waiting on the porch, though." He grunted in pain when Logan grabbed him by the back of his shirt.

Logan whipped him around, grabbing him tightly by the front of his shirt. "I'm only going to say this one time, Seth, so make sure your ears are listening. You will make no moves on that beautiful woman whatsoever. Have I made myself clear?"

"Geez, Logan. I've never seen you react like this. I was just joking. I got the hint the first time. Not to mention Kat already made the comment how...how close you two seem. Lighten up, bro. Let me go," Seth said calmly, holding his hands up in surrender.

Logan gently released him and wiped the wrinkles from Seth's shirt, then stepped back. He ran another frustrated hand over his face. "Sorry, Seth. I don't know what came over me. Just...don't go there."

"I won't. Like I said, I was kidding. Stacy and I are done, but, you know, it's hitting me harder than I expected." Seth shuffled his feet a bit, then glanced at Logan. "You like her a lot. You've never reacted that way toward me. Or that way about a woman. Ever. You barely know her."

"I know plenty, Seth. She barely knows herself. But I know all I need to. Just drop it."

"Okay."

"Is everything okay, Logan?"

Seth turned around as Doni twisted her hands nervously, darting glances between the two of them.

Logan took two long strides and stopped right in front of her, almost reaching for her hand. "Everything's fine, honey. Nothing to worry about. Doni, I'd like you to meet my brother, Seth."

Logan looked at Seth and gestured toward Doni. "Seth, this is Doni. That's what she likes to be called. Kat almost had her going with Kit."

"Well, thank goodness that didn't happen. The way her brain operates sometimes, I just don't know what she's thinking," Seth said with a laugh as he held his hand out. "Nice to meet you, Doni."

Doni gave him a shy smile and tentatively shook his hand. "Umm...yes, Seth, nice to meet you as well."

"Seth and I will grab the bags. Why don't you go inside and see what Kat's up to? Rest your feet a bit, maybe." Logan shoved a hand in his pocket before he grabbed her in front of his brother.

"Are you sure everything's all right? Did something happen? You looked upset, Logan. You're not leaving, are you?" She suddenly panicked, looking up at the sun that was starting to dip down toward the horizon.

Logan couldn't resist when he saw the fright beam out of her eyes, her entire body shaking. He pulled his hand out of his pocket and grabbed her hands to stop the nervous twisting. "I'm not leaving. Nothing happened. Just a word or two between brothers, honey. Nothing serious. Please, don't worry about a thing."

"You looked so upset. The sun's going down and..." A small smile appeared as the shaking stopped with her hands. "I'll wait for you inside. I trust you."

"Hey, Doni. I broke up with my girlfriend. I said some things that I didn't mean. I'm feeling a bit raw right now. She meant a lot to me. Logan's not going anywhere," Seth blurted.

Doni glanced at him, frowning a bit. "I'm sorry to hear that, Seth. Logan's a very kind man. I can only assume you are as well. I imagine she has no idea what she lost."

"Wow, thanks. That makes me feel better," Seth said with sincerity.

"I'll go see if Kat needs my help with anything." Doni glanced at Logan.

He couldn't seem to look away from Seth. Did she really make him feel better with such simple words? His brother normally brooded for a long time when he broke up with Stacy. Those two dated off and on so much it was hard to keep up.

Turning to Doni, he smiled tenderly. "Sounds good, sweetheart. We'll be right behind you with the bags."

Doni nodded and reluctantly let go of his hands. Logan walked to the truck as soon as she entered the house.

"So, Kat's mentioned a thing or two about her, but I hadn't realized. What was that, Logan?" Seth asked, joining him by the truck.

"She hates the dark, Seth. Like, really hates it. Perhaps she relies on me too much, but I'm okay with that. Just the thought of me not around when the sun goes down freaks her out." Logan grabbed a bag from the back of the truck as Seth grabbed the other one.

"Freaking out is an understatement. She was shaking like an earthquake."

"Just one, Seth. If you heard one tiny nightmare of hers, you would realize why. Based on those nightmares, I know she was held in a tiny, dark room. Dark. She's entitled to freak out as bad as she wants."

Seth, mimicking him, ran a ragged hand over his face. "I suppose you're right. I thought she liked to be called Doni."

Logan headed toward the house as Seth kept in step with him. "Yeah, she does. What's your point?"

"You called her honey and sweetheart. The only time you called her Doni was to introduce us."

Logan stopped walking and glared at Seth. "I repeat, what's your point?"

"You know, for being known as such a softie around these parts, you sure harden up real quick when it comes to talking about that woman. I have no other points to point out to you," Seth said as he continued to the house.

Logan slowly followed him, having no response.

"So, are you going to visit me tomorrow? Or are you staying with that hunk of junk all day? Dr. Matthews still wants to see you one more time to see how you're healing," Kat said to Doni as she stood by the front door with a hand on her hip and gestured with her head toward Logan, who was putting dishes away in the kitchen.

"I'm standing right here. I can hear you, you know. Why am I a hunk of junk?" Logan asked as he wiped a plate dry and put it in the cupboard.

"Because you're my big brother and I can call you whatever the hell I please." Kat glanced back at Doni, her eyebrow raised, waiting for an answer. "Well, do you wanna see where I work or what? I'm way cooler than he is."

"How about we meet for lunch?" Doni said with a small smile. "You are definitely cool, Kat."

Doni chose to ignore the comment about Dr. Matthews. She didn't want to go into the clinic. She wasn't even sure she wanted him examining her again. Her nerves jumped at the prospect.

He had been nice, reminding her of a stern, yet sometimes goofy grandfather. He had gray hair sprinkled in between the black that covered his head in tiny waves. He had wrinkles that lined his eyes when he smiled. Although, he didn't look that old. Maybe grandfather was the wrong thing to compare him to, but he reminded her of someone. It sat there in the back of her mind, huddled in the corner, refusing to come out. The thought didn't frighten her. He didn't scare her, just the thought he was a doctor did.

Kat stepped closer to Doni. "Are you afraid of the clinic? You still jump a little when the word...doctor is said."

Doni suppressed the urge to jump right in that moment. "I...my first day in town...and..."

Kat laid a reassuring hand on her shoulder. "I won't pressure you. But sometimes facing your fears head-on is better than taking two steps back. The more you let that fear consume you, the more your memory is going to stay buried."

"I know, Kat. I just..."

"I get it. Don't worry. Lunch is cool." Kat took a step back toward the door. "Bye-bye, Logan."

Logan turned his head as he placed another plate back in the cupboard. "Bye, Kat. Thanks for cooking."

"Anytime lug nut." Kat looked over at the couch, piercing a hard glare at Seth. "It's getting late. Perhaps past your bedtime."

"Considering I haven't had a bedtime in over fifteen years...I think I'm good, Kat." Seth barely glanced at her as his eyes stayed glued to the baseball game on TV.

Kat cleared her throat. "Maybe you need to cry some tears over Stacy."

At that, Seth whipped his head at her. "I'm not shedding one tear over her."

Kat gave him a look that could fry an egg without heat and a subtle tilt of her head toward Doni. "You dated for over two years, on and off. Perhaps one little tear would suffice."

Seth took a deep breath and stood up from the couch. "Yeah, whatever. It's getting late anyway, and I gotta work early tomorrow."

"Do you want to join us for supper tomorrow?" Logan asked.

"No. I got plans with Evan. Told him I'd help put in new brakes on his car. Let's quit talking about Stacy already. We're like oil and water. We just don't mix."

As soon as he stepped within reaching distance of Doni, she lightly touched his shoulder. The pain in his eyes hurt her. He reminded her so much of Logan. "They may not mix well, but sometimes they draw a beautiful picture within the turbulence. Two years is a long time. Something held you two together. Don't forget the good times. Memories are precious, Seth. Don't hate her." Doni dropped her hand from his shoulder, then suddenly panicked. "Unless she cheated. Then you can hate her."

Seth produced a slow grin. "She didn't cheat. But thanks, Doni. You're right. We did have some good times. I don't know why we keep breaking up. I'm done. I'm not going back to her."

"I don't like seeing you unhappy. You look so much like Logan sometimes, and I hate it when he looks unhappy," Doni said, blushing from the admission.

She could see the similarities to Logan. While Logan was taller with brown eyes, short brown hair, and the softest hands known on the planet, Seth's hands were much rougher. She had felt the calluses, the hard work displayed in his grip when they shook hands earlier. His eyes were a pale green, his hair brown, but held a slightly lighter tone than Logan's. He also wore his hair long, combed back in one long slick position. It made her wonder how he got it to stay that way. Gel? Hairspray? Did men use hairspray? Her blush increased as those silly thoughts ran through her mind.

Seth stepped closer, pulling her into a hug without asking. "My brother found a beautiful, amazing woman. He's a lucky man. You ever need me, just ask." He let her go and nodded at Kat. "Lead the way, sis."

He gave a delightful wink to Doni and a quick wave to Logan. They both retreated from the house, making Doni and Logan alone once more.

"That's the second time you made Seth feel better. Those two are like oil and water. They fight so much, I have no idea how they made it two years together," Logan said, putting a cup away this time.

Doni walked leisurely to the kitchen. "Why do they fight?"

"I don't know. Seth never really says. He always avoids talking about it. When she's around they always seem happy, but occasionally they bicker even around us. Little things like who's driving and who's drinking that night. No reason to argue over something like that. I sometimes see jealousy in his eyes when another man looks at her. And when I glance at Stacy, she eyes the other guy just to piss Seth off. I honestly don't know what their problem is."

"He said she didn't cheat." Doni grabbed a towel lying on the counter's edge and picked up a fork from the drip-dry.

"I believe him. I'm sure she does it just to piss him off. Like I said, I don't know why they fight like they do. It's his problem, and if he doesn't want to talk about it, I'm not going to pry," Logan said, pulling open the silverware drawer for her to put the fork away.

"Do you like her? For him, I mean."

"I don't mind her. When they're happy, they're a decent couple. But they fight too much. Honestly, I think he needs to grow up a bit. He's twenty-five. There's no need to make each other jealous. He does it, too."

"Why aren't you married, Logan?" Doni picked up another fork, her attention focused on the pronged device as if it were buried treasure.

"Never found a woman worth marrying." Logan grabbed the fork, brushing her fingers.

"Have you had a serious relationship before?"

Logan put the fork away and grabbed a spoon this time. "Never been married, but I had one serious relationship when I lived in Minneapolis. We dated for about two years, and when I got the feeling I needed to leave the city, she wasn't willing to follow. I couldn't take living in the big city anymore. I like my hometown. Not sure why I ever left. It was a good experience, but I wouldn't leave again."

"Well, she was dumb for not following you. Even after a week I can say that with certainty."

"Is this part of you seducing me?" Logan shoved the silverware drawer closed with his hip.

"No. Would you like it to be?" Doni glanced at the drip-dry. All the dishes were gone.

"It sends a warm feeling through me to hear such words." Logan caressed her cheek, just as suddenly dropping it. "I wish I could ask you the same questions. What happens if you're married?"

"I'm not. And no, I don't remember. Just a very, very, very strong feeling I have. At this point, the way you make me feel, if I am, I think I'd still follow you. I'm not dumb." Doni kept eye contact even as she wanted to look away from his gaze.

His hand went back to her cheek. "No, you aren't dumb, honey. About tomorrow, when are we going to see Dr. Matthews? He's a persistent man. It would be good for you to see him again. Maybe it'll help those memories come back."

"I'm fine. I don't need to see him again."

"Think about it. He can come to the house. I'll stay with you the entire time."

"Sure, Logan, I'll think about it."

She lowered her eyes because she didn't want to think about that right now. His eyes portrayed how much he wanted her to, but she had another fierce problem burning through her mind.

"I said I was going to seduce you, Logan. I don't know how to do that. I guess I lost my memory on that sort of thing as well. I'm getting tired. Do you want to lay down with me?"

"I think you have a fine understanding of how to seduce. You're breaking me as we stand here." Logan didn't wait for a response as he grabbed the other side of her face and pulled her in for a kiss. It was slow, deliberate, and sweet. When he pulled away from her succulent lips, her eyes opened unhurried as her body jolted closer to him.

"I know we have a sort of pull toward each other...but...but I'd never make you do something you don't want to do. If you're really worried about me being married, I'll stop my silly talk."

Logan grabbed her around the waist without a thought or care. "I can't say I'm not worried. But I also said the moment you went into my arms it didn't matter. You've been in my arms how many nights now. Maybe just for sleeping, but as each day passes I find it harder to resist you. You don't have to touch me to seduce me. You do it simply with your sweet, innocent words, honey." He waved a hand over her hair and down her back. "I know you don't like feeling confined. And the dark isn't your favorite. I want you comfortable. I want you to feel safe. Where do you want to sleep? My room or the living room?"

Her hand that rested on his hip trembled. "Your room is big...and the dark...doesn't bother me."

"Honesty. Remember? Don't go backtracking on me now, honey. I can keep the bedroom door open, or we can make a bed in the living room. No matter where we sleep, I can keep a light on."

"Kat says I should face my fears."

"Kat ain't here. I'm the one who holds you as you cry out those fears. I sure in the hell don't want them to increase because you're feeling uncomfortable where you're sleeping."

"How did I get so lucky to break into your cabin? I don't deserve you, Logan. I don't," Doni cried as she pressed her face into his chest.

"You deserve the world. If you let me, I'll give it to you."

"Oh, I'll let you. Quit resisting me, Sheriff." Doni pressed her face harder into his chest.

"I'm done resisting, honey. You've done your seducing, and I'm a goner. Tell me where to set up camp. I'm ready for bed," Logan whispered, then pressed a light kiss to her neck.

Doni trembled from the soft kiss, sinking further into his embrace, wanting to melt into him. "Can we try your room? I want to try."

"Anything for you. We'll leave the door open."

Doni leaned away, squeezing his shirt behind his back. "Then I'm ready for bed. I still don't think I do this seducing right. Can you show me what you would do?"

Logan ran a flustered hand over his face and chuckled. "You're still seducing me with your words, honey. I don't think we're going to have one little problem when we hit those sheets."

8

Logan turned on the bathroom light, closing the door halfway. “How’s that? You want me to open the door a little more?”

Doni shook her head. “That’s fine. It’s silly, really. The dark shouldn’t even bother me.”

Logan hopped in bed and pulled her close as he leaned on his elbow. “It’s not silly. We both know why it bothers you. Don’t be ashamed of that. It’s not your fault. Anything that happened to you is not your fault.”

“Are you su—”

Logan pressed his lips to her mouth to stop the mad words. He didn’t coax her to open but managed to get his point across when he felt her relax a bit.

“Don’t ever think you did something to deserve what happened. I won’t let you think like that. Nobody deserves that. Don’t ever talk like that again, Doni.” Logan brushed a hand over her hair to sweep a bit off her cheek.

“Doni? I feel like a child being reprimanded by a parent. Call me honey.”

"You needed a bit of reprimanding. Tomorrow might be tough."

"Why?"

"I told you—people gossip. I have a strong feeling a lot of visitors will stroll through the sheriff's office tomorrow. They're curious about you. About us. I'm not really known around these parts to date women."

"Really. You date men?"

He chuckled as he stole another quick kiss. "I mean, I haven't had a girlfriend or taken any women from town out on a date in a long time. If I do indulge with a woman, it's always from another town. It doesn't bother me to tell people to mind their business, but sometimes it's easier to avoid that by just making sure I give them nothing to talk about. I can say with complete certainty that people know I am quite taken with you. They'll be swarming the sheriff's office tomorrow. Can you handle that? I don't want anything upsetting you."

"Right now, being in your arms, I can say it won't upset me. Tomorrow might tell a different story. Why don't you date anyone from town?"

"Because it's a damn small town and I know everyone in it. Not one woman appeals to me. In my younger years I dated a few, but they were never the one." He ran a tender hand down her arm and back up, skimming the side of her breast. "I've known you about a week, and the feelings I have for you are stronger than for any woman I've ever dated. That's the only reason I keep forgetting I'm the sheriff and that you're in my bed."

"You make me feel safe, wanted, and special. You're so attentive to my needs. That feels new. I don't think any other man ever treated me like you do. I want you, Logan. Most importantly, I just want to make sure you always hold me. Don't ever stop that."

He pulled her closer into his embrace. "I'll never stop holding you. I like it too damn much."

She squeezed him, running a soft hand down his back.

"Are you sure, honey? Are you sure you don't want to wait?" he asked as he pulled away to see the reaction in her eyes. He needed to make absolutely sure this was what she wanted. "Once I take a little piece of you, I may never let you go."

"Take me, Logan. I don't want you to ever let me go." She pressed into him as she trailed a hand to his chest.

"Damn, honey, you're so beautiful." He pressed his lips to hers as she opened without resistance. As his tongue tangled with hers, he moved within her arms until he hovered over her delicate body. The kiss deepened like it had on the porch, making him press into her, begging for the clothing to disappear.

Removing her shirt with ease, he chuckled. "Nasty barrier between us."

Such a gorgeous woman. Her body was soft and inviting, yet he hesitated. Even though the bathroom provided light, the bedroom still had a hint of darkness. It made no difference because he saw them without effort. Some bruises had yet to fade.

"I don't want to hurt you." He pressed a tender kiss to a bruise just under her breast.

"It doesn't hurt. Your touch soothes. When you walk away is when it flairs to pain," she whispered as she grabbed his hand and pressed it to the same bruise he kissed. "Soothe my pain away, Logan."

"Damn, honey, you have no idea what you do to me."

Peppering kisses all over her abdomen, wherever a

bruise or scratch still lingered, could take all night. He wanted to take every ounce of the pain away.

Having touched every injury he could see, he dove in where he'd been dying to explore for over a week. Her nipple became hard as a rock as his mouth covered it with delight. Her blissful moan sent a rippling fire throughout his body. His hesitations before he entered the bedroom disappeared the moment she uttered that soft, beautiful moan. While he loved and doted on her breasts, taking turns with each one, he brought his hand down to her waist and slipped a hand under her panties, pushing them down somewhat as he did.

So wet already. He groaned as he rubbed a finger over her soft mound and dipped in. She arched her body with a soft cry of pleasure as he pulled his finger out and delved back in again. As she moved with his hand, after a few small strokes, he dove in with two fingers, bringing the pleasure out of her with a slow effort.

He lifted his head, taking in her spirited face. Her eyes were closed, her hands clenching the bedsheets as he worked the magic with his fingers. "You're so beautiful. You feel so beautiful."

Before she could utter a word, he kissed her lips, continuing the slow assault on her body. The more she moved beneath him, the harder he became. He pulsed with the need to consume her with a desired frenzy, but he waited. He wanted her completely sated with pleasure before he took for himself.

Soon, he felt her moving under his body, the movements becoming faster, her breathing becoming more ragged. He grabbed another kiss, plunging his tongue deep as his fingers deepened inside her. Suddenly, she bit his lip lightly as the waves of desire exploded throughout her. He didn't remove his hand until her body relaxed underneath him.

"Oh, Logan...I want more," she whispered as he bent his head, kissing her neck.

"Let me help you with that," he said with a smile as he removed her panties.

She smiled back as he removed his boxers and moved over to his nightstand, pulling open a drawer. "Your need to help...yes, I like this need of yours to help right now."

"Well, I am the sheriff. I aim to help," he said with a grin as he ripped open the condom package.

"I want to help, too." She grabbed the condom before he could protest and gently covered him. He couldn't suppress the groan as her hand slid up with a slow caress. "Did I help you properly, Logan?"

"Oh, honey, you can help me anytime." He shifted over her body, positioning right where he wanted to be. Any lingering doubts he had completely vanished. He wanted her. He had a strong feeling he would for the rest of his life.

He kissed her hard as he pushed into her slowly. She inhaled deeply as her body protested at first, feeling his hard presence. "I won't hurt you. Slow and easy, sweetheart. I promise." He pulled out, then pushed in again, a little further this time.

"I know you won't. It feels good, Logan. Don't stop, please," she said, running her hands down his back to his butt. She grabbed on, helping the slow process as he entered her inch by inch. When he pulled out and started slowly again, she grabbed his butt harder, meeting his slow thrust.

He groaned into her ear as he completely entered her. "Oh, honey, you feel so good. I may not last long. I need you now."

"Need away, Logan."

At first, he slowly moved within her, taking his time. But the more he moved, the more she moved with him, his movements became faster. He needed this passion. She matched him every time he thrust deeply. She felt so good beneath him. His mind went over every memory of her sweet smile, her soft laugh, and caring words.

As he felt his body tingling with burning desire, he knew the next round he would cover every inch of her body with kisses. He needed to soothe the pain of every wound that littered her body. A sudden impulse that he knew he would accomplish before the night was over.

She held on tightly, her pleasure rising in tune to his as he pumped one more time before they came together in glorious bliss. He fell onto her delicate body with heavy breaths. Two kisses to her neck, then he lifted onto his elbows.

"You should've seduced me a long time ago. I've never felt anything like that, honey."

"Now you tell me," she said with a small laugh. "No regrets?"

"No. And as soon as I get rid of this condom, I'm going to soothe every little scratch and bruise on your beautiful body. You might not get any sleep tonight."

"Soothe away, Logan."

LOGAN PARKED the truck and switched the ignition off before turning toward her. "You ready? Promise me you'll let me know if you feel uncomfortable. I don't want you to feel overwhelmed."

"I promise. Are you leaving me at the office while you go—"

"No, honey, I won't leave. I have paperwork to go over, which I'm sure Derek left for me to handle. I'll only leave if it's a dire emergency."

Doni clasped her hands together, wringing them almost too roughly. Logan grabbed her hands. Perhaps this was a bad idea. "There's nothing to worry about. You don't have to be here if you don't want to."

She lightly squeezed his hands. "I need to do this. I need to find some answers. I need...I need to quit relying on you. It's not right."

"You can rely on me anytime. Not just because I'm the sheriff, but because I care about you. What happened last night...if I didn't care, that would've never happened. You can have the need to do anything you want, find answers, get over your fears, meet new people, but I draw the line at not needing me. Do you hear me, honey?"

She nodded as her eyes widened in surprise. Logan glanced out his window to see what grabbed her attention. Mrs. Dunburry, a bulky woman with gray hair and a sharp gait was headed straight for his truck.

"Get ready, darling, it's about to start." He let go of her hand, but not before he gave her one last squeeze for strength, and exited the truck without a trace of his apprehension for her.

"Mrs. Dunburry, good morning." Logan gave a quick perusal to his right. Doni had exited the truck without a fuss.

"Sheriff, how are you this bright, sunny morning?" Mrs. Dunburry rushed out, fixing her attention quickly to Doni. "And you, my dear, to whom do I have the pleasure of meeting? I don't believe I've ever seen the sheriff arrive with such a beautiful woman on his way to work. Have you, Sheriff?"

Logan lifted a brow, amused at her not-so-subtle tack.

"You know, Mrs. Dunburry, I don't believe I have. This is Doni. I'd explain who she is, but I think we all know you know that already." Logan's eyes crinkled with charm as Mrs. Dunburry didn't even flinch at the outspoken words.

"Your mother taught you better manners than to point that out, Sheriff. I shall pretend I heard nothing." Mrs. Dunburry pierced her lips in mock disgust, turning her eyes back to Doni. "You, my dear, are the talk of the town. In a good way, of course. I run the little lovely boutique just a few shops down from the Sheriff's Department. Now, if you ever need a break from this wily man, you just mosey on down. We're not shy around these parts."

Doni shyly smiled. "Thank you, Mrs. Dunburry, for the kind welcome. I would love to see your boutique at some point."

"Oh, wonderful. I'll see you later. I'm off now. I have to open the shop. I just happened to see you two sitting here and had to introduce myself."

"It's always a pleasure to see you, Mrs. Dunburry," Logan said, placing a hand on Doni's back without thought.

Mrs. Dunburry's eyes zoomed to the tender touch, her smile widening to a degree that Logan had never seen before. He almost removed his hand, but knew it didn't matter now.

What did it matter if the whole town saw a simple public display of affection?

Not that a simple hand on her back showed much affection, but nonetheless, it spoke volumes in this town. She was living under his roof, for goodness sake. He imagined many rumors were already flying at that fact. Might as well let them get the facts straight right off the bat. Doni was important to him, and he had no issues showing that. Not after last night. He knew once he fully consumed her body, he wouldn't be able to walk away.

"Sheriff, a pleasure, as always. Have a lovely day. I'll see you later, Doni dear." Mrs. Dunburry abruptly turned around without waiting for a reply and headed toward her shop to the right.

Logan guided Doni to the left, gliding his hand from her back to her hip, shifting her perfectly into his arms as they walked along. "You know, she didn't just happen to see us sitting there. She was lying in wait, I'm sure. It's going to be like this all day. Nosy busybodies. If it'll be too much, say the word."

"She was nice, Logan. Strangely, I was nervous until she spoke. She was refreshing. I can handle this. If I get to the point where I can't, I'll let you know."

He almost stopped in his tracks, but his feet kept moving, albeit a bit slower. "So, you're going to visit her later? Is that what I'm hearing?"

"Perhaps. Is that okay? I..." Doni hesitated, stopping right before they reached the door. "I don't know what it was, but...she reminded me of someone. It's right there on the tip of my mind, wanting to reach out and shout it to me. I think talking to more people, seeing more of my surroundings, things will come back to me. That's what we want, right?"

The eagerness in her eyes reached out and tugged at Logan's heart. "Right."

"So you're not mad?"

"I would never be mad about that. I just don't want you to be overwhelmed or anything, that's all."

She placed a soft hand on his chest, right over his heart. "I'm not sure what I did to ever deserve a man like you. I swear you will be the first person I go to if it's all too much."

Logan felt like saying more, but chose a simple response. “Then I hope you enjoy your time with Mrs. Dunburry. If you’re dying for gossip about the town, she’s your go-to gal. Do you like gossip?” His lips curled into a devilish smile, thinking as he asked, his sweet Doni didn’t seem like the type to indulge in such nonsense.

“I don’t know.” Her lips curled to mirror his features.

He dropped his hand from her hip, pulling it up to her cheek in a smooth, natural way that had become second nature to him. He loved feeling her skin, especially her cheeks that reminded him of porcelain. So delicate. So breakable.

“You haven’t said that in a while. I thought we got past the phrase ‘I don’t know’, but by the devious look in your eyes, I’d say you were doing it on purpose. Watch it, honey. I might just kiss you right here and really give the town something to talk about.”

She took a step closer. “I truly don’t know. Perhaps I enjoy teasing you a bit.”

“Well, do the teasing inside, girly. I’ll have you know, Sheriff, I’ve already gotten a suspect call coming from Mo-Mo’s. I know for damn sure it had nothing to do with his shipment of supplies that are late in its delivery this morning,” Charlotte said with one hand on her hip and the other holding the door open.” If you two are done with the not-so-subtle public display of affection, which I might add I’ve never seen you do, Logie, then perhaps we can start the day. I hear you like coffee, Doni. A dash of milk with a spoon full of sugar. It’s getting cold. I’m Charlotte.” With that, she stepped to the side still holding the door open.

“The queen of all queens that I told you about, honey. Don’t worry. Her bark doesn’t turn into a bite. Right, Char-

Char," Logan said, raising a brow as he walked by her with a tender smile, one hand guiding Doni in front of him.

"Don't call me Char-Char, Sheriff," Charlotte said, following them inside and rounding the counter with quick precision.

"Then don't call me Logie. Why was Mo calling exactly?"

"Wanting the scoop on you and her, but of course, he claimed it was about the deliveryman being late. Don't worry. I nipped it in the bud. Coffee's still getting cold, Doni," Charlotte said, piercing a long stare at Doni, who stood frozen in place. She snapped her fingers in earnest. "Doni? Is she all right, Logan?"

He turned toward Doni, noting the shocked expression on her face. It's as if her lips had halted in mid-speak, forming a circle that could catch flies all day.

"Sweetheart, what's the matter?" Logan grabbed her by the shoulders, pulling her gaze away from Charlotte as a pale-hue covered her skin.

"Shit, darling, you're really starting to scare me. What's going on? Talk to me, don't scare me like this."

His heart plummeted to the floor when she continued to stare at nothing in particular, her eyes glazed with shock. Silence reigned in the room, making him regret bringing her. He knew this would be too much for her and hated himself for letting it happen. Would he be able to pull her back from wherever her mind had wandered? As he called her name again, no recognition in her eyes, he feared it might be impossible.

9

"Charlie, the red princess," Doni finally blurted.

Logan's face contorted in confusion and relief. "What are you talking about? Who's Charlie?"

"I remember we used to call her Char, the red princess. She loved the color red. She always wore red in her outfits, that's why we called her the red princess. She loved the title. It made her feel special, superior even, almost wanting you to bow down to her. I laughed in her face when she actually said it to me one time jokingly. Funny thing, I don't think she was really joking. I hated her. She was such a bitch." Doni said the last bit in a whisper, then turned her head to Charlotte. "Not that I think you are. You're not. That's not what I meant."

Charlotte waved a hand in the air with nonchalance. "Please, I can be when I really want to."

"What else do you remember?" Logan asked, his heart beating a little faster at the first, true memory she finally had. He liked that she had a memory, but he didn't like how it pulled her away from him.

"That's it. Just bits and pieces of her. Mostly nasty ones.

I'm sorry for scaring you. When you said Char-Char, it suddenly assaulted my mind. Just this memory, zapping into me that I...I didn't know what to do but absorb it."

"Quit apologizing for things. You have nothing to be sorry about. This is a good thing. Remembering things is a very good sign." Logan rubbed her shoulders, trying to ease a bit of her tension that had formed from the sudden onslaught. "What's Charlie's last name?"

"I don't know." She smiled lightly. "Before you say anything, I didn't say that in a teasing manner. I don't remember her last name or anything else personal about her. Just fragments of interactions."

"Well, get over here and drink your coffee before it gets spitting cold. The day's a-wasting. Moment's over. She's fine, Sheriff. You have a few phone calls to make, paperwork to complete, and you know, crap, just waiting for you on your desk, just how you like it. She'll be fine with me."

Charlotte's lips lifted into a gentle smile that told him she would look out for Doni. He knew she saw the worry plastered all over his face about letting Doni out of his eyesight. And he *was* worried. He wouldn't deny it if she asked.

Walking away was the last thing he wanted to do. He didn't want to go to his office while she stayed up front for all the vultures to get to her before he had a chance to stop them. He kept eye contact with Charlotte, seeing the affirmation in her eyes that she would keep Doni safe. He trusted her. Charlotte could be ruthless when she wanted to be.

"You're right, Charlotte." Logan glanced back at Doni. "Are you okay?"

"I'm fine. I could use that coffee, and you heard Charlotte, you have things to do. Don't be late on my account. My first memory was a little shocking. I'm better now. The next memory should go better. See, meeting new people will help."

"Don't overdo it. Just...take it easy. You're still healing and whatnot," Logan said, rubbing a hand down his face in a quick fashion.

She grabbed his hand before he could make another sweep, this time through his hair. "Quit worrying. I know I act fragile, but I'm not. I can handle this. Each day I feel myself getting stronger. Please, don't worry."

He almost pulled her into his arms but stopped short seeing Charlotte in his peripheral vision. "You know me so well already. I'm going to worry anyway." He squeezed her hand and glanced at Charlotte. "Don't let it become a circus in here. No one's allowed in the door unless it's official business. Are we clear?"

"Crystal. Now shoo. We have things to do." Charlotte motioned with her hands that he should venture away from their domain.

Logan squeezed Doni's hand one more time before reluctantly releasing it. "My office is down this hallway, last door. Come visit me later."

"Okay. Go on. I'll be fine." She gave him a sweet smile that spoke of bravery, yet he knew better. She was terrified but putting on a good show for Charlotte. Her strength never failed to amaze him. So beautiful.

He nodded, then walked away before he did something stupid. Like whisk her back to his truck, to his home, and right into his bed. That idea sounded more appealing than whatever waited for him in his office.

DONI WAITED until he rounded the corner and then made her way behind the counter by Charlotte. She grabbed the mug that Charlotte held out and took a sip. "Mmm...not too cold yet. Thank you. How did you know how I like my coffee?"

"It's a small town. Not much stays a secret." Charlotte started whipping her fingers on the keyboard, then turned her head sharply at Doni with a small cunning smile. "Plus, I talked to Kat. She told me."

Doni chuckled. "I like Kat. She's been great. Logan told me how much work you've been doing combing through missing persons. Thank you. You have no idea how much that means. I feel so lost."

"I can imagine. I feel like I know you so well. Your face is ingrained in my mind I've looked at it so much this past week. I feel terrible I haven't found anything." Charlotte sighed deeply, then straightened her back into a tight posture. "We'll find who you are. Logan's one of the best sheriffs we've ever had. Not to mention, he's fallen hard for you. Thought I'd never see the day. He's quite a catch around these parts. So many have tried to wrangle that man in. None have succeeded."

"He's a wonderful, kind, generous man. I can see why he's a catch. Have you tried to nab him yourself?"

Charlotte laughed, a deep rich laugh. "Damn, girl, and here I thought you were a timid little thing. Coming right out and staking your claim. I like that. But to answer your question, no, I've never tried. He's a great boss, a great person, but never held my interest in a sexual way. Which is a pity. He's a damn fine-looking man and such a sweet guy. I tell him all the time he's a damn softie. I like a little hardness in my men. He'll treat you right. If not, I'll hang him from his balls."

Doni smiled at Charlotte's candid words. "I have no worries about how he'll treat me. Thanks for your kindness in defending my honor."

"Us girls have to stick together." Charlotte winked, turning back to her computer. "So, your eyes will gloss over after a while going from photo to photo, but I have a decent routine down. I set up another computer for you right next to me. I've already gone through the state of Minnesota and nada. Although, Kat mentioned to look outside based on her little game she played with you. I've also completed the Dakota's, nada as well. I just started on Wisconsin. Do you want Iowa or Illinois?"

Doni took a seat next to her and scooted her chair closer to the desk. "So we're basically starting around Minnesota and working our way out?" Charlotte nodded once. "I'll take Iowa."

She saw the horrible picture of her taped to the wall in front of them and grimaced. "Can we at least take a new picture of me? I look frightening in that one."

Charlotte chuckled as she grabbed the picture, crumbled it up with ease, and tossed it into the wastebasket without looking behind her. "Who needs a picture? I have the real thing right next to me. Let's get to work. I bet you're dying to know who you are."

Doni smiled, shaking her head with vigor anticipation. The mystery surrounding her was a little overwhelming. She did want to know who she was, but then again, it scared her senseless. What would happen if she didn't like the answer they found? The fear of finally knowing almost outweighed the want to know.

The morning flew by, and before Doni knew it, Kat whisked through the front doors. "Okay, how bad has it been today?"

Doni glanced up from the computer and gave her a small grimace. "Not too bad."

"Then what was the nasty face for?"

"Really, Kat. It wasn't too bad. A few people tried to butt their noses in, but I stopped them short. I take my job seriously," Charlotte said, leaning back in her chair and stretching her arms above her head.

Satisfied with that, Kat shook her head once with relief. "Good. Ready for lunch? I actually think the clinic has been super busy today. People must think I'll dish out better than the real thing."

"I'm sorry, Kat." Doni stood up with the frown more prominent.

"Better me than you, Doni. Don't worry about a thing. Are you coming with, Charlotte?"

Charlotte shook her head, standing up as Doni walked by her. "No. I brought my lunch, and I have to man the fort here. You two have fun."

Doni smiled, hesitantly glancing toward the hallway that would lead her to Logan's office. He had ventured out quite a few times, checking on her, making sure she was comfortable. Each time she gave him a warm smile and reassuring words. She didn't want to tell him she felt a bit apprehensive, a bit claustrophobic by the few visitors that straggled in. She knew he needed to work and didn't want to be a burden.

She needed to be strong. For him. He liked it when she was strong. And she wanted more memories to flood her brain. They didn't, though. Not one. Only one lame memory of a woman she remembered as being callous and shallow.

What a horrible first memory!

What did that say about her life? Was that why she

couldn't remember? She lived such a horrible life that it wasn't worth remembering.

Kat must've seen her slow movements because she grabbed her hand with quick anticipation. "Let's go. I'm starving."

They started down the sidewalk in comfortable silence, even as Doni's mind and emotions tumbled in crashing waves. Kat held open the diner's door, making her way to a table before anyone could guide her there.

"Seriously, how bad has it been?" Kat asked as she grabbed the menus from behind the stand holding the salt and pepper shakers, handing one to Doni.

"Well, as Logan likes to call them, nosy busybodies, only a few ventured in. They made silly excuses why they walked in, but Charlotte didn't let any of them speak to me. And really, I kept silent the whole time. It was a bit unnerving. What's the big deal? Is it because I have no idea who I am? Or because I'm with Logan?"

"Are you with Logan? Or just staying with him?" Kat asked as if it wasn't a serious question, just mere curiosity.

"I..." Doni stopped speaking when a petite woman with light blonde hair and pale blue eyes walked up to the table.

"Hey, Callie, we need a few more minutes to look over the menus," Kat said, tapping the menu with a strum of fingers.

"No problem. Can I get you something to drink?" Callie asked as she glanced between the two, but made no obvious effort to linger her gaze on Doni.

"Ice tea for me. Doni?" Kat said, glancing at her.

"Water's fine," Doni replied, avoiding eye contact with Callie, who nodded once and walked away without another word.

"She's not a gossiper. She's been in the spotlight before

and would never do that to you," Kat said, noticing the way Doni frowned as she watched Callie walk away.

"I decided I don't like the gossip either. What's the point?"

"Nothing better to do, I guess. Who knows? Some people can't help themselves." Kat tucked her menu away, obviously already knowing what she wanted. "Back to my question about Logan. You can answer now."

Doni almost dropped the menu. "Is it bad if I like your brother?"

"No. I like you, Doni, I do. I'm just curious how you feel. I know how Logan feels. It's super easy to read him. He never gets like this over a woman. We're friends. I'm being a nosy busybody. I can't help myself anymore." Kat shrugged as she gave her a silly smile.

"Well...I sure hope I'm not married or with anyone. I'll feel slightly bad for...hurting their feelings. I consider myself to be with Logan now. Does that answer your question?" Doni focused her eyes on the menu and what food sounded good to her. As her eyes scanned the options, nothing jumped out. Although, her eyes were having difficulty adjusting as she waited for Kat's response.

To her surprise, Kat started giggling. "Oh, geez, did you sleep with my brother already? Could he not keep his hands to himself?"

Doni's eyes shot up above the menu. Kat's eyes twinkled with laughter and kindness. She started giggling right with her. "No. I think it was the other way around. Do you hate me?"

Kat grabbed her hand, squeezing in reassurance. "Hell, no. Welcome to the family, Doni."

"Really?"

Kat let go of her hand, waving it carelessly as she rested

her elbows on the table. "Please, don't sound so surprised. You might not remember who you are, but you have a beautiful personality. That says enough. You make my brother happy. It's been a long time since I've truly seen him happy. And you play cards with me. Nobody ever plays with me." Kat started to pout, then busted out laughing as Doni joined her.

Doni laughed for a good minute before her face fell somber. "I honestly don't know what I would've done if Logan hadn't found me. If he hadn't walked into the cabin, being so nice and considerate. I think I'm coping better than I would have if someone else had found me. I don't even know how I am coping. That's the problem. I don't think I am. I'm hiding. My memories are hiding. What happened to me, Kat? I..." Doni's voice trailed off as she noticed several patrons a few tables down giving them frequent glances.

She watched as an elderly woman constantly leaned toward her husband, her lips moving rapidly. She couldn't see the man's face, but the frequent shaking of his head told her that his wife was saying things he thought were slightly ridiculous. The woman's hard stare never wavered from Doni, making it known she was whispering about her. She was the talk of the town. She knew this. But suddenly, it really bothered her. The woman's judgmental eyes made her feel weak, guilty even.

Kat snapped her fingers in front of Doni to distract her gaze. "Don't mind them. Remember, they have nothing better to do."

"Was I being loud? Did they hear what I said? What will that do to Logan? Oh, my! Why does he even put up with me?" Doni cried softly as she buried her face in her hands.

A strong pair of arms wrapped around her, pulling her close. She stiffened briefly, then immediately relaxed. She would never, no matter how horrible her memories were, forget the touch of Logan. She pressed her head into his chest as he leaned in, whispering, "Honey, please don't say such things. I don't care what people say or think. I only care what you say or think. I hate hearing you talk like that."

Doni kept her face buried into his chest as he wrapped his arms tighter around her. He glanced at Kat, who had turned her head to glare at the elderly woman. After pinning her with a nasty gaze, enough to make the woman blush with embarrassment and turn away, Kat looked back at Logan.

"Next time, Kat, please let me know you're leaving the building. I can honestly say I had a small heart attack when I walked out by Charlotte and she said you two left without a word good-bye," Logan said softly.

"You knew we were having lunch," Kat said with a shrug.

"Yeah, I know. But..." Logan lifted a hand, almost running it down his face, but settled on running it down Doni's head in a soft caress. "This wondrous woman I'm holding means the world to me. She promised to tell me if things became too much, and it's looking right now like it's getting to be a little too much."

Logan kissed the top of Doni's head. "I'm just as scared as you, honey. Maybe not for the same exact reasons, but scared, nonetheless." He raised his eyes back to Kat. "Just tell me next time."

"I'm sorry, Logan. It didn't really cross my mind. If it makes you feel better, I dragged her out before she could even think of saying good-bye to you. It's my fault." Kat reached a hand across the table, touching Doni lightly on the back. "Are you okay, Doni? I didn't mean to make you upset. That wasn't my intention. I can be a little pushy sometimes. I shouldn't be. Damn, I'm sorry, Doni."

Doni sniffed a few times before she lifted her head from his chest. She gave Logan a quick, reassuring glance before piercing her eyes at Kat. "It's okay, Kat. I'm just having a minor meltdown. Maybe it's a lot to handle. I thought...I thought I could handle it. I can...can handle—"

"I'm taking you home." Logan's tone of voice issued no arguments would be had.

"But, Logan, you have to work. I have to help Charlotte. I shouldn't let them get to me." Arguing with him wouldn't change his mind. She knew this. But going home alone sounded horrible. He had to work, and he'd most likely drop her off. She made tiny little circles on his chest as she remembered feeling his hard body last night, exploring the wonders that she knew she hadn't fully tapped into yet. So much to uncover.

She didn't get enough exploring last night. He had dominated the evening with the need to kiss away her pain, a tortured necessity that she imagined he wouldn't have allowed to be swayed from doing. She hadn't minded in the least.

"Charlotte will be fine on her own. You look tired. You should rest some. I won't have anyone upsetting you."

Doni heard the weariness in his voice. As much as she wanted to go home, she knew he had a job to do. "I...I told Mrs. Dunburry I would visit."

Logan kissed her forehead, chuckling. "Honey, Mrs. Dunburry is the worst of them all. I know she didn't bother you much this morning, but if you go there later, she'll eat you alive. I changed my mind. I'm not going to let that happen. I don't want you going to see her. Not yet, anyway."

"Well, won't she talk about how I said I would come and now I'm not?" Doni said hesitantly. She would hate it if anything came back to make Logan look bad. Her image didn't matter. She was nothing anyway. But Logan was the sheriff. He had an image to uphold, and his image with her by his side looked like a mangled picture colored by a two-year-old.

"I'll set her straight," Kat said, eyeing Callie, who started to make her way to the table with Kat giving a quick shake of her head to wait a moment. Callie nodded, slowed her steps, and turned around without hesitating.

"I don't want—"

"I can see the wheels turning in your mind. I don't care what people say about me. I already told you this. And neither does Kat. She has already set Mrs. Dunburry straight a few times, and one more time isn't going to kill her. I'm taking you home. We'll get lunch to go," Logan said firmly.

"Well, drop me off. You need to go back to work." Doni held in a breath before releasing it slowly. She could do this. She could handle being alone. At least, she hoped so. No time like the present to try.

"Honey, that is never going to happen." Logan raised a finger, lightly brushing it across her lips before she could utter a protest. "I'm not leaving you alone. Remember the conversation we had in the truck? I can work from home just as easily as from the office. If a crisis comes up where they need the sheriff in attendance, then I'll go. I still won't leave you alone. Kat, Seth, or someone else will always be with you. Until I find the person who hurt you, you can't be alone. Okay?"

"Okay, Logan," Doni said, nodding once. She hadn't realized her heart was racing like a jackhammer until he refused her offer of staying alone. She really didn't want to be alone. The thought terrified her. Would she always be like this? How long before he became annoyed and bothered by it?

"Did you get a chance to look at the menu?" Logan asked.

"A little, but I don't know what I want yet. I'm not even sure what I'm hungry for," Doni said, turning a bit from his embrace and picking up the menu again.

"Their club sandwiches are super delicious. They put it on this focaccia bread, mmm, that just hits your taste buds with flavor. I know how much you liked those rolls the other night," Kat suggested.

"That sounds fine. I did enjoy that," Doni replied, closing the menu.

Kat slid out of the booth. "Great. I'll go order. What do you want, Logan? Anything?"

"I'll take a club sandwich as well. Thanks, Kat."

Logan pulled Doni closer, kissing her neck briefly. "I hate seeing you upset."

"I'm not upset."

"You know what I mean. I worry about you."

"Funny, I worry about you," Doni said with a crooked smile.

"Why? I'm fine. You're the one hurt. I just hate...the thought..." Logan leaned closer to her ear. "I have this sudden need to kiss every bruise and lingering pain away again."

She shivered in his arms as his tender words scorched her skin with anticipation. "Oh, Logan. I don't deserve you."

"Wrong. It's me who doesn't deserve you."

Doni caught the older woman's stare again as Logan lightly kissed her neck. She looked shocked by that and murmured to her husband again.

"I don't think she's saying nice things. She's been like that the entire time. It's not making you look good. As the sheriff—"

"Honey, stop," Logan said gently. He sighed, brushing a hand over his face. "We're already the talk of the town. That was definitely started this morning by Mrs. Dunburry. I can't help myself. I can't help when I want to give you a kiss or place a hand on your back. I'm not going to stop myself when the urge comes. Not anymore. There's no point." He grabbed her hand, linking his fingers with hers. "Regardless of what that woman is thinking, you are good for me. Let her look. Let her whisper. Let them all gossip. Because the only thing that matters to me is what you think of me."

Doni smiled, her words halted on the tip of her tongue when Kat slid back into the booth.

"Callie said about five minutes, if that. I made it easy. I ordered a club sandwich, too," Kat said, swiping a hand across her face to remove a strand of hair that wavered into her eyes.

"Sounds good," Logan replied.

Within five minutes, Logan had their food in one hand and Doni's delicate hand in his other. He pulled her out of the diner, turning to Kat. "Are you coming over tonight?"

"I can't tonight. I promised to help at the soup kitchen in Mulhene. And that cute guy who handles the ladle so deliciously is going to be there." Kat sighed wistfully, fanning a hand over her forehead as if she was picturing his face.

Doni giggled. Kat dropped her hand and gave her a mischievous smile. "He's so dreamy. I've volunteered at the soup kitchen for five years now, and sometimes, I think it's just because of him."

Logan rolled his eyes. "Seriously, Kat."

"Seriously."

"What's the cute guy's name?" Doni asked, smiling at her.

"Oh...Johnny. Doesn't that just sound dreamy?" Kat

closed her eyes, emphasizing the act of picturing him in her mind. She suddenly snapped her eyes open, pinning a sweet gaze at Doni. "I'll be over tomorrow night. Can't miss my volunteering tonight, though."

"In the name of love, I don't want you to either. Have a wonderful time, Kat. Do you want to play some cards tomorrow?" Doni asked eagerly.

"You're on. Try convincing lug nut to play with us," Kat said, gesturing her head at Logan as she turned toward the clinic. "Take it easy the rest of the day. You're still healing, Doni. Make Logan pamper you. You deserve it."

Doni lamely waved good-bye, the brief spot of happiness dissipating as Kat continued on her way. *Take it easy the rest of the day. You're still healing.*

Logan tugged lightly on her hand to follow him to his vehicle. She was sick of resting. Her wounds, her aches, her pains, for the most part, were better. But the mere thought of venturing out into the big world, or in her case, in this small town, made her sick as well. She wasn't strong enough like she had hoped she would be. A few gossiping whispers, strange glances her way, and she caved into a pathetic child.

Yet, every time she felt worthless, felt a complete abandon of sorrow sweep through her, Logan swooped in with his sweet words and tender touches. She knew she could handle anything as long as Logan stood by to help her through it.

That's what scared her the most. She relied way too much on him. What would happen when he realized it? Where would she be then? She should stop it. Get it together. Remember who she was. Anything! But nothing would come.

Did she want to remember so she finally had the

answers to what happened to her? Or because she wouldn't need to rely on him?

She squeezed his hand tighter and smiled when he lightly squeezed back and gave her a look that spoke volumes. A look that stripped her bare, making her wish they were already home. A look that she shouldn't treasure because it made her want to rely on him even more. The thought of losing this amazing man made her cringe with fear. Having no memories was a good thing. At least for the moment.

10

LOGAN BRUSHED another tense hand over his face as he slipped his phone back onto his belt. He instinctively grabbed the soothing hands that wrapped around his chest. A long, silent sigh escaped before he leisurely turned around, pulling Doni closer.

"What's wrong? The first call had me slightly worried. This second one even more," she whispered into his chest.

He kissed the top of her head before releasing another silent sigh. "I don't know what you heard, but Seth's coming over."

"Why?"

"I have to leave."

Her body shook as she quickly glanced around, looking for the nearest window. The sunlight streamed through the big bay window in the living room. Yet, the tiniest hint of darkness settled right after.

Logan cupped her chin, gradually bringing her to meet his eyes. "Please, try not to worry. You'll be safe with Seth. I have to go, honey. I want to promise I'll be back before dark...but I can't."

She buried her head into his chest. "Please don't, Logan."

He squeezed her tighter as a rush of dread swept through him. "I have to. Oh, sweetheart, if I could stay I would. I have to go. I..." He kissed the top of her head again as he tried to formulate the right words. "Just because I haven't gone out searching in the woods doesn't mean my deputies stopped."

Her head slowly lifted to meet his gaze. "What are you saying?"

"Bolt's been out searching every day. He found something. I have to go."

"What did he find?"

He kissed her lips, savoring the sweet taste. "I think he may have found where you were held. It's about two miles north of my cabin. Until I see it for myself, I'm not going to say anymore. I have to see it. Seth's coming over, and I need to leave. I need you to know why I'm leaving. You'll be safe with Seth."

The tremors leaving her body broke his heart. He couldn't stop them or figure out how to quash them. Everything in his heart told him to stay, but his mind told him he had to go. He needed answers to catch the bastard who laid a hurtful hand on her. He just needed a calming peace, and he'd never get that with the unknown hanging over them. She was *his*. But she would never truly be his until the truth came out.

"I can try calling Kat instead. If that will make—"

"No, Logan. She was really looking forward to tonight," Doni said with short breaths.

He didn't have the heart to speak the truth that Kat had been making up a story to lift her spirits. And for a brief moment that afternoon, it worked. Even before he could set her straight, she whispered, "Try really, really hard to get back before dark."

Logan didn't need to glance at the clock to know it was nearing nightfall already. Instead, he gave her a smile and a light kiss. "Can you do something for me?"

She shrugged.

"Seth still seems pretty down about breaking it off with Stacy. Can you help get his mind off it? I hate seeing my brother like that. You have this way with him. Even better than me and Kat."

To his relief, a brief smile tinged her lips. "I can try."

"Good." He kissed her again. Her soft lips sent desiring tingles that exploded throughout his body. He would never get tired of the way she made him feel. If he could sear it into his mind, wrap it up like a present waiting to be opened at every available opportunity, he would.

Ten minutes later, Seth barreled through the front door. "I came as fast as I could."

"Let me get Doni and tell her you're here." Logan's steps faltered as he started for the hallway. "She's having a rough time, Seth." He ran a tired hand over his face. "Today wasn't a great day in town either. Damn gossipers. Try to keep her occupied...with anything. This is the first time I won't be here when it's dark out. You might have a hard time. Thanks for coming, I know you were helping Evan." Logan finally grazed his eyes to Seth, seeing nothing but concern and understanding. He knew he could always count on his brother.

"She'll be fine. We'll be fine. Don't worry about interrupting my evening. I know how much she means to you. Evan understood."

"Seth, have you ever felt a fear so immense you thought it might break your heart concerning Stacy?"

Seth fidgeted before answering. "Shit, Logan, that's a hard question."

"Not really."

Seth hesitated. "I guess I have to say no."

"Well, my answer would be yes. Telling me not to worry is like saying just rip my heart out. I told her I had to leave and that you were coming over. No matter what I said, she ran to the bathroom a few minutes later. She hasn't left since. She's terrified. I'm terrified for her. Call me right away if it looks like she needs me. I'll come back regardless."

"I'll do my best, Logan. I won't say *don't worry* again, just *get this bastard*. How's that?"

Logan nodded, then made his way down the hallway to his room where Doni had holed up in the bathroom. He knocked on the door once, waiting a brief moment with no reply. Normally he would leave her be, but the fact he had to leave, and the fact his concern had skyrocketed the minute the call came in, had him twisting the knob.

She stood in front of the sink, her hands clenched to the rim as she leaned forward, gazing into the mirror as if her life depended upon it. She made no reaction to him opening the door or to his soft footsteps toward her. The first clue to indicate she knew he entered her domain was the slight intake of breath as he wrapped his arms around her waist.

"What are you doing, honey?" he whispered into her ear, lightly kissing just below it.

"Trying to figure out who I am so you don't have to leave," she said with a slight stammer.

"I know you're scared about me leaving, and trust me, so am I. I want you to remember everything. But even if it all magically came back to you right now, I would still have to leave."

Logan shut off the four-wheeler and hopped off. Derek disengaged his four-wheeler as Bolt walked up to them.

"Show me, Bolt," Logan said with a sharpness he never used toward his deputies. He wanted to apologize, but he couldn't seem to. How was Doni doing? That's all he really could think about.

"It's over here. I don't even know how I saw it. Maybe it was the metal handle reflecting with the sun." Bolt stopped in front of a steel door with a large metal handle attached to the right side. Several huge piles of leaves were scattered around the door, some still resting lightly on top. "This wasn't meant to be found, Sheriff. Like I said, I don't know how I saw it. How's Doni?"

"Hanging in there. Seth's with her right now. Did you dust the handle for prints like I asked?"

"Yep." Bolt shuffled his feet, moving some of the leaves in his haste. "There weren't any. I couldn't find one."

Logan sighed, clapping a reassuring hand on Bolt's shoulder. "Not your fault. Just means we're dealing with a smart individual. No time like the present. Let's see what's inside."

Logan reached down, grabbed the handle, and pulled. Grunting slightly, he braced his feet to get a better grip. The steel looked rusted in spots, but not enough to show weakness as it gave Logan a hard time lifting. When he finally slammed it to the other side, a dank, horrid smell washed over him.

Damn, talk about dark. His hand shook as he grabbed for the flashlight strapped to his belt. He knew in that moment his beautiful, strong Doni escaped from this very place. There was no question to it.

"You found nothing else around the area?"

"Brief cursory glance, no. I dusted the handle for prints like you told me to, looked around, but mostly stayed by the door. I listened for any sounds coming from below, and I didn't hear anything. I also didn't want anyone surprising me. I won't lie. It crossed my mind waiting for you, Sheriff," Bolt said with a shudder, glancing down into the dark hole that lay waiting for exploration.

"I can go first," Derek offered, also eyeing the deep, dark hole.

"I got it." Logan pulled his gun from its holster, positioning his flashlight above the weapon, then followed the shallow light down the path of the rickety stone-like stairs.

Logan almost stumbled on an uneven step, except the extra light coming from behind him helped to straighten his stance, as well as his unbridled emotions. The only thought to keep him sane as he continued down into the darkness was that Doni sat in his house with his brother, completely safe.

No one could harm her. Not anymore.

"IT'S BEEN A LONG TIME. When do you think he'll be back? Soon?" Doni asked for what seemed like the hundredth time as she paced in front of the big bay window.

Seth blew out a silent breath as he tried to formulate the right words to calm her down. So far, he sucked at the simple task. Since she left the bathroom right before Logan left, she had yet to stop pacing in front of the window. Any time a single word left his mouth, it didn't matter. She kept walking on the same path. He wouldn't be surprised if a formation of her path emerged with vibrancy.

"Doni, I'm not gonna lie here anymore. Not that I was, mind you. He won't be back before the sun sets. Grab a seat next to me and let's just get lost in this game. Minnesota is in the playoffs. I could use the help in cheering."

Her pacing didn't cease as he'd hoped. Not one sign of a reaction from her. It tore at his heart to see her eyes glued to the window as the sun made its descent.

Logan tried to warn him, but he really didn't think it would be this bad. He should've known. His first clue should've been the moment he met her.

"Doni, come sit by me. Please?" he tried again. The only response to pierce his ears was the small haunting footsteps she continued since walking out into the living room. He figured he should be glad she was pacing in the living room and not back in the bedroom hiding out. What would he do if he had to try comforting her in his brother's room?

LOGAN SWUNG his flashlight and gun slowly back and forth as he made his way down the hallway. Each time his foot made solid contact with the ground, he cringed with revulsion that Doni ever stepped foot inside this place. He heard the echoing footsteps behind him, extremely glad to have the company. What about Doni? She had no one. All alone, no one to comfort her. Maybe having no memory was the best thing for her.

"Nothing yet?" Derek asked, his voice rumbling throughout the walls.

"It's dark as hell, Derek. But no, nothing yet."

They ventured about fifty more feet when Logan finally saw more than just a wall flicker back at him. He slowed his steps. "I got something. It's another door on our right."

Derek slowed his steps as he took position by Logan in front of the door. Bolt waited for them outside. Logan didn't like the unknown. He didn't want anyone to come behind them unaware. He felt better with one of them outside, guarding the door.

Logan wanted to take a deep breath, he wanted to forget where he was, he wanted to run a terrified hand over his face; instead, he grasped the door's handle and pulled. A screeching, creaking sound echoed around the darkness.

"Shit, how many times you think she heard that?" Derek muttered as his hand shook with discomfort for the first time, his light flickering around the ground.

"I really don't want to know." Now or never. He walked into the tiny room, still holding his weapon steady, although he scrunched his nose at the horrid smell. Like walking into an outhouse that had never been emptied or cleaned.

Their flashlights swept the room, taking it all in. Just like the hallway, the floor was made of dirt, as were the walls. It reminded Logan of building a snow fort in the winters when he was a kid. Instead of bright white snow surrounding him in peace, dark, damp dirt surrounded him in horror.

Poised opposite the door hung a set of chains that were strapped to the wall. The moment Logan's light hit the chains, Doni's horrifying cries at night hit his ears. Every trembling tear that fell from her eyes broke his heart a little more. He couldn't even imagine her trapped against the wall with no chance of escaping.

Before his body could freeze in terror, he kept shifting the light around the room. Besides the chains that said more than words could describe, the room was completely bare. He finally put his gun away.

"The only question that keeps running around my brain

is how in the hell did she escape?" Derek asked in a whisper. To Logan's ears, his gentle words roared in the tiny confines.

Logan looked at him, unable to erase the chains from his mind. "Sheer will, bravery, and...a strength that none of us probably possess."

AFTER WATCHING the sun dip down and Doni pacing a deep hole into the floor, Seth finally stood up from the couch. Each step he made to the kitchen displayed the worry. What the hell should he do? Yanking open a cupboard, he stared until his eyes hit the prize.

The tea kettle.

He hated tea. The taste itself, just thinking about it, made him cringe with disgust. But he knew Kat liked it. He could only assume Doni would as well.

A few minutes later, he had a nice cup of tea waiting to soothe Doni's nerves. He picked up the cup with hopeful anticipation and walked over to her. She had briefly stopped her pacing to stare aimlessly out the window.

"Hey, Doni. I made you some tea."

Doni's eyes trained onto Seth, then glanced at the cup in his hand as confusion marred her features.

"Do you want to try it? I suck at making tea, but for you, I thought I would try," Seth said, his fingers itching to fidget.

"You shouldn't worry about Stacy. You deserve better." She grabbed for the tea with shaky hands.

Seth's mind went blank. A second later, he decided to go with it. "Yeah, maybe. I was with her for two years. It's hard to let something like that go."

"My mother always told me that if you don't know you love someone within six months, they aren't the one. She's not the one, Seth. You deserve better." She walked to the couch and carefully sat down.

Seth had no idea if it was the tea, the talk about Stacy, or complete numbness that overtook her. He didn't care. He decided to keep rolling with it. Did she realize she'd made a comment about her mother? He didn't think so, and didn't want to remind her about her memory loss and why Logan wasn't here.

"She has this annoying laugh that grates on my nerves sometimes. But there were times when she wasn't feeling well, and I would purposely try to make her laugh. You don't think that's love?"

Doni's brows crinkled in contemplation as she took a small sip. She made a nasty face as she followed through on her swallow. "No, I don't think that's love. Her laugh grates on your nerves? If you loved her, it would be music to your ears. I think that was just you being a nice boyfriend."

Seth plopped down next to her, taking care not to spill her tea. "Hmm...I guess you have a point. She's a great girl. We had fun. Maybe that's all it was...fun. Not sure I'm ready to settle down anyway."

"Then the best thing you can do is walk away. Better to be a lame duck than an ugly one my brother always says." Doni took a sip of tea, cringing again.

Seth almost asked what that meant, as he had no clue, but the words wouldn't pass through his lips. Did she even realize she continued to slip memories of her family? Her mother, and now her brother. What was going on? He was no psychologist, but maybe her fear of Logan being gone was so deep that her memories were slipping out. Which made absolutely no sense the more he sat there and thought about it. *What a dumb thought!* He rubbed his hands on his lap while he processed the next best thing to say.

"Maybe that's why I walked away. I knew deep down it was just a comfortable thing to be with her. Plus, I think..." The rubbing on his legs increased.

When he didn't finish, she glanced at him. "You think what?"

He shook his head with slight agitation. "It's nothing."

With her free hand, she grabbed one of his. "It's definitely something. We're friends. You can talk to me. I won't tell anyone."

He gradually brought his eyes from their hands to her troubled face. "It's dumb. We used to make each other jealous. Nothing ever happened. I never touched another woman, and she never touched another man, but we could be mean just by looking, flirting even. Petty, I know. Childish. I have no excuse."

He lightly squeezed her hand, suddenly ashamed for touching her like this. What would Logan think if he walked through the door right now? Would he think he was hitting on Doni? He felt like a leech, taking the comfort she offered. But sadly, enjoyed her soft touch and refused to push her away.

"For some reason, I still think you haven't told me what you were going to say. It's okay, Seth. You don't have to tell me."

He cleared his throat as he loosened the grip on her hand. "There were times she smiled a certain way or said a certain thing to..." He let go of her hand as he ran his hands through his hair in frustration. "I tried to pretend it was nothing, but I think she liked someone else. More than me. I think...I think that's why I always tried to get back with her. I wanted to be her sole focus, and I don't think I ever was." He pulled his phone out of his pocket, fiddling with the screen. "You wanna see a picture of her?"

Doni nodded, holding her hand out as Seth gave her the phone. A smiling brunette with shoulder-length hair and bright hazel eyes stood happily with her arms wrapped around Seth, her head peeking out from behind his shoulder.

Her finger hovered above the phone before she said, "May I?"

"Sure."

She continued to scroll through the pictures. Most of his pictures contained him and Stacy taking goofy selfies, or just some of Stacy by herself. Seth always managed to capture her beauty.

"Who's this?"

Seth leaned over as he glanced at the screen. "My friend Evan."

A sudden sadness cloaked Doni's eyes. "You were supposed to help him with something. I can't remember. Instead you're stuck with me."

He nudged her in the shoulder as he gave her a light laugh. "I'm not *stuck* with you. I was supposed to help him with his brakes, but this is more important. I like hanging out with you."

"He doesn't mind?"

"Na, he understood. I'll help him tomorrow. Or the next day, or whenever the hell we get to it. It's not an emergency to get the brakes done. Don't worry about it, Doni."

She nodded once and continued scrolling. He had a ton of pictures on his phone. Most were friends from high school, or at least the ones who hadn't happened to skip town the minute the diploma hit their hands. Others were co-workers or his family. Some pictures dated back a few years. She stopped scrolling again.

"I know her. Umm...Callie, I think. She works at the diner."

Seth leaned over to get a better look. A small smile touched his face. "Yeah, that's Callie. Nice girl. I haven't really talked to her in quite a few years. We say hi to each other, but we don't hang out. Not like we did that day. We used to be good friends."

"What happened?"

"I guess Stacy happened," he replied with a deep sigh.

"You're better off without her. You deserve better. I don't just say that because you're Logan's brother. Although, you do remind me a lot of him. You're sweet, kind, and considerate in your own way. The best thing to do is move on and find someone who speaks to your heart."

"That's great advice, Doni. I am moving on. I'll try to stay friends with Stacy, but I won't go crawling back to her. Or hell, even let her crawl back to me. We're horrible. We both do it. I don't know what's wrong with us."

"Relationships are a finicky thing. Can anyone ever understand them? Geez, I constantly questioned myself dating Brent. He always—" She stopped mid-sentence, the horror of what she said clear on her face. "Oh, my...Brent."

She dropped the teacup from her hand, the warm liquid splashing over her pants, down the couch, and onto the floor. Her other hand released his phone as it landed between the two of them. The horrified expression frozen on her face made Seth's words stick in his throat.

"What will Logan think? He's going to hate me." She abruptly stood up, running from the room.

The last thing Seth heard before his brain finally told him to get up was a strangled cry and a slamming of a door. "Oh, shit."

11

"MAN, these lights suck. Can't see worth a damn," Derek muttered as he continued to fingerprint the door to the "terror chamber" as he'd been calling it.

"Just keep at it. Nothing's going to pop up anyway. I have this nasty feeling there's nothing worth a damn inside this room for evidence. How in the hell are we going to figure out who took her if they left nothing behind?" Logan ran a tired hand through his hair.

That's all he had been doing this evening. If he wasn't running a hand through his hair, it was running down his face. His agitation and rage for the treatment that Doni suffered wouldn't simmer down. No matter how hard he tried to picture her sweet smiling face safe at home, he saw a damaged, broken Doni chained to the wall. The images wouldn't disappear.

Derek had offered to process the room, but Logan declined. He needed to stop picturing her chained to the wall whenever he glanced at the chains. He couldn't do that if he wasn't staring at it and he couldn't help but stare. He figured the longer he stared, the sooner the horrible picture he conjured in his mind would dissipate. Because the room remained empty. Doni was safe at home. However, the longer he stared, the more the picture morphed from a disturbing fragment to a grotesque horror.

"It's been a week. Whoever it was cleaned up the moment he knew he lost her. The best thing for us now is..." Derek stood up from hunching down near the floor, making no mistake to forget one inch of the door. "She needs to remember."

Logan came closer to Derek, the light enhancing his menacing glare. "I don't want her to remember. Not this. She can remember anything but this." His hand made another trail down his face. "Her nightmares...I don't even want to hear them tonight. Shit, I can see myself having them."

"Let's see if Bolt found anything outside. Are you done in there?" Derek asked, putting his supplies back into his kit.

It's like Derek knew he needed to get out of this place. "Yeah, let's get some air." Logan didn't wait for a response as he made his way out of the dark tunnel and into the fresh night air. He had collected samples from the chains to confirm Doni had been chained to the wall, but her terror of the dark was enough evidence for him to know she had been locked in that room. Despite searching every inch of the room with his flashlight, he didn't see any other useful evidence to tag and bag. If there had been anything else in the room, someone had taken it with them.

Bolt stood near his four-wheeler. Without hesitation, he made quick long strides toward him as he tried to flee from the weight that sat heavily on his shoulders. "Find anything, Bolt? Any little thing?"

Bolt looked up from his phone and backed up a step from the intimidating stance coming from him. "Uh...no, Sheriff. I didn't find anything."

"Damn it!" Logan shouted as he turned around in frustration, stalking away from Bolt to get some air. He was surrounded by the peaceful night, the fresh woodsy scent floating through his nostrils, yet his chest refused to draw in a decent breath.

DEREK WATCHED Logan storm off and joined Bolt by the four-wheeler. He looked at Derek with a bit of confusion and a tremendous amount of concern. "Is the sheriff all right? I've never seen him act like this."

"Shit, Bolt. I don't know if he's all right. I'm not even all right. So I'm going to say, no, he's not. It's hard being down in that dark pit. I was only thinking one thing down there. What did she go through? She was locked in that room, chained, beaten maybe, and...who knows what else. It's obvious. It's so obvious that I can't believe my eyes. But the sheriff has fallen hard for her. If I was thinking about her chained and locked up and scared out of her mind, imagine what the hell he was thinking. The lack of evidence isn't helping either. It's dark out. Maybe we'll find something outside tomorrow in the daylight. We didn't have much daylight left when we got here."

Bolt shook his head with confidence. "I don't know. I checked real good."

"I'm not saying you didn't. I'm just saying we need to double-check when the sun is on our side for time."

Bolt shrugged yet squared his shoulders with defiance. "Fine, but I didn't miss anything. I did find out who owns this part of the woods."

"That's something at least. Who owns it?"

"Oh, you're gonna like this. Mr. Barten himself, the old cranky bastard."

"Oh, joy. Can't wait to tell the sheriff that one. He'll love talking to him," Derek muttered as he set his stuff on top of the four-wheeler. "I'll be right back."

He made his way over to Logan, noticing how badly Logan's hand shook as he replaced his phone to its spot on his belt. "You all right, Logan?"

"I have to go. Secure the area, and we'll come back tomorrow to make another sweep," Logan said distractedly as he made his way to the four-wheeler.

"Okay." Derek followed him, wondering why the sudden need to leave. "Umm…so Bolt found the owner of this area. You aren't gonna like it."

Logan hopped onto the four-wheeler with a weariness that appeared to age him within seconds. "Just spit it out, Derek. I really need to go."

"Mr. Barten."

Logan cranked the engine. "Don't call me unless it's an emergency. I don't need to give you the definition of an emergency, do I?"

"You just take care of Doni." Derek stepped back as Logan raced off into the darkness, a small sliver of light leading his way.

Seth stopped pacing in front of the bay window when the front door opened. "I tried everything. I hated calling you, bro. I totally screwed up."

"It's fine. To be honest, I expected a call much sooner. What happened? Where is she?" Logan asked, glancing around the room as a tired hand combed through his hair.

"She's in the bathroom. She locked the door on me, and now she's refusing to respond. Don't go yet. I gotta say something first." Seth shuffled his feet a bit before looking at Logan. "She stood in front of the window pacing a hole into the floor. I made her tea and offered it to her. Suddenly we were talking about Stacy."

"She doesn't like tea. I'm sorry about Stacy. That's my fault."

"What do you mean it's your fault?"

"I told her to talk to you about Stacy. Make you feel better. I was being sort of selfish, though. I said it in the hopes it would make *her* feel better while I was gone. You know, something she had to do. I'm sorry. I need to go check on her."

Seth grabbed him by the shoulder. Logan jerked at the contact. He swung around with an expression that spoke volumes.

"Geez, Logan, I'm not gonna hit you. It's fine you told her to do that. She did make me feel better. She's really good at putting my relationship with Stacy in a perspective that I should've considered a long time ago. And oddly, I think it was making her feel better. She actually took a seat on the couch, and we talked for a while. I didn't grab you to hit you. I grabbed you to stop you before you talked to her. I have to tell you something."

Logan rubbed a hand over his face, trying to compose himself and rein in his emotions. "I can't take much more, Seth. I can't even tell you what we found. No words can describe the...just tell me."

Seth blew out a silent breath. "I don't know if it was the distraction of talking about Stacy or the tea... I don't know. I would tell her something, and she would respond a few times mentioning something like my mom always said, or my brother always said. She didn't even realize she said anything."

"That's good to hear."

Seth shifted his feet as he finger-combed his hair. "Yeah, this last part might not be good to hear. She remembered something about...a guy named Brent. I'm pretty sure her boyfriend. That's when she spilled the tea, said you would hate her, and ran to the bathroom. She hasn't responded to me since. She didn't even care she remembered something. The only thing she cared about was the thought that you would hate her. Don't hate her, Logan."

Words almost failed him. "I would never hate her, Seth."

Logan walked away without another word and made his way to the bathroom as fast as his feet would carry him. His brain had turned to mush the moment he received Seth's call. He never should've left her. But he had to. He repeated that as the knowledge of his choice still refused to sink in.

How in the hell could he do his job as the sheriff and take care of the woman who was swiftly building a spot inside his heart? It felt impossible to manage both. For the first time in his life, he was on the verge of putting his job second. Even the mere thought of doing that befuddled him. He was the sheriff. That should always come first. Always!

Since the moment he met her, he had been putting her first. Who was he kidding? She wasn't building a spot inside his heart. She had already taken it over and surrounded him with such love he couldn't function correctly.

He knocked quietly on the door. "Honey, it's Logan. Can I come in?"

Silence answered. He pressed his ear to the door, hoping to hear any tiny sound coming from inside. A cry, a whimper, a movement of any kind, but he heard nothing. The silence was worse than anything else. His heart raced as he grabbed the handle and twisted lightly. Resistance hit his hand. Seth told him she locked herself in. Why did he expect it to magically open?

"Sweetheart? Please open the door."

He knocked again, barely tapping on the door. Scaring her with loud noises might be bad. Or did he need to make loud noises and snap her out of whatever funk she was in? He had no clue what was going on.

He didn't care about this Brent guy. He didn't matter. No other man concerned him. The only thing that mattered was she would never walk out of his life without him fighting to the death. She was worth fighting for.

He pressed his head against the door as the heavy weight of guilt and sorrow flooded his veins, seeping deep into his bones. "Honey, please open the door for me. I'm sorry for leaving you. I don't hate you. I will never hate you."

He twisted the handle again, mocking himself into wishful thinking. "I need you to open the door." The knob rattled as he shook it harder. "Doni, open the door. Please don't do this to me. Whatever it is you're thinking, we can talk about it. Please, don't shut me out. Open the door, sweetheart."

After another minute of pure silence cloaking the room, he pushed away from the door and ran to the kitchen. He barely missed colliding with Seth, who was pacing in the kitchen.

"Is she all right? Did she say anything?"

Logan politely pushed Seth out of the way and dropped to his knees in front of the sink. "She won't answer me, and she's not opening the door. I don't hear anything inside the bathroom. Not one sound, Seth." He grabbed one of his small toolboxes from the cupboard and slammed it onto the counter. "Shit, I've never been so scared in my life. No sound. Nothing. Just nothing."

"She wouldn't hurt herself." Seth's voice didn't convey the confidence it should have.

Logan grabbed the small box that held his tiny precision screwdrivers. "I hope not, Seth. But honestly, she's been through a lot. She's been coping better than most people would in the same situation. I should've never left."

Seth followed him as he ran back to the bathroom and quickly picked the lock. He slowly opened the door. Fragments of glass littered the floor. Doni was huddled in the corner between the toilet and the shower. Her head leaned against the wall with her eyes closed as she held her hands tightly to her chest, a slow trickle of blood making its way to the floor.

"Doni!" Barely registering the sound of glass crunching beneath his feet, he rushed to her side and grabbed her hands. Relief overwhelmed him when he realized it came from her right hand. It didn't appear to be too serious. "What happened, sweetheart?"

He didn't wait for a reply as he scooped her up and carried her out of the bathroom. She started to cry. He didn't care. Any sound from her lips sounded like music to his ears. The silence had been horrible. "It's all right, darling. I swear, everything's all right now. I'm not mad. I don't hate you. Do you hear me?"

She responded by crying harder, burying her head into his chest as he walked out of his room and down the hallway to the other bathroom. Seth popped his head out of the bathroom.

"I grabbed the first aid kit for you. Should I call Kat? The doc—anyone else? I'm sorry, Logan. I didn't hear the glass breaking. If I had, I would've broken down the door, I swear."

"I know, Seth. It's fine. No need to call anyone. It looks like a small cut. If I think it needs stitches, then I'll have you call Kat. Go make some coffee," Logan said, dismissing his brother.

Seth nodded and walked away. Logan shut the door and looked around the bathroom wondering how he could clean her hand without putting her down. It wouldn't be possible. He kicked his leg up, knocking the toilet seat down. The loud slamming noise barely penetrated her senses. He sat down on the toilet and held her, gently rocking her as he whispered sweet encouraging words.

It felt like hours when in reality, only minutes had ticked by. Her sobs lessened from small cries to scattered breaths to even breathing. Even then, he continued to rock her with his soft voice echoing around the room.

Finally, her silence bothered him again. "Talk to me, honey, please."

"I'm sorry, Logan," a tiny, frightened voice answered.

"That's not what I want to hear. You have nothing to be sorry about. Absolutely nothing."

"Did...did Seth say anything?"

He rested his chin on top of her head as he grasped her tighter. "He mentioned you had a few memories of your mom and brother. Small things, but that's good." He kissed her hair, inhaling her enchanting aroma. "He also mentioned another memory that you had of a guy named Brent. Probably a boyfriend. And that's good as well."

A sharp breath escaped as she lifted her eyes to his. "Why would you say that? You don't want—"

He grabbed a kiss to silence her words. "I feel like we've had this conversation a few times. Where are you?"

She looked confused as she glanced around. "In the bathroom."

He grinned as he kissed her lips. "Try again."

The confusion intensified as she glanced around again. "Minnesota. Did I blackout or something? Are we somewhere else?"

"No. Stop worrying and thinking in those terms. Where are you right at this moment?"

A few seconds ticked by before she whispered, "In your arms?"

"Yes. In my arms. Right where you belong. I don't care about this Brent guy or any other guy. You're mine, and I'll do anything to keep it that way."

She hid her head into his chest. "I don't deserve you."

"Please don't do this again, honey. You scared me. Scared the life right out of Seth. I will never ever hate you. Your memories are going to come. Some might scare the hell out of you, and some might not make you feel a thing. We'll get through each one. But not like this. Not with you hurting yourself." Logan looked at her hand as he stood up. "Let's clean that hand now."

He tried to release her and experienced a strange déjà vu when she refused to loosen her grip. "You have to let me put you down. I don't want your hand to get infected. Let's clean it. Please, honey."

For a brief second, he thought she retreated into herself again and decided to make this task more difficult than he wanted it to be. Then, her arms relaxed and a heavy breath escaped. He tenderly let her down and grabbed her hand as he turned on the water.

After finding the perfect temperature, he washed her hand and inspected it to make sure no glass was wedged inside her wound. A long, thin cut ran along the side of her hand near her pinkie. He didn't think she would need stitches, but he hated seeing the small cut and the tiny nicks covering her knuckles and part of her fingers. The water washed away the blood, cleaning the wound. How in the hell could he wash away her fear?

Quickly wrapping her hand with a towel, he then grabbed the first aid kit. A little bit of ointment, gauze, and her wound was neatly fixed. Stitches didn't look necessary.

"I didn't mean to break the mirror. I hope you don't think I intentionally hurt myself. I wouldn't do that," she whispered. "Are you mad at me, Logan?"

His eyes made a path from her hand to her shirt where the mangled evidence of her injury glared at him. He finished his ascent to her beautiful, worried face. "Honey, I will always help you when you get hurt. I'll be honest. It's hard as hell to look at you like this. Your bruises are finally fading, and now I see this." He raised her hand and closed his eyes in tortured pain.

Gently letting her hand go, he opened his eyes and cradled her face. "I'm not mad. However, I am worried. I need you to promise me you'll never lock yourself in the bathroom, or any other room for that matter, again. Not knowing if you're okay, hearing that horrible silence...I just can't handle that. I don't care about the mirror. That's fixable. If you get hurt, well, then we have a big problem. Please, talk to me next time. Let me in."

"I promise."

"Good. We're fine. I'm not mad. I don't hate you. Never."

He kissed and hugged her as he poured his heart into the kiss. "Let's change. I can't stand the sight of your blood. Seth made you some coffee."

"Can I say again that I don't deserve you?"

"No. You're never allowed to say that." For her sake, he

smiled and grabbed her uninjured hand. "Come on, let's get that coffee."

DONI SAT down at the table. Logan took a seat next to her.

"I'm sorry, Seth," she murmured when he placed a hot steaming cup in front of her.

A chair dragged across the floor. Seth plunked down with a rough sigh. "You have nothing to be sorry about. Are you okay? That's what has me worried."

She grabbed the mug, giving a weak smile. "I'm fine. It's just a small cut. Thank you for the coffee…and the nice talk we had. You're not mad at me, are you?"

"There's nothing to be mad about. You've cured me of Stacy. How can I possibly be mad?"

A small laugh escaped as she took a sip of her coffee. "You're too kind. Just like Logan. Thank you, Seth."

"Anything for you, Doni."

"It's getting late. Or more like it's been a long day. You could probably still use some rest, honey." He tossed an arm around her shoulder soothingly, kissing her cheek.

She leaned into him, closing her eyes as she pictured lying in bed and wrapped in his sweet embrace. "I am tired."

"Why don't you change for bed and I'll walk Seth out, okay?" Logan suggested.

"I just changed." She laughed, then her expression turned to instant horror. "I made a mess. I need to clean the bathroom. I can't believe I broke your mirror. Oh, Logan, I'm sorry."

She tried to bury her head into his chest by throwing her body closer to him as Seth said, "I already cleaned it. You're safe to walk in there barefoot if you want. Don't worry about the mirror. Logan doesn't care."

"Seth's right. I don't care about the mirror. I care about you. Go get ready for bed. Take the coffee with you."

She lifted her head, the uncertainty still lingering. "Okay, Logan." She trailed her eyes to Seth, who had the same tender look in his eyes that Logan held. "Thanks for cleaning my mess."

She dropped her eyes to the mug, tracing the top with her finger. "I really didn't mean to hurt myself. After...my memory, I just wanted everything to come back. All of it. I kept staring at myself, just seeing this woman. I don't know who this woman is. I just got so mad that I punched the mirror. I didn't think about what would happen after I punched the silly thing."

Seth stood up and gestured for her to stand up. "Come here. Give me a hug. It'll make you feel better. Quit saying you're sorry. You didn't do anything wrong. I'm sure it's not easy remembering things, so you're entitled to a few minor meltdowns. No one's mad."

Doni let loose a small chuckle and stood up, walking into his arms.

He hugged her tightly, his breath tickling her neck. "I think I already said this, but my brother is a damn lucky guy. Quit worrying about what happened tonight. It's fine."

"Okay, Seth," she whispered as tears puddled in the corners of her eyes. Before she broke down in front of them, she let go and made her way down the hallway, forgetting all about her coffee.

"Shit, I'm sorry, Logan," Seth said.

"For what? Making her feel better. Being a good brother. I think everyone needs to stop saying sorry around here." He stood up and headed for the front door. "Come on. I need to talk to you, and I prefer to do it outside. I want to make it quick."

Stepping outside into the cool night air, the darkness, for the umpteenth time that night, swathed him with a crushing blow. He never had a problem with the dark. Not until he stepped into that horrifying room. Just standing on his porch, he could picture those deadly chains hanging with despair. Without notice, Doni's beautiful face entered, chained helplessly to the wall.

Inhaling a deep breath, he turned to Seth as he closed the door. He needed to make this quick. If the dark was creeping him out, he could only imagine the terror Doni was going through in his bedroom. He wasn't fooled. She probably retreated into herself the moment she walked out of the kitchen.

"I—"

"I'm not mad, angry, disappointed, or whatever the hell you got going on in your head. Just knock it off already, Seth. I have enough to deal with trying to make Doni feel better. I'm not really in the mood to make you feel better as well. You're a big boy."

"Right. I'm sorry. Or not. Or shit, what did you want to tell me?" Seth asked as he brushed his hair back.

"Look. Don't take this in the wrong way, personal, or anything dumb like that. I'm just trying to do my job here." Logan looked at the night sky one more time. This was harder than he thought.

"What? I swear I didn't mean to make her upset. I know she got hurt because of me and—"

"This isn't about Doni, or at least not in the sense you think. You know we found where she was held, right?"

"Yeah."

"I'm not accusing anyone of anything, but I'm going to do my job. Do you hear me?" Logan said with more force than he intended.

"Damn, Logan, just spit it out. You're talking in circles here. I have no idea what you're trying to tell me."

"I have to go talk to Mr. Barten tomorrow since that's where the bunker or chamber or pits of hell, whatever you want to call it, was found. It's on his land."

Talk about screwing this conversation up. He needed to step back inside the house and out of the darkness. It was slowly creeping into his skin and hollowing him from the inside out.

Seth took a step back as the confusion became a bit more prominent. "All right. Good luck talking to him. You know how he can be."

"I know. And I hope you know I'm going to have to talk to Evan as well," Logan finally uttered with regret.

"What the hell does Evan have to do with this? He's my best friend. Okay, so his dad's an asshole. A cranky old bastard who barely gives him the time of day, unless he's feeling inclined to get on his ass for some stupid reason or another. He would never hurt anybody. Never." Seth clenched his fists. "The fact you would even think it necessary boggles my mind. And you insist that you're not accusing anyone of anything."

"I'm not accusing Evan or his dad of anything, but the fact is that shit was found on their property. A little girl was murdered in my town, on my watch. A woman...a woman I've come to care for deeply was kidnapped, held against her will, and had to escape on her own. I'm to the point I don't care if I'm offending anyone. I'm going to do my job. My job dictates that I question the property owner and the surrounding family members still in town. I'm not saying Evan did anything. I know him. I know he's your best friend, but maybe he saw something. Maybe he doesn't realize it. I'm not doing my job if I don't talk to him."

Seth released a heavy breath. "You know how this town operates. I hear what you're saying, but just talking to him... the rumors will spread. He's guilty just for you having a word with him."

Logan ran a tired hand over his face. Damn it, he didn't want to let down his brother like this. "I can't help the rumormongers running around town. We questioned Dr. Matthews and nothing came out about that."

"Yeah, he's the damn doctor. I'm sure people just thought you talked with him about Doni's condition. They won't think anything good if you talk to Evan."

"I'm sorry if that happens. I truly am, but I'm just doing my job, Seth. I didn't have to tell you, but you're my brother. I'm telling you because *you are* my brother. I wanted you to have a heads up. Keep it to yourself, please."

"Whatever," Seth muttered as he rushed down the steps and headed for his truck.

"Seth?" Logan called out, taking a few steps toward him.

"'Night, Logan. Thanks for being such a wonderful brother," he yelled as he slammed his door shut on Logan's worried face. He cranked the engine, heading out of the driveway before Logan had a chance to stop him.

12

LOGAN SHUT his office door with a soft thud, twisting the knob to make sure it locked. Why he suddenly felt the need to lock his door was beyond him? He never had before. But the moment he started to close the door, he felt an insane urge to lock it.

He didn't trust anyone anymore. How could he when his town was falling apart with violent crimes sprouting out in every corner? Overreacting slightly? Yeah, maybe, but he couldn't shake the nasty feeling that overcame him anytime he thought of Doni hurt, tortured, alone, and chained to a dark, damp wall.

His sweet Doni. He couldn't get his mind off her, who sat happily, hopefully anyway, back at home with Kat. He couldn't stop thinking about Seth, who currently refused to take his calls, both last night and still this morning. And he couldn't get his mind off the fact that he knew with complete certainty someone in this town hurt Doni.

Was it Mr. Barten, his son Evan, or another person in town?

Finding the answer was like solving an impossible

riddle. He wouldn't stop until he did. And apparently, burn a few bridges along the way.

He stopped in front of Charlotte's counter and waited for her to get off the phone. Two minutes later, she hung the phone up and gave him an amiable smile. "Yes, Sheriff?"

"I'm heading over to Mr. Barten's residence. Only contact me if it's an emergency. Mrs. Boomerton's flower debacle is not an emergency," Logan said dryly, as he attempted to keep his irritation in that he had been delayed earlier.

"She can be quite persuasive, Sheriff. I'll try my best, but if what I heard correctly is true, she's still having a difficult time."

"Your humor does not impress me at the moment, Charlotte. I mean it. Don't call me. Don't call Derek. Don't call Bolt. Nobody. Mrs. Boomerton can handle her own little flower problem. It's not our problem."

Charlotte exhaled noisily, garnering an annoyed look from him. "I like it better when you're a softie, Logie. Can you go back to being that guy? You're being a meanie right now."

"When I find the bastard who hurt Doni, then yes, I'll go back to being a softie. Okay, Char-Char."

"Fine. I'll take what I can get," she said as he briskly walked away.

Logan pulled into the Barten's residence, shutting the vehicle off with more force than necessary. The urge to throw his phone through the windshield had him gripping it harder as he forced himself to clip it back to his belt. He needed to stay strong, not lose his cool.

He acted like a jerk back at the office, even a bit last

night with his own brother. This case, Doni herself, was starting to get under his skin. He needed to solve it. Insisting it was all for Doni's sake would be a lie. Part of him needed to solve it for himself.

He hated the idea this happened in his county on his watch. He hated the pain she endured nightly. Perhaps solving the case wouldn't lessen her pain to the threshold he wanted, but maybe enough for her to have a surge of memories to put her more at ease.

Last night, the silence, the sight of her huddled in the corner, terrified in the bathroom, covered in blood. The defeat on her face. He had seriously thought she harmed herself intentionally. He couldn't convey the torture that brought to his heart. So, he *had* to solve this case.

Everywhere he turned it proved to be difficult. Even Derek's most recent phone call didn't ease his mind. Absolutely nothing was found around the site in the woods. Nada.

He needed hope and a whole lot of luck to find something within this interview, or interrogation if he wanted to be a real ass. It wouldn't take much for the situation to turn into that sort of thing. He knew Mr. Barten wouldn't hold back. He proved that thought the moment he heard a loud bellow directed his way.

"What the hell I got the sheriff on my property for? I ain't done a damn thing. Get in your ol' fancy vehicle and git out."

"Good morning to you, too, Mr. Barten."

"I said git off my property," Barten grounded out, spit flying.

"I'll leave after I've had my say. Have you heard about the woman we found in the woods? No memory, bruised, beaten, locked away..." Logan asked, gauging his reaction to every little word.

"I ain't got time for such nonsense. Marybeth don't let me, damn woman, never gettin' off my back. What's some crazy woman got to do with me?" Barten made a grunting noise, then hocked a loogie near Logan's feet.

Logan wanted to take a deep breath. He wanted to run a hand down his face in agitation. He wanted to punch Barten in the face for his demeaning words about Doni. Instead, he responded, "Well, the fact that we found where she was held, chained to a wall, locked deep underground, on *your* property, makes it your business. Do you happen to know anything about that?"

Barten just stared at him. He wondered, for the first time, what Barten did all day. He rarely left the property, now retired from the paper mill a town over, and it didn't appear that time was on his side. He looked old, worn out, and every day his age. By the looks of it, he hadn't showered in some time.

His pants were stained with black and brown marks, Logan wasn't sure from what. His plaid fleece buttoned-up shirt held tattered edges and dirty spots all over. His white scraggly beard held the remains of whatever meal he recently devoured, and his hair peeked out in oily waves under a raggedy ball cap.

After taking his time to look him over, he suddenly didn't think it was too far off that he would hold a woman against her will. He looked every bit like a backwoods maniac that one would find in a cheap B flick movie.

Finally, Barten decided to answer with another loud coughing sound and spit directed at Logan's feet. "Ain't got a damn clue what you talking about. Git off my property now. You had your words."

"Have you seen anyone around your property lately?"

"Not sure I'd tell you if I had. Damn woman probably had it comin'. Probably dressed like a whore and got treated like one. Ain't no woman worth nothing else, 'cept my Marybeth. She gonna whack you with her paddle if you ain't git off my property. Better yet, I should pop you with a bit of buckshot. I ain't one to repeat myself, Sheriff."

"Not that I think you will, but don't make any future trips anywhere, Mr. Barten. I just might be back. And if you threaten me again, I'll lock you up. Perhaps your son Evan will be more helpful. Or how about your other son Wayne? Have you heard from him lately?"

"You leave them outta this. They ain't done nothing wrong. I'll say any damn thing I wanna say. I have a mind to get my shotg—"

"Don't test me, Mr. Barten. Not today. You won't like the results. I'll be back if the need arises. You have a pleasant day," Logan said, walking back to his truck before he decided to arrest the man for the simple fact—he was an asshole.

Logan fired up the engine, glancing in his rearview mirror the entire time he drove out of the driveway. Barten never moved one inch, his scowling face a permanent memory in his mind. Fifteen minutes later, he pulled into the mechanic's shop on the edge of town and got out of his vehicle to talk to Evan. Hopefully this conversation would go better than it had with Barten. And it should, he knew Evan pretty well considering Seth was his best friend.

Evan saw Logan right away and wiped his hands on a rag that he had looped through his belt. "Morning, Logan. Are you having some car trouble?"

"Nope, not today. Are you here alone?" Logan asked, making a quick cursory glance around the garage.

"Yeah, slow morning. Working on a few cars, but nothing strenuous at the moment. Barry went two towns over for some parts we need. Is there a problem?" Evan asked, sniffing his nose as he wiped a hand underneath it.

"Look, Evan, I'm just doing my job. Please, take no offense. I had a word with your dad today, and well, I didn't get very far."

Evan laughed with disgust. "You honestly didn't expect to, I hope. He's my dad, and I never get very far with him. Probably the reason I never go over there and try to avoid him at all costs. What did he do?"

"Nothing. At least, nothing that I can prove. Look, you heard about Doni, right?"

"Yeah, of course. Seth told me about her. He had to leave yesterday in the middle of helping me with some tough brakes to hang with her. I get it. She's going through something. You're working the case and worried about her. That's the impression I got from Seth."

"He came over last night so I could go check out a lead. We found where she was held, and we found it on your dad's property." Logan figured he should quit fooling around and get straight to the point. "I'm not accusing your father of anything, and I'm surely not accusing you of anything. Does anything about a cellar of sorts in the woods on your dad's property ring a bell to you? We had a hard time finding it."

Evan rocked on his feet like he wanted to take a step back. "You think my dad...me...had something to do with Doni?"

"I don't think anything right now. I'm just doing my job following leads and asking questions. If you think this is easy for me, it's not, Evan. I've known you a long time, and I know you're a good guy. You're one of Seth's best friends, but

I have to ask questions. Please don't make this harder than it should be."

"I have no idea what you're talking about. My dad likes to hunt. I don't like the woods. You know I'm not the outdoorsman type. I don't know anything about this cellar you're talking about. And my dad wouldn't share anything like that with me. Wayne's his favorite. He always went hunting with him. I'm the no-good, piece of shit, worthless son, who can't do a damn thing right. I'm pretty sure that's word for word coming from his mouth."

"Have you heard from Wayne? Last I knew, he hightailed it out of town ten years ago and hasn't been seen around here since."

"Best thing he ever did was hightail it out of here. He wasn't any better than my dad with the way he treated me. He's probably sitting in some prison. Maybe running his name will tell you where he is," Evan said with a deep loathing.

"Have you seen anything strange around the property? Seen anyone who doesn't belong? Anything helpful for me, Evan?" Logan asked, trying to keep the slight desperation out of his voice.

"Like I said, Sheriff, I don't really go near my dad. If I see something, I'll let you know." Evan wiped his hands on his rag again.

His voice told Logan he had nothing else to say, which for some reason, raised Logan's suspicions from none to high. Evan was hiding something. Logan knew it with every breath in his body, but trying to pry it out of him right now would never happen. He knew when to retreat and develop a better plan.

"Thanks for your time, Evan. Like I said, I meant no offense. When's the last time you saw your dad?"

"Does it matter?"

"I only ask because he mentioned your mom a few times, in the sense that she was still around. Just wondering about his health." Logan shrugged, trying to get back on better ground with his brother's best friend.

"Honestly, Sheriff, I'm not really sure I'd care if he was sick. He always talks to Mom like she's there since she passed away. I wouldn't doubt it if she is hanging around haunting him. He was just as much of a bastard to her that he is to me. I have work to finish."

Logan nodded once and headed back to his truck. Evan turned around to the shop and wheeled himself under a car as if Logan hadn't been asking difficult questions. He tried to call Seth as he drove away and groaned in frustration when Seth still refused to answer.

LOGAN ENTERED the house with a smile on his face, the first one of the day to grace his features. Doni immediately dropped the rag and flung herself into his arms. He embraced her with as much enthusiasm as she displayed. He could get used to this sort of routine. A long day at work just to come home to a beautiful, delightful woman who was excited to see him.

"How was your day, honey?" Logan asked, grabbing a kiss before he followed her into the kitchen.

"Nice. Kat and I played some cards, did our nails, watched some TV, and you know, girl stuff." She picked her towel back up and continued the chore of putting the dishes away.

Kat walked into the kitchen and went straight for the fridge. "Need something to drink, Logan?"

"No, not yet." He leaned his long body against the counter and watched as Doni fluttered around the kitchen as if she belonged there.

"How was your day, Logan? You look tired," Doni commented as she put several plates away.

"A little, it was a long day. Not much headway either," Logan muttered, crossing his arms as the sudden urge to run his hand down his face came over him. He knew it was a quick giveaway on his emotions and he didn't need to fuel Doni or Kat with how he truly felt.

"Do you want to talk about it? What have you found? Did you go back into the woods?"

"Nothing for you to worry about. Why don't I grill some steaks? I'll go start up the grill." Logan pushed himself off the counter and headed for the sliding door adjacent to the kitchen table.

KAT WATCHED as her brother started the process of getting the grill prepared and didn't miss the rigidness in his movements.

"I think he had a bad day. You think he found something terrible out? Maybe something bad about me," Doni said between short breaths as her face fell into a frown.

Kat gave her a quick hug for reassurance and guided her to the pantry. "You were dying to make some cookies earlier. I think now is a wonderful time to do that. Logan loves cookies and it just might cheer him up. I do think he had a slightly rough day, but I guarantee it had nothing to do with the fact something bad popped up about you. He wouldn't hold anything like that from you. Trust me."

Doni inhaled a deep breath and opened the pantry. "You're right, Kat. I'm being silly."

"I'm going to have a quick chat with Logan. You get started on those cookies." Kat received a small smile in return and headed outside.

She shut the glass door and stepped into Logan's face just as he grabbed for the charcoal bag. "What the hell is wrong with you?"

The bag juggled in his fingers before he gathered a firm grip. "Can you not scare the hell out of me? Geez, Kat. What are you talking about?"

"Your attitude, that's what. You were all smiles and charm when you walked in the door and then just as suddenly you were abrupt and rude. You shut her down and walked out. That is so unlike you. She thinks you know something and it's something bad about her. Do you know something?"

Logan set the bag of charcoal down as he moved the grill over a spot. Not that the grill needed to be moved. "No. I didn't lie. We didn't make any headway. I didn't mean to make her think otherwise."

"Charlotte called today. She said you were a meanie. What's that about? And Seth—"

Logan held his hand up, then shifted the grill over another inch. "I don't want him mad at me. I'm just doing my job. He won't even answer my calls."

"He's being dumb and when he realizes that, he'll apologize. Look, Logan, you're the sheriff, yes, but the whole weight of the world is not on your shoulders. You are one man. I know you didn't mean to act that way toward Doni, but maybe you need to take a step back and take a deep breath. Ask for help. Or let the help in when it's offered."

Kat turned her head and saw Doni working busily at the counter. "I told her to make cookies. She tries really hard to be brave. For you, I imagine. This case is about her. She wants to be included. Try being a little more forthcoming with your answers next time."

"I know the case is about her, but generally, you don't share a case with a victim," Logan snapped.

"Is that what she is to you? A victim? If you weren't my brother, I would slap you silly for saying such a thing."

"Damn it, Kat! I can't see her like she was last night. When I opened that bathroom door, I thought she hurt herself. The blood...the silence...I just can't see that again. All that from a small memory that still gave us no clue. Okay, a guy named Brent she may or may not be dating. Not much to go on. No damn evidence in the woods. Mr. Barten threatening me with buckshot. Seth pissed for supposedly accusing his best friend of being involved. It's just all too damn much right now. I need to be a meanie, as Charlotte likes to put it, or I'm going to explode," Logan said as he whipped around toward the yard breathing heavily.

"I think this was you just exploding, Logan. Do you feel better? You need to let it out. You can't shut people out. Not me, and especially Doni. I understand that last night scared you. It scared Seth, or he wouldn't be so obtuse right now. She needs to face her fears. I've said it before. I'm saying it again. Holding back from her is not the answer. Let us help. Talk to us. Don't come rushing outside to get the grill going."

"How are we going to eat if I don't get the grill going?" He turned around and grabbed the charcoal.

"This is why I hate having conversations with men. You get absolutely nowhere. You dumb men never listen. Clean your ears, Logan," Kat retorted and stomped back inside the house.

LOGAN CONTINUED to work outside while he pondered everything Kat said. He did act like a jerk. The entire day, not just with Doni inside the house. He couldn't, nor wouldn't, apologize to anyone. He wasn't that sorry acting that way toward them. Nosy busybodies that needed to mind their business. People needed to cooperate when he tried to do his job.

But he knew he needed to apologize to Doni. He should never act that way with her. She was fragile, yet, so brave. Kat was right. He needed to trust she could handle it. One breakdown shouldn't make him discredit her bravery altogether.

He stepped inside the house and made his way to the fridge as Doni tossed a pan of cookies in the oven. Kat sat at the kitchen table fiddling with her phone, throwing a quick, angry glare his way. He suppressed the urge to roll his eyes, knowing she was right and he was wrong. Without a word to anyone, he grabbed the steaks and walked back outside.

When he knew the steaks were good for a few minutes before they needed to be turned, he headed back in the house with an apology on his lips. Doni stood in front of the sink washing her recently dirtied dishes from the cookies. She didn't even glance his way when he opened the sliding door. He couldn't tell if that was indifference or intentional. He didn't wait to find out as he slid behind her body and pressed a soft kiss to her neck.

"Forgive me, Doni. I was a jerk before. I hated seeing you

the way you were last night, and I guess I'm afraid to share anything in fear of how you'll react. I don't want to see you hurt in any way ever again. Physically or emotionally. I just can't stand it. I promise I won't do that again. Please forgive me."

Her body stood rigid as he waited patiently.

"You're mad at me." He said it as a statement, yet it hung in the air like a question—a heavy burden between them.

She finally rested her back against his chest. "I'm not mad. I never was. More so worried than anything else. I know I scared you. I scared myself. I promise I never meant to hurt myself. I was staring at myself, the unknown swirling around me, and I just got so angry. I punched the mirror without thinking. I was frustrated."

"And I believe you."

"Did something happen today? Did you find something?" she asked as her body became stiff again.

"I swear I found nothing. That's why I've been so cranky today. I need to find something, but not a damn piece of evidence is popping up. I'm sorry for that as well, honey."

She grabbed his hands to loosen his grip and turned in his arms. "Don't ever be sorry about that. You're doing everything you can. Try not to be so hard on yourself."

"That's what I said," Kat piped in.

Logan turned around to face Kat, bringing Doni within the crook of his arm. "Okay, okay, I hear you, lovely ladies. I'll try to snap out of this meanie funk I landed in." He kissed her cheek.

"Now, if only Seth would get his head out of his ass," Kat muttered as her fingers flew over her phone with quick precision. "He won't even answer *my* calls or texts."

"I'm not upset by the way he acted. I expected it, actually. Evan's his best friend." Logan glanced at the clock.

Another minute or two and he would need to flip the steaks.

"Did you find anything out about Wayne?" Kat asked.

"Who's Wayne?" Doni interjected.

"He's Evan's brother. He hasn't been around town for ten years or so. He wasn't good news back then and still isn't. Evan didn't have much to say other than telling me he knows nothing and saw nothing, but he did suggest I run Wayne's record," Logan said with a hint of sarcasm.

"Really? He had to cock an attitude. Like you don't know how to do your job," Kat said.

"Don't worry about it, Kat. I already have Seth mad at me. Let's not make this bigger than it needs to be. Keep your loud mouth out of it. I can handle Evan."

"Well, does he have a record?" Doni asked.

Logan chuckled. "A mile long. He's been in and out of jail since the day he left. He's bad news. Tracked him all the way to Florida—"

"Florida?" Doni interrupted, a strange look crossing her features.

"Yeah. Does Florida ring a bell? Something feel familiar?" Logan asked with hope.

"No. I don't know why I interrupted you," Doni replied with a shrug.

Logan knew better than to press. "Well, he was released from another stint in jail about two years ago down in Florida, and I can't track him after that. It's like he dropped off the face of the earth."

"Or up to no good..." Kat offered, glimpsing at Doni so briefly only Logan saw it.

"Barten was no help. He's an asshole, but I don't get the feeling he's involved. Evan, well, probably not him either. But Wayne, I don't like just thinking of him. We tracked a few reports of *strangers* roaming around town, according to the information given to Charlotte by concerned citizens, which panned out to be nothing. So, we really have no lead to go on from here. Doesn't mean I'm going to quit. I'll figure this out." Logan clasped Doni's face as he kissed her with a tenderness that spoke volumes. "I have to flip the steaks. The cookies smell delicious. I can't wait to taste one."

13

LUCKY, MINNESOTA
SHERIFF'S OFFICE
7:45 AM

A KNOCK SOUNDED.

Logan barely made it into the office peacefully or with a chance to catch his breath, as every early riser in town felt the need to stop him offering so-called tidbits of juicy information or questions pertaining to Doni. Most wanting to know why she hadn't been back into town since the first time she appeared. Logan really wanted to answer with—because of you. Instead, he smiled his friendly sheriff smile and replied with a nonplus answer that had them shaking their heads at his retreating back. Now, he still couldn't sit down at his desk without being bothered.

"You busy, Logie?" Charlotte asked, walking in without an invite. Her hands were positioned behind her back, a thousand-watt smile on her face, and her posture suggesting she wouldn't be leaving until she had her say.

"Apparently not." He leaned back in his chair and took a

sip of coffee he managed to grab from the break room before attempting to hide in his office.

"Oh, so you're still in meanie mode," Charlotte stated, changing her hands from behind her back to her hips.

"Char-Char, I just got in. Barely unscathed. I can't even sneak into my own office without everyone hounding me."

"Well, you are the sheriff," she replied, raising a brow that dared him to argue with her. "But, let's move on, shall we? You need to talk to Bolt."

"About what?"

"I get why you're a bit uptight lately. Worrying about Doni and all. Makes sense. I'm letting your little attitude slide for the moment. Bolt's, however, not gonna let slide. He's acting a little too arrogant for my tastes. Do you know he's already been out in the woods again this morning taking another look around? He states with the utmost certainty he missed absolutely nothing. And if there's a shred of evidence, he'll be the one to find it since he found the cellar. He swears he can find more evidence to bring down the bastard who took Doni. I don't like it."

He took another sip of coffee. "Am I missing something, Charlotte? I'm okay with him being persistent. He did find where Doni was held."

"I'm not an idiot. Don't you trust people around here?"

"You lost me."

"You locked your door yesterday. I needed to get a file from your office, and I couldn't get in. You never do that. Bolt's acting funny. Do you suspect him of something? Because, honestly, I'm not really liking his attitude lately. It's suspicious. You all searched that woods, and out of nowhere, he magically finds that little hidey-hole. Now he's out there searching again with a fine-tooth comb. I swear if he comes back with so much as a teeny-tiny speck of evidence, I'm going to consider him guilty."

He closed his eyes as he ran a tired hand over his face, breathing in a bout of strength and patience. He didn't leave the house tired this morning. In fact, he left today feeling much better than the day before, especially after last night. He had loved Doni several times, showing his apology first, then how much she meant to him. Right before he got up to shower, she decided to show him how she felt. Why couldn't the morning continue in such beautiful bliss?

"I'll be honest here, Charlotte. I don't know why I locked my door. I just felt the need. Right now, I'm taking Bolt's enthusiasm as a good thing. I can say I don't trust the people in this town, but if I can't trust the people I work with, well, we're in a shitload of trouble."

"Fine, but don't say I didn't warn you," she said, shooting him a stare that would get any other man to drop to his knees in pain. Logan didn't even bat an eye.

"Thank you for the warning, Char-Char."

"Don't get that attitude. I just might make you prepare the coffee in the mornings. And we both know how much you like my coffee," she said, nodding her head as if he should agree.

"Now that we had that wonderful talk. I do need you to do something for me. Since you're such a wiz on the computer and all."

"Oh, now you're trying to sweet talk me. Such a typical man. Back and forth."

"I can't have your illusions falling short on how men behave," Logan said with a wink.

"Cut your crap. What do you want?"

"I need you to get me the contact information for the

FBI," Logan said, as he started to organize his desk from the clutter he let pile up in the two short days of work.

"Excuse me? Can you run that by me again?"

He glanced up with no expression for her to decipher. "I need the contact information for the FBI."

"The FBI?"

"Yes, Charlotte. The F. B. I. You know the federal agency that swoops in when local law enforcement can't handle it anymore and needs some assistance," he replied, hating to admit he needed the help. But he refused to worry about his pride. The only worry he had room for was Doni and her well-being.

Kat had been right last night. He needed to ask for help. He didn't think she meant to this extreme, but what the hell. With more resources at their disposal, the likelihood of identifying Doni became larger. That's all that mattered. She needed this.

"I can't believe you want to call in the Feds. You got this. You're almost there."

"Almost where? We have shit to go on, Charlotte. I have no suspects unless you want to count Wayne, who hasn't been documented anywhere in the last two years. Or how about Evan, who happens to be my brother's best friend, and I've known the damn kid almost my entire life considering he was at our house more than his own home. Or, yeah, his dad, who still thinks his wife is around and can't wait to tell her every little thing I did while on his property. It's not going to hurt to have some outside help. Doni needs it. This isn't for me. This is for her."

"Well, don't expect me to welcome them with open arms. I'll be half-cordial, and only for Doni's sake." Without another word, she turned around, slamming the door on her way out.

"Oh, boy, what a great day this is going to be," Logan muttered as his phone rang with a piercing annoyance. He threw an exasperated look at the phone, catching Brittany's file out of the corner of his eye.

Ten years old. Already gone.

He blew out all of his frustrations with one heavy breath.

Life wasn't that bad. It could be worse.

TAMPA, FLORIDA
FBI FIELD OFFICE
VIOLENT CRIMES/TRAFFICKING DIVISION
9:38 AM

HE SAT MUNCHING on his cold, day-old fries, eyeing the crime scene photos that were scattered across his desk. He popped another fry into his mouth when a long shadow covered his mess he liked to call home these days.

"You are the only person I know who can eat and look at grotesquely, horrifying pictures at the same time and not throw up," Agent Deke Sumnter said. He stood directly in front of the tall lamp that gave off just enough light to help him see everything splattered across his desk.

"Can you move, please? I can't see my grotesquely, horrifying pictures when you're standing in the way."

"No, I can't move. How about you act like a normal person for once, open the damn blinds, and let some light in. Or better yet, turn on the actual office light. I know it's been a rough three months. You have every right to act the way you are, but you're starting to turn to the dark side, and it's a bit concerning, Danny."

Agent Daniel O'Rourke finally looked up at his partner of five years, friend for ten, and waved a hand in his face. "Move, Deke, I can't see."

"All right, moving this conversation along. A call came into Quantico—"

"Good for Quantico. We're in Florida."

"Knock it off. Just listen for once. A call came into Quantico from a small town I've never heard of. Lucky, Minnesota. The sheriff found a woman in the woods, injured, lost, and absolutely no memory of who she is or what happened. Nothing. Nada. He's asking for assistance."

Danny shoved another fry into his mouth, chewing loudly just to piss Deke off. "Don't care. We have plenty of cases we need to solve right here, right in front of me. It'd be great if I could see to continue my work."

The shadow moved away as did the pesky footsteps. Danny almost smiled, something he hadn't done in the past three months, until a bright light illuminated the room, making him cringe and close his eyes. "What the hell! Do you mind, Deke?"

"The only reason I know this is because Laurel, you remember Laurel? Tall blonde with to-die-for legs and tight little ass we always enjoyed gawking at. Well, never mind, that's beside the point. This request came across Laurel's desk, and she immediately called me with the information. She has a damn good memory. I mean, we haven't been to Quantico in how many years. Very good memory."

Danny opened his eyes, blinking a few times to adjust to the light he wanted off with a passion. He couldn't stand the light. It made him see how pathetic he was, how much of a failure he'd turned into. "Turn the damn light off!"

"No, you need to get used to the light. You need to snap out of it. You need to put back on the Danny face I once knew. You need to start acting like an FBI agent instead of a dead man walking."

"And what, pray tell, do I need to do all of this for?"

"Because we're flying to Lucky, Minnesota to help out the local sheriff."

"Get out. I'm not flying anywhere. I'm busy trying to solve this serial case sitting in front of me. Butchered women. Gotta get this serial killer off the streets," Danny said, waving his hand around the desk, grabbing another fry as his hand hovered near that area.

"I thought I could talk you into it, nicely, of course. I see you're going to make me do this the hard way. With shock value." Deke grabbed the folder he had tucked underneath his arm, opened it slowly, and laid a photo over all the other photos littering his desk. "Here's the woman the sheriff found."

Danny's hands shook as his eyes zoomed onto the photo. His brain couldn't understand or decipher what his eyes were seeing. A pale face, bruises, scratches, and the most forlorn look he could ever imagine stared him down. He reached for the photo.

"Aubrey."

Lucky, Minnesota
Logan's house ~ Outside on the porch
3:45 PM

A cool breeze swept through her hair as she watched a rabbit scamper across the yard. Her lips curled up in delight. Nature in its finest. How could you not appreciate the simple things in life?

As she enjoyed the quiet afternoon, it made her think back to the cabin, and those few precious days she and Logan sat outside enjoying nature. A memory.

A memory she would never forget.

Doni's thoughts turned darker with the knowledge that she had so few memories. She needed to start remembering because she didn't like seeing the stress or the worry cross over Logan's features as it had the night before. She understood his reasoning for apologizing, but it hadn't been necessary. She's the one who should be sorry. If she could remember what happened, then maybe he wouldn't have such a difficult time. Perhaps she would be able to point him directly to the person who hurt her.

If only she could remember and not freak out in a manner that made him think she would harm herself. That had been an accident. Nothing but a dumb accident that she would never repeat. Ever. One minute she was staring at her face so intently into the mirror, and the next minute, she was slamming her fist into her reflection. She only wanted to remember.

The rabbit shot across the yard in the opposite direction. She had no idea what the rabbit found so entertaining, but she could see the enjoyment with each hop it displayed. The rabbit seemed rather small. Not that she knew the average size of a rabbit, but it didn't look like its small stature was holding the rabbit back from doing what it wanted to do.

So why in the world was she sitting here holding back? She had no memories. Why wasn't she doing something to change that?

That's it. That's what she had to do. Finally, a sense of direction, a fresh outlook on where to proceed. She needed to talk to Logan. He wouldn't like what she had to say.

Lucky, Minnesota
Sheriff's Office
3:48 PM

Deke pulled the door open. A beautiful woman sat behind the counter, yet her expression didn't appear inviting.

"I'd ask how can I help you, but I can guess just by the doom and gloom outfits and slicked back hair why you're here," the woman said as she stood up.

Deke had an urge to touch his hair at the comment, but refrained as he and Danny walked to the counter. As his hand rested on the counter, his black hair, a bit on the longer side, took that moment to slide down the side and hang over his forehead. Just seeing the fire in this woman's eyes had him combing it back in one smooth move. "I'm Agent Sumnter, and this is my partner, Agent O'Rourke. Your name is..."

"We would like to speak to the sheriff," Danny said with a clipped tone.

"Let me see some badges first. Just because you look like FBI, talk like FBI, and smell like FBI, doesn't mean I'm just going to believe you are with the FBI," the woman said with a sweet smile.

"Just exactly what does the FBI smell like? And I didn't catch your name." Deke leaned closer.

She sniffed once, cringing after the fact. "Like that."

Her head snapped to Danny, who smacked his badge on the counter. "I want to speak to the sheriff."

She inspected both of their badges with the eyes of a hawk. Satisfied, but the irritation still prominent, she wrote their badge numbers down on a notepad. "Just in case you do something worth reporting. I won't need to ask. I can just call your supervisor like that." She snapped her fingers with a flick of her wrist and laid their badges on the counter for the taking.

"I'll have you know, you called us, not the other way around," Deke said with a charming smirk.

"Correction, Agent Sumnter, was it? The sheriff called you. I would never do such a thing."

"Again. I would like to speak with the sheriff," Danny said with little patience.

"Well, if you will—" The woman stopped speaking when the doors opened and a man barreled through with a harried expression.

"Where's Logan, Charlotte? I need to talk to him."

"He's busy, Seth." She pointed to the man to turn around and walk back outside.

"His office, then. Thanks, Char-Char," Seth said with a wink to further irritate her and continued down the hallway.

"Seth, you get back here."

Deke gave her a sultry smile as she leveled an evil eye at him and Danny.

"Don't move. I will go get the sheriff."

Deke enjoyed the way she swung her hips in anger as she walked away from them. "I have a feeling we're not welcome here."

"Gee, what gave you that impression," Danny mocked as he took a step to follow her.

Deke stopped him. "Patience. She'll be right back.

LOGAN STOOD up and rounded his desk when Seth whipped open his door.

"I'm sorry, Logan. I was an ass. I'm done now."

"I know, Seth. I didn't want to do what I did. I just—"

Seth held his hand up. "I know. Trust me, I know. You did it for Doni. Thinking of her made me realize how dumb I was acting. How is she?"

"She's fine, better."

"I really should stop by the house and talk to her as well. I had this sudden epiphany. Or hell...I just saw Stacy, and it made me think of Doni. I really acted like an ass. I needed to clear the air with you."

"Air's cleared. It doesn't matter. You know Doni would enjoy a visit."

Charlotte walked into his office, the steam almost visible coming out of her ears as she glared at Seth. "Don't you ever walk past me without permission. I said he was busy and I meant it." Charlotte then shot a glare at him. "The FBI's here."

"The FBI? Why are they here?" Seth asked, confused. "Those two suits in the lobby?"

"I called them. I don't have much to work with here. I figured I could use all the help I can get." Logan smiled at Charlotte, trying to lessen her disposition just a little, receiving a deeper scowl in return. "Send them back, Charlotte, please."

She turned around and stormed out of the office, her hips swaying with anger.

"Do you really think you needed to call the FBI? You can handle this. I shouldn't have given you a hard time."

"Seth, this isn't for me. It's for Doni. I want to catch this bastard, and I want her to have closure. Maybe her memories will come back..." Logan's voice trailed off as he watched two men walk down the hallway.

"Gentlemen, I'm Sheriff Caldwell. Thank you for coming. I didn't expect you this quickly," Logan said, offering his hand as they stepped inside his office.

"I'm Agent Deke Sumnter, and this is my partner, Agent Danny O'Rourke. We have a good reason for coming quickly," Agent Sumnter said, shaking hands with Logan.

Agent O'Rourke stood next to Agent Sumnter, eyed Seth briefly, then turned his attention to Logan. "Where is she?"

Logan jerked slightly. What was with the attitude? His appearance didn't speak highly of him either. While he was dressed in a nice black suit that only held flight wrinkles, it hung from him in a homely manner. His face looked tired, shadows rimming his eyes and a hint of sadness that seeped out as he stared at Logan. There was something familiar about this man.

"She's not here, if that's what you're wondering," Logan replied.

"I want to see her."

Logan stepped back and rested against his desk. "I thought we'd have a chat about the case and what I have so far. Talking to her right now would not be the best thing. Maybe a brief summary of the case would be best."

"No, Sheriff, the best thing right now is for me to see her," Agent O'Rourke said as he clenched his teeth, making his gaunt face appear more menacing.

"I think we're getting off on the wrong foot here. I agree with you, Sheriff Caldwell, a brief discussion would be best," Agent Sumnter said.

"Damn it, Deke. I want to see her. I have to see her. And—"

"Look, don't make me argue with you in front of these

two because I will. Damn if we aren't. I know how you're feeling right now. I know how you've been feeling the last three months. A few more damn minutes isn't going to kill you. Settle down, Danny. I'm not sure how much more I can stand from you before I knock some sense into you. With my fist, I mean," Agent Sumnter said, showing him a fist with the utmost respect.

"Are you two brothers? You work together in the FBI?" Seth asked with mild curiosity.

"Who are you?" Agent O'Rourke countered.

"He's my brother. You're asking to see her like you know who she is. Do you know who she is?" Logan straightened, his relaxed posture suddenly gone as tension took its place.

Agent O'Rourke ignored his partner, who put his hand out to stop him from moving, and stepped into Logan's face. "Yes, I know who she is. She's my sister, and I want to see her right now."

14

A HEAVY SILENCE swallowed the room as Logan and Danny stood toe-to-toe with Danny's words hanging in the air. Logan's throat clogged as so many harrowing emotions overwhelmed him. The world just shifted, and the ground was about to consume him in one fell swoop. An announcement that should sound happy and joyous yet felt like nails to his heart. He had a sense of dread that she would suddenly slip from his life without a backward glance.

Her brother found her.

"Well, I didn't see that one coming. Makes more sense now," Seth finally said, breaking the silence.

Danny made no effort to move. "What makes sense?"

"Your attitude. I get it. She's your sister, but you can't just waltz in here and say, "Hi, sis, long time no see." You just can't," Seth replied.

Danny took a step back from Logan and turned toward Seth. "Why the hell not? She's been missing for three months. Three long, agonizing months. She needs me."

"Wrong. She needs *my* brother. You'll see that soon enough. She doesn't remember you. She doesn't remember her own name. Demanding to see her and thinking she's going to run into your arms with happy longing is just asking for disappointment. Think about it. What is her name, by the way?" Seth asked.

"Look here—"

"It's Aubrey. I think we all need to just have a seat and talk about this. Let's all calm down," Deke said, interrupting Danny.

"Aubrey. I like it. It's a beautiful name. It fits her. Don't you think, Logan?" Seth asked as he looked at him.

Logan finally moved his gaze from Aubrey's brother to Seth, unsure of where to go from here. He couldn't get a handle on the turbulence swarming his mind, but he knew he needed to snap out of it and just go with the flow. "It is a beautiful name. My brother makes a very good point. Just dumping her with this information wouldn't be good. I agree with you, Agent Sumnter, we should all have a seat and talk this through."

"Good. Let's do that." Deke took a chair near the desk, dragged it back a bit and gestured for Danny to take a seat. "Come on, Danny."

Danny's only response was a scowl.

"Well, I'm going to go. I have something I need to do. I'll stop by later at the house, Logan." Seth headed for the door.

"Where are you going?" Logan asked, a strange suspicion hitting his senses.

"Not running to Doni...Aubrey, if that's what you're thinking. Just something I gotta do."

"I'd feel better knowing if you don't mind," Logan said, unable to let it go.

"Will you be honest with me?"

"Of course. When have I ever held back?"

"I talked to Kat. When you talked about Evan last night,

she got the feeling you weren't saying something. Is there something I should know? Was he involved?" Seth asked as he took a step back, almost as if Logan already answered and he couldn't take it.

"This is all fine and dandy, this little family issue you have going on, but I don't have time for any backwoods family drama. I want to see my sister," Danny said with irritation.

Logan ignored him as he kept eye contact with Seth. "I have no idea if he's involved, but I had a small feeling he was lying to me. That's it. Nothing but my gut talking to me."

"Okay, well, I'm off to have a talk with Evan. If he's hiding something, I'll let you know. He might be my best friend, but if he had even a small part in hurting Doni, he'll be the sorriest man alive." Seth turned to leave.

"Don't do anything stupid, Seth. Let me do my job." Logan wanted to stop him from leaving, but he knew his brother wouldn't listen to a word he said.

"Don't worry, I know you're the sheriff and would arrest me if I did something stupid." Seth grinned as he grabbed the door handle. "But you're also my brother, so you'll bail me out just as quickly." With those parting words, he shut the door.

"Doni? Evan? Does any of that involve Aubrey?" Deke asked, taking the seat he offered Danny.

"Yes. I think it's time for that chat." Logan walked back to his chair and sat down with anxious energy. He gestured to the other vacant chair in his office. "Please, have a seat. I really don't want to continue down the path of hostility with you, Agent O'Rourke. I know she's your sister and you want to see her, but hear me out first. She's not just a person who stumbled into my cabin, injured, scared, and confused as hell. She means something to me. I'm not asking for myself. I'm asking for her sake."

Danny's angry stance didn't encourage Logan that he would actually comply with his request. Just as suddenly, his features fell into despair as he sighed heavily and sank into the chair. "I'm ready to talk, Sheriff."

"WHAT'S GOT you in such a flurry? Logan will be home soon. You know he'll be home before it gets dark out," Kat said as Doni scuttled about in the kitchen.

Doni stopped measuring the flour and glanced at the bay window to see the sun still shining. She hadn't even considered what time it was. Her focus had been centered on making a cake and how to bring up what she wanted to say to Logan. She knew he would resist. Talk about having her work cut out to convince him about her plan.

"I just thought a cake would be nice, that's all."

Doni went back to her task, measuring flour, sugar, cracking eggs, and anything else the recipe she found online required of her. She'd pulled out the blender when the front door opened. Logan walked in, followed quickly by two other men she had never seen before. A bizarre sensation flooded her senses until Logan snapped her out of it with his mellow voice.

"Hey, what are you making?"

She set the blender on the counter and met him halfway, melting into his arms that opened immediately for her. "A cake...for you. Who's with you?"

"Some people I want you to meet. You made cookies last night, not sure I deserve cake today as well."

"Of course you do." She kissed him briefly on the lips.

He grabbed her hand and pulled her toward the living room where the two men stood waiting. Kat stood up from the couch.

"Umm...so I took your advice from yesterday, Kat, and I called in some help. This is Agent Deke Sumnter and Agent Danny O'Rourke from the FBI," Logan said.

Doni couldn't help but notice how Logan pronounced their names rather slow and the subtle glance toward her as he did.

"This is—"

"I didn't mean for you to do that. I meant us—me, Doni, Seth, you know, that sort of help. You don't need a bunch of stuffy Feds running the show around here," Kat exclaimed, interrupting Logan as he was about to finish introductions.

"Why is everyone in this town against the Feds except for the sheriff himself?" Deke asked, his brows dipping, indicating he was very annoyed by Kat's statement. The look on his face felt so familiar to Doni.

She gazed at the two men, a funny feeling sitting in the pit of her stomach. Logan's voice rumbled softly next to her. "Could at least one person today be nice about this fact? Why do you sound so pissed, Kat?"

"You're the sheriff. You don't need them." Kat enunciated each word carefully.

"While I appreciate everyone's utmost confidence in me, I found it prudent enough to call them," Logan replied, clearly exasperated.

"I'm not sure how I feel about it either," Doni said quietly as she squeezed his hand.

Logan lifted her hand, pulling her closer. "Trust me, it's the best thing I ever did. Believe me when I say that. I did it for you."

"I trust you, Logan." Doni smiled and gathered another hug from him.

Kat rounded the coffee table and shook her finger at Deke and Danny. "My brother's the sheriff. You will not shove your little badge in his face and just take over. Do you hear me?"

"Do you have a name to go with that feisty attitude?" Deke asked with a wily smirk.

"Bitch...if you don't adhere to what I just said."

Danny busted out laughing. "Thank you."

The smile that lit his face made Doni's heart sore for a moment. Then he dropped the smile just as quickly.

Kat lifted an eyebrow and raised a hand to her hip. "Are you laughing at me?"

"No. I laughed because I thought it was funny as hell. And thank you...because I haven't laughed like that in a long time." Danny glanced at Doni.

Why was he suddenly looking at her so intensely? The look unnerved her, making her take a step closer to Logan.

Logan must've realized she was starting to get uncomfortable as he squeezed her hand in reassurance and then directed his attention to Kat. "Settle down, please." He glanced at Deke and Danny. "That's my sister, Kat. She can be quite vocal, just like everyone else you've come across today. And this...this is Doni, as she likes to be called."

"Hi. You can call me Danny."

Doni wanted to back up again when he spoke. Instead, she mustered up some bravery and softly replied, "Nice to meet you, Danny. Are you sure I should call you that...being a federal agent and all?"

"I want you to. It's fine. You can call this guy Deke, or Decker, as some of his friends like to call him," he said as he pointed to the man standing next to him.

That man seemed much friendlier as he offered her a bright smile. "So, what are you making? I didn't hear, but if it's something sweet, I'm a fan."

"Chocolate cake. I should finish that," she said, yet she couldn't seem to move.

"Special occasion, hankering for it, or just trying it out?" Deke asked.

"What's it to you?" Kat threw in.

"Are you going to be like that all night? Do I need to arm myself with a bulletproof vest?" Deke asked with mock sincerity as he placed a hand on his chest.

"Maybe. I haven't decided," she shot back.

"Kat..." Doni waited for her to glance her way. "Minnesota nice, isn't that the saying? I'm sure these gentlemen... where are you from?" Doni looked at them.

"Florida. Tampa, to be exact. Although, I was born in Maryland, spent some time in Virginia at the FBI Academy, and then got sent to Tampa. Deke here was born in California, then Virginia for the Academy, and off to Tampa, just like me. If you were wondering about it all," Danny rushed out before Deke could respond.

Puckering her brows with confusion, she tried to make sense of everything. Why did he have to explain all of that to her? She didn't ask for an entire history. But his words swirled around, the wheels turning in her mind as the funny feeling started to become larger.

"Florida?"

"Yeah. Have you ever been there?" Danny asked.

Something like hope seemed to fill his eyes as she thought about it. "I don't know."

"The cake, honey, I'm dying to try some," Logan suddenly said.

"Right, the cake." She turned to leave, then stopped. "I

suppose you're going to want to talk to me about what happened. I mean, that's why you're here."

"Yeah, but no rush. Cake does sound good. We can always talk later, or tomorrow is fine as well. We did just go through a whole day of flying and driving," Deke said with a friendly laugh.

This was her chance. She might have better luck convincing Logan of her plan if the FBI agreed. "Well, I suppose you'll want to see what Logan and his deputies found yesterday. You know, where I was...you know, held." She blew out a small breath, knowing that it didn't come out as confidently as she wanted it to.

"Yes," Danny replied with a bit of hesitation.

"Good. I can't wait to see it myself," Doni said and walked away to the kitchen. Phew! She said it, and without stuttering or tripping over the words.

"What did you just say?" Logan asked with a sharp tone.

She grabbed the blender and turned it on. "I said I can't wait to see it myself. These silly memories aren't coming on their own. I decided a nice little push might help."

"And when did you decide this?" He shook his head as he walked toward her. "Never mind. It doesn't matter. You're not going anywhere near that place. Nowhere near it."

"It's a good idea. I'm sure the lovely agents agree, right?" She glanced at them with a small smile while she continued to beat the batter.

"Umm..." Deke managed to say.

"I think going alone with the sheriff for the first time would be better. If you don't mind, Au...Doni," Danny said.

"I do mind. I want to go." She shut off the blender and grabbed a spatula. The batter fell into the pan slowly, taking its time. Scraping the bowl, she tried to speed up the process. The nerves, the shivers were about to start. She could feel her bravery wavering.

"Forget it, honey. It's not happening. Not now. Not tomorrow. Not after one time with the agents alone. Never," Logan said, stepping closer to her as she opened the oven and put the cake in.

She shut the oven door and put her hands on her hips as she looked at Logan. She tried to force her hands not to shake. To put on an air of confidence. To be brave and strong. Except when she spoke, it sounded slightly weak. "I'm going."

Logan closed the distance between them and grabbed her face with a tender caress. "It's not happening. I'm not going to argue. It will never happen. Your memories will come. Just give it time."

No. He wouldn't stop her. She shoved his hands away and circled around him. "That's not fair. I want to help. What's it going to do for them to see it? You've combed the area and found nothing. Unless a suspect pops up, even with the FBI here, you'll gain nothing. My memories, they could give you everything. Don't you see, Logan? Why are you being so stubborn?"

"One of my many wonderful traits I possess. I never had a need to be stubborn with you until now," Logan said firmly.

"Well, lucky for you, I just realized I possess that same wonderful trait," she said, posing with her hands on her hips to emphasize her determination. A stance she saw Kat display often when her brothers tended to annoy her.

"I'm not having this discussion anymore. I don't give a damn what they say," Logan said, pointing at Deke and Danny. "They say sure, it's still no. You're not going."

"They have more say. They're federal, and you're not."

Kat sucked in a harsh breath as Logan looked at Doni as if she slapped him. "Federal or not, it's never happening. I refuse to see you break down, and who knows what sort of reaction you'll have. I'm not taking that chance. A simple memory of a guy named Brent, your boyfriend, sent you hiding in the bathroom and hurting yourself. I can't see that again. I won't."

Logan didn't wait for a response. He turned around and stepped outside, shutting the door with quiet ease.

"Your boyfriend's name isn't Brent, it's Richard. You dated Brent in—" Deke stopped talking.

"How do you know that? Do you know me? Do you know who I am?" Doni exclaimed, bordering on hysteria.

DANNY WATCHED as Kat prepared the coffee. He really didn't have the energy for coffee, but he figured she was just doing something to occupy the time.

He now understood the sheriff's hesitancy of springing the news on his sister. The shock in her eyes as Deke tried to explain everything to her wouldn't leave his mind. It played like a song on repeat. And like an imbecile, he stood there frozen in his spot, watching as the terror spread across her face.

Not happiness.

Not relief.

But pure unbridled terror.

Deke managed to tell her what her real name was, where she lived, and who her brother was. The brief look she had given him hadn't revealed any clues on what she thought besides the fear in her eyes. Then she ran out of the room before he could say one word.

He wanted to curse the sheriff for coming back into the house as she fled. Instead of getting the chance to console his own sister, that responsibility fell to the sheriff. The feisty woman Kat, as Deke had called her, had provided the sheriff with a one-liner explanation and he immediately ran after her. The damn sheriff hadn't even given him a chance to go.

He should be the one consoling Aubrey, not the sheriff. But he knew deep down, she wouldn't have accepted anything from him. She didn't know who the hell he was.

No sound.

No sight of them.

It made Danny nervous.

His eyes wouldn't leave Kat's movements as she moved around the kitchen. Watching her do the simplest things kept him calm. Otherwise, complete despair might consume him that he couldn't even comfort his sister. Directing his attention on this interesting woman seemed like the best solution.

She was easy to read as well. Her irritation and frustration came out in every tiny movement she made. Even something so little as when she reached into the cupboard above the coffeepot to grab three coffee mugs. The door swinging open with force. Or the loud knock to the counter as she slammed the mugs down. She clearly didn't feel the need to hide her emotions.

"Kind of late for coffee, don't you think?" Deke asked as he sat next to Danny at the kitchen table.

Kat glanced at him with one brow raised. She picked up a cup, waggled it with mockery, and opened the cupboard to put it away.

Before she could close the door, he corrected himself.

"Whoa, whoa, I didn't say I didn't want one. I just said it's kind of late."

"You have a big mouth. You should learn how to curb it. It seems to get you in trouble and create a situation into a huge fiasco," Kat said firmly as she slammed his cup back onto the counter. "It might be late, but I need something to do. I'm worried about Doni...Aubrey, sorry. It might take me a bit to get used to her real name."

"How did you come up with calling her Doni anyway?" Danny folded his fingers together to curb his nervous energy. It was hard to watch her when she was talking and focusing on him and Deke. He'd rather have the silence.

Kat leaned against the counter, crossing her arms. "Well, her favorite saying when I met her was 'I don't know.' I figured we needed to call her something, and I came up with some names using the letters from 'I don't know.' She liked Doni the best. Now I see why."

"I don't understand."

"You know, for such spiffy hotshot FBI guys, you two are really dense." Kat rolled her eyes as Deke gave her a charming smile while Danny burrowed his brows. "Your name is Danny. You're her brother. She can't remember who you are yet, but when given some choices, she picks Doni. Pretty darn close to Danny if you ask me. She wants to remember. Don't forget that."

Kat turned around to the coffeepot. His fingers relaxed as she went back to preparing the coffee. This was much better. Calmness again.

Then the front door opened, directing his attention that way.

Seth, the brother. Yeah, he didn't like that guy. Of course, who was he kidding? He didn't like any of these people. They stood between him and his sister. Perhaps he shouldn't think like that, especially since she had no clue who he was, but he needed to hate somebody, and he couldn't hate Aubrey.

"Are you here to cause problems, or did you get that stick out of your ass?" Kat asked.

"Stick removed." Seth joined them in the kitchen, grabbing a chair across from Danny and directly next to Deke. Kat nodded, grabbing another mug from the cupboard.

"Where have you been?" Kat asked briskly.

"Talking to Evan," Seth mumbled.

Kat whipped around, her eyes digging into his soul and ripping it into shreds with one simple glance. "And?"

"He wouldn't say anything to me. And damn if it doesn't hurt. My best friend is holding something back, and I want to hate him for it, but..."

"But..." Kat prompted him to continue.

Danny's curiosity piqued, leaning forward a little, waiting for his answer as well. They had talked quite a bit with the sheriff before heading to see Aubrey.

"I think it has to do with his brother. I don't think he's protecting him out of love, more like fear. Wayne was a scary-ass dude back when he was eighteen. Can you imagine how he is now?" Seth said with a shudder. "I wanted to beat it out of him, but I just couldn't. He would never hurt Doni. I just can't believe it. I can believe him withholding information about his brother, though."

"Well, I hate to burst your bubble, but if he withheld information in an investigation, we will lock him up," Deke said matter-of-factly, referring to Logan's attempt at gaining information from Evan. "And we already started the search back in Tampa for Wayne. If he can be found, we'll find him. He sounds like a wonderful suspect to us, that's for sure."

"Well, just know, he's dangerous and a piece of work

whenever you come across him. Just be careful," Kat said, turning back to her coffee task.

"Gosh, that sounded like you care," Danny said sarcastically.

Without turning around, Kat retorted, "Don't kid yourself, I don't care about you. I care about Don...Aubrey. Once she remembers, she'd hate it if you got hurt."

Danny felt thankful that her back was turned. Her words affected him more than he cared to admit and he hated her seeing that. Refusing to dwell on why, he trained his thoughts back to Aubrey. How was she doing? He could kick Deke in the face for his stupidity and blowing the whistle like he had.

"Where's Logan and Doni...ah, shit, I meant Aubrey?" Seth asked, glancing around the kitchen and the living room that sat bare.

"Einstein next to you blabbed everything to her. She didn't take it well. Logan's been with her since. Not sure how she is right now," Kat replied, bringing the cups over to the table and taking the open seat next to Danny.

Seth slowly turned his head to Deke, who suddenly looked embarrassed. "It was an accident. It just slipped out. Logan was getting upset and mentioned a boyfriend named Brent. He was wrong. I corrected it by saying his name is Richard."

Seth burned his tongue gulping too much coffee at that statement. He spewed a bit of the coffee back in the cup as he coughed a little. "So she had a wrong memory? She has a boyfriend?"

"Why does that make you sound so shocked and disappointed?" Danny asked quietly, the same menacing glare he had in Logan's office back on his face.

Seth held his stare for a while when Deke responded,

"Her memory wasn't wrong. Just old. She dated a punk-ass kid named Brent when she was a senior in high school. Little twerp almost got his balls shot off."

Kat glanced at him with surprise. "And how did that almost happen?"

"He was a little too touchy-feely to Aubrey's liking. She mentioned it to us, and we had a little chat with him. Happens a lot actually, us having a chat with the men she dates," Deke said, glancing at Seth as he said it, lifting his coffee for a sip.

"Meaning a lot get too touchy-feely with her?" Kat asked with a smirk.

"Meaning we don't like any man she dates, including the current asshat she's seeing," Danny answered, eyeing Seth just as Deke had.

He wasn't an idiot. There had been clear intimacy between Aubrey and the sheriff. And what had the sheriff said back in his office? *She's not just a person who stumbled into my cabin, injured, scared, and confused as hell. She means something to me.* What did she mean to him? Thinking about it just raised his anger level.

"How come you keep saying we? You both act like her father instead of a brother and...and whatever you consider yourself to her," Kat said, throwing a hand in Deke's direction.

Deke made eye contact with Danny, who nodded his head to continue. The fury rolling in his veins made it impossible to speak.

"I met Danny in the academy. We were both newbies looking for the excitement, the rush of starting with the FBI. Not too far into our training, Danny got a call. His parents were killed in a car accident. Aubrey was only fifteen at the time. He suddenly had sole custody of his sister. I mean, she was fifteen, it's not like she was a child, but she still needed structure and guidance. I sort of stepped in and helped him. I have three sisters and a brother. I'm no expert at raising kids, but I knew enough about rebelling and such. It took a while to settle Aubrey down. She took the death of their parents hard."

"My sister is all I have. Maybe I can get a little overprotective, especially with the men she dates. Hell, none of them are good enough for her. I'll probably never think any man is good enough. She did go through a rough patch when our parents died, but she's better now. Or she was before..." Danny took a sip of coffee. "Deke is like a brother to her, while I feel like a parent sometimes. I'll do anything for my sister."

"So this asshat she's dating, Richard, you said. Why don't you like him?" Kat asked, looking at Danny.

"I told you. I don't like anyone she dates. Nothing in particular he did. He's arrogant and a jerk to boot. He never lets his superiority get in the way when he storms into my office demanding to know where we're at in her case. I don't know why he bothers either because I never see an ounce of worry. More like superb acting," Danny said through clenched teeth, taking another sip of coffee.

"I already told you I thought something was off the day she disappeared. She had something to tell me. She mentioned Richard, and not in a friendly way." Deke held up his hand as Kat's mouth started to open. "And please don't ask if we checked him out as a suspect, because yes, we did. With a fine-tooth comb. He's clean. He had nothing to do with it. He had a solid alibi when she disappeared."

"Does he know she's here? Because I can guarantee you, he will not be welcome in this house. Because, you know, he sounds so arrogant. He'll probably set her back even further," Seth said.

"No. We didn't stop to tell anyone but our boss before we boarded our flight. I don't plan on calling him either," Danny replied.

"That's harsh," Kat said with a hint of sarcasm.

"Don't care," Danny said with a firm tone.

"Neither do I." Kat smiled behind her mug as she took a drink.

Small crinkles formed around Danny's eyes, half amusement, half reflecting. Before he could respond, Logan stepped into the room.

"Is she okay?" Deke asked immediately, standing up from his chair.

"Yes, but no thanks to you. What happened to easing her into it?" Logan demanded.

"It was an accident," Deke muttered as he sat back down into his chair, the guilt evident in his posture.

"I don't care what it was. She..." Logan let his body fall against the counter as he brushed a hand over his face. "She really is okay. She cried a little, but nothing too...nothing like last night."

Seth breathed a sigh of relief and leaned back in his chair as he had been sitting on the edge of his seat.

"What is she doing? Can I talk to her?" Danny asked, standing up like Deke had. But unlike Deke, he had no intention of sitting down. He wouldn't take no for an answer. Well, shit, why did he even ask?

"She fell asleep, so no, you can't talk to her." Logan's eyes held a challenge, daring Danny to argue, to walk past him and wake her up.

Tempted to initiate that challenge and maybe knock a

fist into the sheriff's face, he could feel it burning in his bones to take a step forward.

"Fine, I can wait. We were just talking about her boyfriend Richard," Danny said with a slicing tone, changing his mind at the last second. Only because Aubrey's face blurred into his vision.

Logan barely reacted except for a slight twitching of his jaw. "What about him?"

"Nothing. Agent O'Rourke was just explaining how much he despises the man," Kat replied before Danny could, receiving an annoyed look from him.

He never let anyone get the best of him. "Kind of like any man my sister dates. I also said that." Instead of eyeing Logan with the warning, he kept his glare on Kat, unsure of the reason.

"Well, besides what we went over in my office earlier, did something else pop up about him that makes him a suspect? Or was it just talk?" Logan asked.

"Just talk. Are you sure she's okay?" Seth asked, getting up with his mug and walking it to the sink.

Logan gave him a weak smile as Seth clapped a hand on his shoulder, waiting. "She'll be okay."

Seth nodded and headed for the fridge. "Who wants pizza? You have some cardboard pizzas we can just toss in the oven?"

"Doni's..." Kat rolled her eyes. "I mean, Aubrey's cake is cooking in the oven. I should check that, actually. Why don't you order some instead, Seth?"

Seth nodded again as he walked to the sliding door and stepped outside on the porch. Danny found it amusing he didn't even think to ask everyone what they wanted. He assumed the food was more of a formality than a necessity.

He wasn't that hungry, and he imagined no one else was either.

Kat grabbed the potholders near the sink to check on the cake. Logan moved away from the counter and approached the table. "You two are welcome to stay here. My house isn't huge by any means, only a three-bedroom house, but I do have two spare rooms."

"How do you have two spare bedrooms available? Where in the hell does my sister sleep?" Danny asked, standing up again.

"That's a simple answer. With me. And she will until she says otherwise. Not you, but her."

"What kind of sheriff takes advantage of a victim like that?" Danny asked, his fists clenching, just waiting for the opportunity to hit him. The audacity of this man to touch his sister like that.

"Hey, buddy, she's not a victim. She escaped on her own. She's a survivor and her own hero, so watch what you say. My brother would never take advantage of anyone. Just wait until the sun goes down. Just wait until he says he needs to leave for some official business and watch her react to it. You just wait and see. My brother has done nothing but support and help her. So if you're planning on using those fists, you better expect to punch a woman as well because I'll be jumping into the fray," Kat said as she propped her hands on her hips with a potholder dangling from one hand.

"I'm finished talking for the night about everything. We can go toe-to-toe tomorrow. I only came out here to let everyone know she's okay. I need to go back to the bedroom in case she wakes up. Like my sister said, when it gets dark out, and I'm not there, she doesn't take it too well. We even sleep with the door open. She feels confined otherwise. I'm really surprised she sleeps in the bedroom instead of the living room like I offered, the openness, the space, the feeling that she can breathe without fear."

Logan took a short breath and stepped closer to Danny. "You don't have to like me. You don't have to cooperate with me about the case. But please believe my words about your sister. She ran out of the room tonight, not because she couldn't handle what was said, but because she's scared of you."

That made Danny waver in his stance. His fists crumbled as he backed up. "She's scared of me? But I—"

"Not in the sense you're thinking. She can't remember you. She looked at you as Agent Sumnter said you were her brother, and nothing. No recognition. She feels horrible inside and is scared of what you'll think of her. That you'll hate her. I guess I was wrong to hold the information back from her because she took it fairly well. The only thing she is really struggling with is the fact she can't remember you, and you stood right in front of her. Keep that in mind when you have the urge to hit me. I'm the one that stands between you two right now." With those parting words, Logan turned and walked away.

Damn, if the sheriff wasn't right. He did stand between him and his sister. Instead of feeling more anger, he felt nothing but pure anguish as he dropped down into the chair.

15

THE MELODIOUS CLICKING of the door shifted Aubrey's eyes from the serene landscape to her right as Danny walked over to her and gestured at the empty chair next to her. "May I?"

"Of course. I'd like that."

"Sure is quiet out here, nothing like Tampa," Danny said, sitting back while stretching his legs.

"I like the quiet. At least, I like the quiet when I'm looking at something beautiful like this." She bent forward, pointing toward the edge of the woods. "Look, it's Brownie. He's back."

Danny squinted, not that it was too far to see, but a habit he formed whenever he looked at something with interest. According to Deke, anyway. She had no idea since she still couldn't remember anything about him.

"The rabbit? They name the wildlife around here."

She sniffed her nose lightly and sat back as she shot a glance at him. "I named him."

"I didn't mean it in a rude way."

"Well, then you shouldn't say it in such a way." She

crossed her arms and shifted in her seat. “Why don’t you like Logan?”

“The sheriff’s fine.”

“Is this normal? You lying to me?” she asked, watching as Brownie bounced around the yard, something he enjoyed doing since she first saw him.

“I’ve never lied to you, Aubs, never...until now, I guess. I can’t really say why I don’t like him. Let’s just say I’ve never liked any man that you had an affection for. Including Richard.”

“I don’t want to talk about Richard.” She wrapped her arms tighter around her chest and focused harder on Brownie. “He’s a good man. I wouldn’t be where I am without him.”

“Who, the sheriff? You escaped on your own.”

“Maybe I did, but I’ve wanted to escape within myself, and he just won’t let me. He pushes me, yet is so gentle. I know you don’t like me sleeping with him, but...” She finally looked at him. “The first night...I fell asleep on the couch in his cabin. I think he was worried, or who knows what his thoughts were, but he laid a pillow and blanket on the floor near me and fell asleep, too. I woke up screaming, fighting, and fell off the couch. He was right there to make the nightmares disappear. I asked him to sleep near me after that. Then, it was me who asked him to sleep right in his arms, and then it was me who...do you get the picture? Logan’s been nothing but a gentleman. If I ask, he normally gives. I wish you’d be a little nicer to him, that’s all.”

His eyes clouded over with sadness, but he managed to surprise her once again. “I can try. For you, Aubs.”

“Thank you. It’s not much to ask.”

They sat in silence. Aubrey watched Brownie as she tried hard not to dwell on the fact that three days had gone by with no memory, no flashbacks of the man sitting next to her. He would share stories here and there, call her by her nickname Aubs, and any other little thing that he hoped would prompt recognition that he was her brother.

But nothing. She felt doomed to live in a shortened memory life until she died. She thought at times she was meant to wash all those old memories away and start a new life.

His partner, Deke, tried his best as well. But unlike Danny, who had a permanent morose expression, like a dark cloud hovered above him, Deke was all smiles, friendliness, and good-natured humor. She saw him nudge Danny a few times, probably telling him to knock it off. She understood her brother's disposition. He was disappointed and discouraged, and she had no one to blame but herself.

Logan, through everything, stood by her with strength and understanding. When she needed an ear, he was her sounding board. When she needed to cry, he offered a shoulder. When she wanted to vent her frustrations with the lack of memories, he gave her encouragement that it would all come together in time.

Not once did he give his impression about her brother. Not once did he display a rude attitude toward her brother, at least in her presence. Not once did he try to sway her one way or the other concerning her brother. She appreciated it, but it upset her as well. What did he really think of Danny?

And Danny could get downright obstinate with Logan, spewing harmful words that she imagined he didn't do before she disappeared. Logan would look at him, his muscles twitching a bit in his cheeks, but no words would leave his mouth. Not like Kat's.

Kat wasn't one to mince her words or hold back. Logan normally didn't respond to Danny because Kat never gave him a chance. She would jump in Danny's face telling him where he could shove his attitude. Aubrey almost found it comical if it weren't her fault for all the tension filling the house.

"Can we talk about something, Aubs?" Danny asked, breaking up the silence.

"Sure. I like talking with you." She gave him a small smile, trying to express her apologies that things weren't going the way he liked.

"We haven't come up with any new evidence. Can't find this Wayne character, and his brother, Evan, still isn't helping. Without the truth, we can't lock him up for obstruction. We do think he's hiding something, though."

She sighed, shaking her head with understanding. "And it's killing Seth. He just broke up with his girlfriend, you know, and now he's losing his best friend. It's just not right."

"Right."

His tone didn't indicate he cared about that at all, but she did. Seth almost felt more like her brother than Danny did. What would he say to that?

"So, Deke and I have, maybe, a few more days here. Our boss is going to make us come home soon. The case is going cold and stalling. But don't think that means I will stop. I'll never stop looking until I find the bastard who hurt you."

Her face lit up with delight, thinking how much he sounded like Logan. "I know. It's okay if you don't. I understand how difficult it's been. We can just move on."

"Moving on. That's what I want to talk about. I want you to come home with me to Florida. That's where your home is, your job. I think you still have a job. I'm sure if you walk back into the school, they'll give you your job back."

Just like that, joy was replaced with panic. Where was Logan? She whipped her head to the sliding glass door and saw him in the kitchen near the coffeepot. His back pierced her eyes, but just seeing him made her feel slightly better. Not by much, but enough to calm her racing heart a beat or two. "I ca...can't—"

"Aubrey, please, don't just say no." He started to reach for her but stopped when she leaned away from him. "I won't force you. Look, I know the sheriff means something to you. I'm not trying to diminish that. Honestly, I'm not. I may never like the men you date, but I never try to get in the way. That's the truth. But this is different. Maybe being in your old surroundings will help with your memories. Maybe it will all click. You won't know if you don't try. That's all I'm asking. Just try."

Her eyes swung back to Logan, who had turned around and finally caught her look. At first, he smiled tenderly at her, but he must've sensed an agitation from her because his brows fell into a frown and his feet moved forward an inch, stopping just as quickly. He pulled a tiny grin out and gave her a small wink, still giving her the option to make her own decisions. So understanding. How could she possibly leave him?

"Please, Aubrey. I'm not saying you have to forget about the sheriff. Just come home for a while with me. You're my sister. I promised Dad that if anything ever happened to him or Mom, I would take care of you. I have failed miserably at that so far. I'm trying to make it right. You belong in Florida," Danny said with a firm tone.

She slowly turned to him. "Why can't you call him Logan? I know he's the sheriff, but must you refer to him like that all the time."

His expression remained like steel as they stared at one another.

"I can't promise anything, Danny. I'll think about it." She

couldn't stand the look on his face, so she turned to the yard, searching for Brownie, searching for something else to take over her mind. Her eyes hit the woods, the trees standing with elegance, a whispering breeze speaking to her. And suddenly she knew what she had to do.

"Did you hear me, Danny?" She could barely control the excitement and the terror bubbling through her.

His face had lost the chiseled stone look. Now, nothing but emptiness glared back. "Yeah. I was just helping you look for Brownie. That's what you were doing, right?"

"I was. I guess he left. He uses a lot of energy running in the yard."

She smiled at him for the Brownie comment. Perhaps she was too hard on him at times. But when he talked about Logan the way he did, she just couldn't tolerate it. Logan was her world. Danny would have to learn to accept that.

"I'm going to grab a coffee. I'm sure we're going to head out for the day soon. Who's staying with you today?"

"Kat."

His attempt at hiding his annoyance was horrible. "Well, have fun, I guess."

"MORNING...LOGAN."

"Good morning. How's Aubrey doing?" Logan asked as Danny walked over to the coffeepot. He wished he could beat the answers out of him. He saw the terror run over her face outside.

"Fine. Are we ready to leave soon?"

"Yeah, I just want to say good-bye to Aubrey first. Kat just got here. Why don't you say morning to her as well," Logan said, a slight twinkle in his eye as he did.

He knew those two couldn't stand each other. Thank goodness for his sister stepping up and saying the things he really wanted to say. Because if some of those nasty words came out of his mouth, Aubrey would start to hate him.

He walked past Danny, resisting the urge to push him in a childish manner and stepped outside. Aubrey glanced at him and stood up from her chair, falling into his arms with an urgent frenzy.

"I wish you had more vacation time. What I wouldn't do to just sit on the porch at the cabin and watch nature pass us by," she whispered into his chest.

"We can go to the cabin any time you want. Vacation is never a problem when it comes to you." Logan kissed the top of her head as he inhaled her sweet essence. "Everything all right?"

She lifted her head and grabbed a kiss. "Yep. Danny was just talking to me. He asked me something."

His heart picked up its pace, but he tipped the corner of his lip up soothingly. "Yeah, what did he ask?"

"If I would go home with him when he finally leaves."

His smile wanted to falter, but for her sake, he maintained its perfect position. A boyfriend, a close friend, hell, even a husband, he would've fought tooth and nail with. But family. He'd never get in the way of family. His family was important to him. Everything to him. He knew how much Danny cared for Aubrey. Otherwise, he wouldn't be the jackass he was half the time, or all the time, really. A part of him would wither and die when she left, but he would never hold her back. Not for family.

"He cares about you. He loves you." Logan kissed her lips, opening her mouth with the tip of his tongue, and took a bit of her sweet essence as a memory he could cherish when she was gone.

"I told him I would think about it. I'm not sure I can leave you, Logan," she said, breaking from his lips as she rested her head against his chest.

He squeezed her tighter, enjoying the warmth that seeped into his bones. "I'm not sure I want you to, but you have to do what's best for you, honey. Don't let it be because of me. Do it for yourself."

"Stop always being so reasonable. Demand I stay."

"Aubrey, I—"

"Hey, you ready to roll, Sheriff," Deke said, popping his head out of the sliding door, unaware of the serious conversation going on.

Logan leaned down and kissed her neck. "We'll finish this conversation later." He let her go reluctantly and turned toward Deke. "Ready if you guys are."

"We are. Bye, Aubrey. Have a good day with Kat," Deke said with a wink and popped his head back inside the house.

Logan started to walk away when Aubrey grabbed his hand and yanked him back for a kiss. She clung to him with a sort of desperation he didn't understand. Then it sunk in. She'd made her decision. Instead of dwelling on the heartache already settling into the pit of his stomach, he kissed her back with all the vibrancy his heart could muster.

"Bye, Logan," she said against his lips, lightly biting his bottom lip before pulling herself away.

"Bye, honey. I'll call you later. I—" He kissed her one more time, hard, yet with tenderness. "Bye."

She sighed deeply at the pain she saw in his eyes as he walked away, then kicked her leg in the air with irritation at his stubbornness not to beg her to stay. Always looking out for her and her feelings. Well, she was feeling a lot right now, that's for sure. Why couldn't he see those true feelings? The blinding terror of leaving his home, his arms, his comforting presence. Could she handle a night alone without him? She couldn't even cope properly when the sun disappeared unless he was near. Would her brother be enough to get her through that fear?

She plopped back down on her chair, brooding. That's how Kat found her.

"Geez, don't put on a happy face for me." Kat stretched her legs, crossing them at the feet as she leaned back in the chair and raised her head to look up at the sky.

Aubrey took in her relaxed posture, but the tired wrinkles around her eyes told her Kat was as affected by the recent events as everyone else. Nobody could escape the tension, the stress, the worry of it all. Not until she remembered everything.

"Danny asked me to go home with him. Logan said to do what was best for me."

Kat trailed her eyes from the brilliant blue sky to Aubrey's lost expression. "That would make me frown, too. What are you planning to do?"

"I don't know," Aubrey said with a shrug.

Kat chuckled, slapping a playful hand on her shoulder. "Girl, you're still using that damn phrase. Do I have to go back to calling you Doni?"

Aubrey pierced her lips in a gentle smile. "I do kind of miss it, actually. It feels more a part of me than Aubrey does. I still don't know who I am, Kat. I'm surrounded by my brother and his memories, by Deke and his friendship, yet I don't know them. I know you. I know Logan and Seth. That's what I know."

Kat shook her head as she raised her eyes back to the sky. "You have time to think about it. Maybe Logan won't come right out and say it, but I will. I hope you stay. I'll also understand if you go. Knowing who you are is important. I'm sure your brother made a good case why it's best to go with him."

"He did."

And for the next hour, they sat in silence, watching the morning slowly pass them by. Aubrey imagined they thought about the same things, or maybe not. Everyone had problems. A normal person tried to solve their own problems. She hadn't tried that. She was sitting back, curled up in her cocoon of safety, and watching as everyone else tried to solve it. No more. She needed to take her turn. Right now sounded like a good time to start. If only she could muster up some bravery.

"Can you help me with something, Kat?"

Kat opened an eye, peeking over at her. "Love to. If I sit here any longer with my eyes closed, you might start hearing some snores."

Aubrey chuckled, flexing her fingers over the chair railings to calm down. "You have to promise not to tell Logan."

Kat sat up straight, turning her whole body to Aubrey as her brows dipped. "You're not gonna leave without saying good-bye, are you?"

"I'm not leaving, but I want to do something and I can't without your help. I suppose I could've tried and left you here sleeping, but I want you to come with me."

"I don't like the sound of this. What are you talking about, Aubs?" Kat said, using her nickname for the first time.

"I need...want to go...I have to..."

"The answer's no. You can't even say what you want to do." Kat stood up and took a deep breath.

"I have to go back." Phew! She finally said it.

"So you are going to leave without saying good-bye to him? That's not right, Aubrey. That's just plain mean."

Aubrey jumped out of her seat and pointed a finger in Kat's face. "Don't you call me mean. I said I wasn't leaving."

"What the hell does I have to go back mean?"

Kat stared at Aubrey for a brief minute, then stumbled back. "For the love of—oh, hell, no. We are not going there. Absolutely not. Logan would kill me if I did that." Kat shook her head as she moved away from the longing in Aubrey's eyes.

"Please, Kat. I have to." Aubrey's eyes lit up with panic but dimmed with strength.

"No. It's out of the question. Not gonna happen. Nope. Sorry." Kat shook her head with vivacity. "It's not happening, Aubrey."

THE CONSTANT DRIP-DROP in his ear did nothing to soothe his nerves. Not that he figured it would. But just one little thing to keep his mind off the knowledge that Aubrey was leaving him had to work. Otherwise, he would become a broken man—right in front of her brother.

He watched solemnly as the other two men, who he wanted to hate with a passion, and Derek, organized everything they had collected for the case. It wasn't the first time they organized. Danny had a nasty habit of rearranging things frequently, insisting that a new fresh look could give them something they didn't see before. He agreed with him to an extent, but figured it was more nervous energy on Danny's part than anything else.

Logan heard the coffeepot weaning down. He turned around, waited another thirty seconds before he grabbed the pot and poured coffee for everyone. He hoped it was suitable for everyone's tastes considering Charlotte decided to give him the silent treatment after he still refused to speak to Bolt and boycotted making the coffee. He really did miss her special brew she could concoct, but not enough to say something to one of his own deputies.

Bolt was just eager, excited, and looking for his chance to shine in the light for once. He knew how that felt. He had that same surging energy when he worked down in Minneapolis. He didn't anymore. If he couldn't trust his own people, he was screwed. Plain and simple. So, he trusted Bolt.

"Coffee's ready. Where are we starting today?" Logan asked, turning back to meet their gazes. Enough brooding. Time to get in the game and worry about his heartache later.

"Damn if I know. We've been over every inch of that forest, possible suspects, and the evidence when she was abducted, which wasn't much. I feel like we're nearing the end. Coldness is creeping in." Deke shrugged, grabbing his cup from the counter, and sipped with a grimace. "I'll make the coffee tomorrow."

"Little too much today? Sorry, my mind is everywhere." Logan walked over to the table. "Did you call down to the lab in Minneapolis this morning? What did they say about processing the dress?"

Deke took another sip, obviously not caring how horrible it tasted. "They said they'd try to push it up for us by a week, but that's the most they can do. They're backlogged horrifically. That's exactly how the beautiful woman's voice put it, too. Horrifically. Even with us calling, pulling our FBI weight, it didn't work like we wanted it to. Like I said, the best she can do is a week."

"Better than nothing, I guess," Logan murmured as he continued to scan the table. Why couldn't one small piece of evidence pop up? Any little piece would do.

Surveillance video photo stills from the grocery store across the alley where Aubrey had last been seen before she disappeared. Photos, text messages, and emails from Aubrey's phone that so far were useless in pointing them in a good direction. They found no enemies, digging deep into her comings and goings. She generally got along with everyone. She was a fifth-grade school teacher and had a few run-ins with disgruntled parents, but no incident that would set a parent off to the extreme of kidnapping.

Danny did say she could produce talons on occasion, but not mean enough for someone to nab her off the street. Deke was the first to voice the concern that it could be connected to one of their cases. Some crazy criminal they locked up looking for revenge. Targeting Aubrey instead of them.

Thankfully, they grabbed all of their work they gathered from the initial investigation before they flew to Minnesota. The list compiled contained their most recent and most violent cases. They ranged anywhere from rapists to murderers to armed robberies. But the most disturbing were a few of the human trafficking cases they worked. They generally stuck to the violent crimes, only helping on occasion with a trafficking case. But Derek was quick to point out the inconsistencies concerning why the trafficking cases just didn't fit. Why take her and lock her up for three months underground in the middle of a small town in Minnesota that most people have never heard of? It just didn't make sense. Everyone agreed.

"Maybe if we would've received a call sooner, we'd have better luck...in all aspects of this case," Danny said with a harder edge in his tone that Logan hadn't heard before.

Logan looked up from the rim of his cup, biting back a nasty comment. Danny deserved it. But his heart couldn't handle it. That's all he needed. Having to explain to Aubrey how he and Danny managed to get into a physical altercation. And it would be physical. The looks he received, the sharp words, all indicated Danny was just waiting to pop him a good one. That would never happen. Not if he could prevent it.

He chose to ignore Danny's comment without a comeback of any kind. It wouldn't matter what came out of his mouth anyway. Apparently, no one else found it necessary to comment either.

"I say we focus on this rapist case from six months ago you had. Just his picture is creepy. It's a really good sketch the artist managed to capture from the victim," Derek said, holding up the sketch. Black and gray pencil etched across the paper, a scraggly beard with beady eyes and a long scar dragging from his left eye to the corner of his lip.

Logan swallowed hard before he answered. "She wasn't raped."

Deke and Danny quickly looked at him. Derek also glanced at him and nodded. "I know that, Logan. But this victim...she says he held her for three weeks before he even touched her...you know, touched her. Beat her a few times, too. It sort of matches what happened to Don...Aubrey, besides the rape part, of course. That's all I'm saying."

"Why the difference in time then? He held out only three weeks on this victim before raping her. Why would he wait three months with Aubrey?" Deke asked, throwing the idea around the room.

"Are we sure she wasn't?" Danny mumbled.

"I'm positive." Logan didn't look at him, just took another sip of coffee.

"Did you have a rape kit done?" Danny asked.

"No, but—"

"Then how in the hell do you know my sister wasn't raped? What kind of damn sheriff are you?" Danny banged his hand on the table, shaking some papers near the edge.

"I'm the kind that had to calm a frantic, scared woman who freaked out anytime I mentioned calling a doctor. She...the look in her eyes, the terror...I can't describe it. She wouldn't listen to me. She wouldn't cooperate. To calm her down I told her it was fine, she didn't have to go, use my bathroom to clean up. She couldn't even manage that. I had..." Logan blew out a breath as the urge to turn around and walk away consumed him. "I had to help her myself. I saw every inch of her bruised and beaten body, and she wasn't raped. It was dumb, I know. Evidence probably washed down the drain, but that wasn't my concern at the time. My only concern was to calm her down. I know you despise me, Agent O'Rourke. Why don't you get it out of your system and hit me already?"

Danny's anger flowed like a raging river, his heavy breaths like rough currents. "I told Aubrey I'd be nicer to you."

Logan released a strangled laugh. "Yeah, you've been doing a wonderful job of that. I get it. Appealing to her senses so she graciously walks out of my house with you without a backward glance. Don't worry, Aubrey, I like the sheriff, you can see him again. Is that the kind of bullshit you've been feeding her? Once you have her tucked away in your domain, I'll never see her again, will I?"

"If I have my way, no," Danny replied matter-of-factly. "Especially since you touched my sister the way you did. She could've been raped. She should've seen a doctor."

"She's terrified of doctors. The mere word doctor puts her in a panic," Logan shouted.

"Bullshit!" Danny slammed his hand on the table. "She's never been terrified of doctors. Hell, she's dating a damn doctor, Richard, or did you forget she has a boyfriend, Sheriff?"

"No, that can't be right. Logan's right. She freaks when she hears the word doctor. You have to be extra careful around her not to mention it. Kat's even been trying to get her to the clinic, see if she can get over that fear, or see why she's scared. She can't even entertain the notion of going to the clinic. I can't imagine she'd date a doctor," Derek said, glancing between the two. Both men stood, breathing heavily, fists clenched, just waiting for the first sign the fight would begin.

"That doesn't make sense. Danny's right as well. Richard is a doctor. They've been dating for five months, that doesn't include the three months she was gone," Deke said.

"You're sure he had nothing to do with her abduction?" Logan asked.

"Oh, now you're questioning my abilities?" Danny asked, disgusted.

The anger swirled around the room, making the air thicker than a foggy night on a deserted road. The dam holding them apart teetered on the edge of bursting. Just one more word to push them over.

"No, just confirming because otherwise I can't fathom why she would date a doctor, and yet, be so terrified it puts her in a panic that I hate witnessing. I don't want to fight with you, Agent O'Rourke. I really don't. I just want what's best for Aubrey."

"We cleared him. He had a solid alibi that night. He was at a dinner meeting with the hospital's board of directors. He hasn't left the state since her abduction. I don't see how it could possibly be him," Deke replied.

"I don't like it." Logan ran a tired hand over his face. "Do you have a picture of him?"

Logan didn't want to know what he looked like. He didn't even want to think about another man dating Aubrey before him. But he had this sudden need to see what he looked like. They talked about Richard, brief comments here and there, but never in depth about the guy. He wished he would've known he was a doctor a few days ago. It looked like some pieces to the puzzle on why she was afraid of doctors were starting to fall into place.

Danny pasted a nasty grin on his face but held his words. He shuffled through the pictures until he found one with Richard in it. "Here. Aubs took this herself with her phone. They were at a charity function about a month before she disappeared. He's the guy on the right. The other guy is a colleague of his...Dr. Antonio Sparks."

Logan suppressed the urge to yank it out of his hand. He stared at the picture, eyeing Richard with the eyes of a sheriff. Clean-cut, hair smoothed to the right and swept back a little, a smile that spoke of money and eyes that shined at the camera-holder. His suit fit his frame perfectly, with a silk handkerchief adorned in his breast pocket. At least, Logan assumed it was silk. The guy appeared to ooze money by the way he dressed and stood with such impeccable posture. The other guy, Dr. Sparks, shared the same alluring persona.

When he was finished glaring at the photo, his eyes turned into a man in love. He wanted to rip the photo into shreds.

Then his eyes started the squinting habit Danny loved to perform.

Derek must've noticed. "You see something of interest, Sheriff?"

"I'll be damned. I think I just found a connection between the good doctor and our wonderful town. She has no memories. The word doctor sends her in a panic. Whether you want to admit it or not, Richard is involved. And now I'm beginning to know how," Logan said, handing the photo to Derek.

"Care to explain," Danny said dryly.

"Holy shit. I see it. Now we just need to find him," Derek said, handing the picture over to Deke instead of Danny, who stood closer to him.

"The guy lurking in the background, near the window. That's Wayne Barten. Doesn't show up anywhere for two years and suddenly he's at a fancy charity function. Same one Aubrey and Richard are at. I'd bet my life on it that Wayne took her on the order of Richard. Why? I don't know yet. But I know it's true," Logan said.

"You just want it to be true, so she doesn't go jumping back into his arms," Danny spat out.

"And you're ignoring the fact because you missed it from the beginning," Logan shot back.

Deke slammed the photo onto the table. "Enough! Both of you."

He looked at Danny with a wicked eye. "Knock it off. Think like a federal agent and not like a brother right now. You're just being a jerk because you feel guilty. Hell, I feel guilty. I've been working her case just as hard as you have and I missed this. Sheriff Caldwell has nothing but Aubrey's well-being at heart. He cares about her more than *dick* here did." Deke slammed his finger over Richard's face to emphasize his point.

He quickly threw his head at Logan. "And you, you're just egging him on. I know you're trying not to, but try harder. It only fuels his anger. No matter how idiotic Danny acts and what he says to Aubrey, you shouldn't worry, even though I know you are. I see the way she looks at you, the way she acts. She's not going to write you out of her life. If any of us should be worried in this room, it should be me and Danny."

"You're right, Agent Sumnter. I apologize for my behavior. I care about her, and I have a strong feeling she's going to go with you two. It just hurts thinking about it. I would never stop her. Family is important." Logan rubbed a hand over his mouth and chin. "I think we need to entertain the notion that Wayne and Richard know each other."

"I agree. I'll call some of our colleagues to question Richard. I also think we should go talk to Aubrey. I know she doesn't remember anything yet, but it can't hurt to show her this photo and see if anything springs to mind," Deke said, picking the photo back up.

"Why don't we grab some other pictures as well? Can't hurt for her to look at some of the pictures she took herself, whether they're a part of the case or not," Derek offered.

Danny didn't respond to anyone, but did start to gather the photos near him and shove them into a folder. Logan watched him for a second before he walked to the counter and set his coffee down. "Let's go. The sooner we solve this case, the better it is for everyone. Most importantly, Aubrey."

16

Bolt shut his phone off. Hell, yeah. The pride in the sheriff's voice was well worth the effort. Just wait until the sheriff saw what he found. He knew his dogged determination looking for evidence would pay off. No way was he just a simple deputy.

What was wrong with wanting a little recognition now and then? He just wanted a bit of respect and awe the sheriff received. It's not like the sheriff did much. The county was too small to do much. Why did the sheriff ever leave the city? Such opportunity sitting at the tips of his fingers. Soon, he'd head off for the city and wow them with his abilities.

He stepped around the tree, grinning like an idiot. He sensed some hostility from Charlotte, although, for the life of him couldn't figure out why. He didn't do anything wrong. Played everything by the book. The sheriff must think so since he didn't say anything to him.

Wait until he could shove this evidence into Charlotte's face. She wouldn't have anything to gripe about then. She always complained about other people being nosy busy-bodies when she was one of the worst. She was nothing anyway, in the grand scheme of things. Nope, this was all about Aubrey.

He leaned against the tree, taking in the forest's beauty and his brilliance as he waited for the sheriff. The look on the sheriff's face would be worth everything. Tapping his foot on the tree's bottom, with a little pitter-patter tune on his thigh, he couldn't stop picturing how excited the sheriff would be.

He was no dummy, though. Alert and ready for action. When he heard the twig snap to his left, he backed away from the tree with a smile. Oh, the excitement was about to rise in intensity.

"Change of plans. Bolt found a backpack in the woods. He's pretty sure it belongs to Wayne. It's not far from where Aubrey was held. We have to check it out," Logan said, putting his phone back on his belt.

"You know, I heard Charlotte grumble a bit about him. Are you sure he knows what he's doing? We've been out there the last few days, and suddenly he finds a backpack," Danny said skeptically.

Logan gritted his teeth as he mustered up some patience. "Please don't knock down any of my deputies. Ever. If Bolt says he found something, he found it. End of story. I plan on checking it out." Logan looked at Derek. "You have an opinion?"

"Nope. Just like you said. Bolt found something, he found it," Derek said with a shrug.

"I'll go check it out. Why don't you head to my house and talk to Aubrey about the pictures? What do you two want to do?" Logan asked, giving Deke and Danny a look, more so Danny that just dared him to say another word about one of his deputies. He was sick and tired of hearing the doubt. Bolt may not be the world's greatest deputy, but he tried.

"We'll head with you. Backpack could indicate Wayne's in the area. You might need backup." Deke clapped Danny on the shoulder and guided him to Logan's vehicle.

"Fine," Danny muttered, shaking off Deke's hand.

"Call me right away if she remembers something," Logan said to Derek, who started walking to his own vehicle.

"You got it. Good luck," Derek said, raising his eyebrows as he eyed Danny.

"Yeah, thanks," Logan mumbled and pulled open his door.

KAT LOOKED BEHIND HER, trying to refrain from placing a hand on her heart. "Did you hear something?"

"Shouldn't I be the one who's supposed to be all jittery and jumpy?" Aubrey asked, looking behind Kat, eyeing the woods around them. "I don't see anything."

"This was a horrible idea. I can't believe I caved."

"Because you're an awesome friend. I have to do this. I just have to, Kat. Logan refused the first time without even thinking about it. I need my memories. You just don't know." Aubrey turned away, taking in the big steel door. "It looks heavy. Moment of truth."

Kat grasped her arm as she started to bend down and grab the handle. "I seriously don't know about this. I don't think you should go in there. This is worse than a horrible idea. This is...I don't know, catastrophic."

Aubrey clutched Kat's hand as she managed a smile that

she hoped portrayed her bravery and not the complete dread that filled every pore in her body. "Really? Catastrophic? What's with the words 'I don't know?' Isn't that my line?"

This entire adventure would've been impossible without Kat. It had taken a lot of pleading on her part to get Kat to agree. They had both been around as Logan and everyone else talked about this place, its exact location, how deep into the woods it sat, the complete isolation that gave the madman plenty of freedom.

Aubrey had no clue how to get to it, even hearing from Logan's lips himself where it was located. But Kat knew exactly how to get to it and where to find the keys to a four-wheeler. She would've tried to brave it on her own had Kat denied her, and Kat probably knew that as well. That's why she finally caved.

"This isn't funny, Aubrey. You have no idea how you'll react. What happens when it all comes flooding back, and you drop into a catatonic state. Geez, Logan would hate me and never forgive me. I'm not sure I'd forgive myself. I really don't think you should go down there."

"You're always telling me to face my fears. Like the clinic...seeing a do-c-cter." Her smile never wavered, despite the wavering of her words. "I'm doing this. You can't stop me."

"You can't even say a simple word without stuttering," Kat said harshly as she dropped her hand from Aubrey's arm and backed up.

"But I said it. That's progress."

"Then let's do slow progress. Let's go to the clinic. Show me you can handle that first."

"No." Before Kat could stop her, she reached for the

handle and pulled. "Damn, this is heavy. Help me, Kat." She turned her head. "Please, Kat."

Kat rolled her eyes and pushed Aubrey to make room. Aubrey tightened her hold near the handle's top, Kat's hands directly below. Together they tugged on the door, grunting and using their feet as leverage.

"Wow, I feel like I need to work out more," Aubrey said between breaths, letting go of the door as it slammed to the other side.

"We'll start a workout regime together. Hell, I'll take a run through the woods right now. Let's go." Kat started running in place, twisting in the other direction.

Aubrey rummaged through her backpack she tossed on the ground and produced two flashlights, flicking the switch for one of them. "Kat, we're doing this." She tossed the other flashlight at Kat.

"I want to hate you right now. I'll go first."

Aubrey's arm stopped her in her tracks. "No. This is my journey. You can come down there with me, but I go first."

"You're brave. You're strong. Congratulations. No need to prove it anymore."

"I get why you're acting like this. And it's okay. I need my memories, Kat. I may be standing in front of you, I may sleep happily in Logan's arms, I may enjoy the talks with my brother, but I am still lost and hidden away from all of you. I won't be truly whole until I get my memories back."

"I could keep going back and forth with you, especially arguing about the words you just said." Kat sighed heavily, flicking her flashlight on. "Lead the way."

Aubrey shined her light into the deep hole, cringing at the darkness that gaped at her. Swallowed whole already and she hadn't taken one step yet. Kat breathed heavily beside her, and she knew right then if she delayed any longer, Kat would get her way and they would leave.

With slow, shaky movements, she carefully climbed down the stairs, letting the darkness consume her. The light trailing ahead did nothing to keep the darkness from entering her mind, almost screaming for Logan, before she clamped the urge and kept moving forward.

When her foot hit the bottom step, she swung her light back and forth hitting two walls rather quickly. Confined. Way too confined. The hallway, barely four feet wide, crushed her. She could feel the walls closing in, and she hadn't taken one step. She just had to push back.

First step.

The walls inched closer.

Second step.

Another inch, another breath, trying to escape.

Third step.

The walls were next to her arms. Her lungs struggled for air.

Fourth step.

She dropped her head between her knees as the walls suffocated her. A hand on her back made her straighten up instantly. "I'm fine. I'm fine. Just needed a breath." Blocking out the black swirling around her, the damp air that crawled down her throat, she picked up the pace.

There's nothing to worry about. You're safe. You're not alone. The walls can't hurt you. The darkness can't take you away. Your name is Aubrey. But who are you?

She repeated that each time her foot connected with the ground, propelling her forward.

"Going slow you freak me out. Going fast is just as freaky," Kat muttered.

"We're almost there."

"Shit, are you remembering stuff?"

"No, I just feel it." Another step forward. "Or maybe just hoping."

Kat almost tumbled into Aubrey when she abruptly stopped. Kat's flashlight fell to the floor, making a clunking sound that reverberated throughout the dark mass that surrounded them. She grabbed Aubrey's shoulders, peering over her. "What is it?"

"A door."

Aubrey tracked her light to the right, landing on another steel door that stood open. Its invitation to enter rang loudly.

Who are you? You're Aubrey, but who's that?

Her light stayed on the doorway for a few seconds as she contemplated, for the first time, if she should really walk in there. Did she want to know what happened in that room? Did she need those memories? Her new memories were so beautiful she almost didn't want to tarnish them with old, ugly memories.

You're safe. You're not alone. Find out who the real you is.

"Do or die," Aubrey said as she took a step forward.

"Really, must you say those words? Down here, in the darkest of the darkest place I've ever been."

Aubrey glanced at Kat, her light still shining through the doorway. "Are you scared?"

"Are you making jokes? Is this really a time for jokes?"

"I would say this is the one time we need it."

"You have a point." Kat let loose a fake haughty laugh. "That better?"

Aubrey chuckled and shook her head. "Much better." She didn't stop to contemplate anymore, to wonder what the hell they were doing; she moved forward again and stepped through the threshold.

Kat walked in behind her and stood close to Aubrey as she shined the light around the room. The room wasn't large—four walls with no windows. A set of chains hung directly in front of them. She took her time covering each wall.

Dirt. Dark. Damp.

She swung the light again, deciding she couldn't ignore the chains.

"Remember anything? 'Cause if you do, you are taking it more remarkably than I thought," Kat whispered.

"Nothing."

"Hmm, well, that sorta sucks."

Aubrey looked at her and smiled. "I'm so glad you're here. You've made this easier. I can't believe I still can't remember."

"You can't force it. Take another look around." Kat gestured with her hands, finally realizing she didn't have her flashlight. "Crap. Can you shine the light in the hallway? I dropped my flashlight when I ran into you."

Aubrey nodded and turned around. She stayed in her spot, more afraid to move than anything else, and shined her light into the hallway. Kat ventured through the doorway and bent down. She stood there a moment, making Aubrey shiver with unease.

"Everything okay?"

Kat glimpsed at Aubrey, producing a small grin, then brought her head forward again. She grabbed her flashlight and shined it down the hallway. "I think we have a problem."

The worry, the concern, the slight agitation in Kat's voice had been there the entire time, but never fear. Until now. "What sort of problem?"

"Can't you smell it? Because I can see it. Unless it's a

ghost. A ghost I can handle. Yeah, let's go with a ghost," Kat said, her words spilling out rapidly.

"A ghost? Kat, what the hell are you talking about?" Aubrey rushed to her side, grabbing hold of her shoulder as she shined her light down the hallway toward their exit. "That's smoke, Kat. Not a ghost."

"Are you sure? Wouldn't a ghost be better? Because otherwise we are screwed. Someone just started a fire, and we're trapped, Aubrey."

"Who would do that? I—" Aubrey's lip froze.

"Come on, Aubrey." She pushed Aubrey inside the chamber, grabbed the door, and slammed it shut.

"What are you doing?"

"The smoke will kill us before the fire even hits us," Kat said as she grabbed her shirt and started unbuttoning it. "We have to stop the smoke from getting in."

"How do you know it's a fire? Maybe it's just..."

"Aubs, there wouldn't be smoke if there wasn't a fire. Come on. Help me block the bottom of the door." Kat yanked her shirt off and stuffed it against the door where it met the floor.

Aubrey had a buttoned shirt on as well, considering she was wearing clothes borrowed from Kat. Her hands started to unbutton the shirt, shaking while she struggled to hold the flashlight at the same time. The light slipped from her fingers when she made it to the second button. It landed with a loud clanging sound. Shuffling in a circle, the dark was suddenly too much for her, accompanied by the frantic sounds of Kat shoving her shirt against the door. She knew the moment she found the flashlight as her foot connected with it. Losing her balance, she flung in the air and landed with a hard thud.

"Aubrey!"

KAT SCRAMBLED on her knees to where Aubrey fell. "Hey, are you okay?"

No sound echoed back as Kat screamed her name again.

"Shit!" Kat rushed back to the door where her flashlight lay and shined it on Aubrey. There was a small dark patch on the side of her head. She gently turned her head. A slow trail of blood ran down her hair. "Shit, Aubrey. Wake up. Don't do this to me."

Kat turned her head back to the door. The smell of smoke had reached inside the room. Her shirt wasn't enough to cover the entire door. A small portion still allowed the smoke to enter. It would take longer, but they could still be in trouble from smoke inhalation. Who was she kidding? They were in deep shit regardless. No one knew where they were.

She looked at Aubrey one more time, knowing she couldn't jostle her and take her shirt off. But she needed to cover the rest of the door. She would probably die down here anyway. Was her modesty that important?

She groaned as she yanked off her undershirt and scooted back to the door, shoving her other shirt to cover the rest of the door. A sigh of relief left until she glanced up. Damn. The top of the door. A small crack of smoke filtered through.

"Oh, hell."

17

Derek knocked again on the front door of Logan's house for the third time. Yanking on the doorknob wasn't helping. The damn thing was locked. It didn't make any sense why they weren't answering. Kat knew better than to leave the house, especially without telling Logan where they were going.

Logan would flip a lid when he found out. He heard about the near heart attack Logan had when they left the sheriff's office to have a simple lunch down at the diner. Logan wanted to know where Aubrey was at all times. Just the thought of her back in the lunatic's hands who hurt her put him in a panicked rage.

Derek knocked again, pounding harder, thinking about the conversation he had with Kat about her first slip-up. She had, in her Kat-like way, told him to mind his own business. He kindly responded the sheriff was his business. He didn't consider Logan *just* the sheriff. He was his best friend, someone he couldn't imagine not confiding in when he needed an ear, or a buddy to grab a beer with after a long day of dealing with crap. If Logan was upset, he considered it his job to correct the matter. Or maybe he just wanted a chance to speak to Kat. Not that she ever saw him as more than just Deputy Graham, at your service.

He gave up knocking, circling the house to make sure they weren't lounging on the porch or in the yard somewhere. Aubrey liked the fresh air, enjoying nature at its finest. If she chose to stay, which he sincerely hoped she did for Logan's sake, he knew she would fit right in around these parts. If you decided to stay and put up roots, you normally had some sort of affinity to nature. Lucky, Minnesota had a lot to offer with its small population, ranging forests, and beautiful hiking trails.

He walked back to his truck with agitated steps when he failed to find them anywhere on the property. He would try saving Kat's butt from a severe reaming by attempting to call her first. If she didn't answer, well, he could already picture Logan's reaction.

DANNY HOPPED OFF THE FOUR-WHEELER, stretching his legs as he glanced around the woods. He saw the backpack he assumed Deputy Bolten had found, but oddly enough, he didn't see the deputy. "Where the hell is your guy, Sheriff?"

Logan inhaled a patient breath, perusing the area in the same fashion Danny had. "I'm not sure, Agent O'Rourke." He eyed the backpack, then glimpsed at the four-wheeler that belonged to Bolt. "Bolt? Where are you? Bolt?"

"Maybe he pursued Wayne?" Deke said, walking up to the backpack. He opened it up and started to dig. "Survival and hunting gear in here. And damn, evidence to lock his ass up."

"What do you have?" Danny stepped closer to the backpack but still kept glancing around the woods.

Deke slowly raised his hand, holding a gold heart-shaped locket. "Aubrey's necklace. Same one she never took off for anything. Unless, of course, the bastard who took her snatched it off her damn neck." He stood up, clutching the necklace with pure rage.

Seeing the necklace, Danny almost dropped to his knees hyperventilating from the thought of Aubrey manhandled, hurt, beaten, and locked away, the picture too much for his mind to handle. His eyes caught the side of Logan's face, which stopped his downward fall. He looked just as shaken as him. And now wasn't the time for them to act this way.

"Well, we need to—" Danny stopped when Logan's phone started to ring.

"It's Derek," Logan said, looking at the screen as he put it to his ear. "What's up, Derek? Did she recognize anyone in the picture?"

Deke stood up and walked to the four-wheeler. He grabbed an evidence bag from his belongings when he turned toward Logan's worried voice.

"What do you mean they aren't there? Kat never called me. Did you try calling her?" Logan asked. He started to pace, walking from one large tree to another.

Danny and Deke watched his agitated pacing, sharing a look of concern. Deke quickly bagged Aubrey's necklace while Danny tried to focus his eyes on their surroundings other than Logan's distressed posture. Why in the hell was Deputy Bolten not waiting for them? Why weren't Kat and Aubrey at home?

It felt like déjà vu when Aubrey went missing the first time. His slight worry when Deke called saying Aubrey wasn't at home when she said she would meet him there after work. The panic that built when they found an officer who found her phone on the sidewalk on her usual trek from school to home. The complete and utter devastation that consumed him when he realized that his sister was truly in trouble. He couldn't deal with that again. Never again. He just found her.

"Okay, we have a problem," Logan said as he slipped his phone back on his belt with a trembling hand. "Derek says they aren't at my house. He tried calling Kat's cell with no answer. She wouldn't ignore him. He called Seth, and he has no idea where they are. He hasn't seen or talked to either of them this morning. He even called Charlotte, who said she hasn't seen them stroll through town. And she would've seen them."

"All right, let's not panic. This isn't the time for that. Let's think rationally about this first," Deke said, combing a hand through his hair.

"Where the hell is your deputy?" Danny shouted.

"Don't go blaming my deputy. He has nothing to do with why they are missing." Logan took a step toward Danny as Deke walked into his path.

"I told you two to knock it off, and I meant it. Fighting does not solve the issue." Deke trained his eyes on Danny, knowing he needed the warning more than the sheriff did, then glanced at Logan. "Would your sister go somewhere without telling you? Maybe they're just having some fun and couldn't answer the phone yet."

Logan dragged a hand down his face. "Possibly. Kat knows how I would feel about it, but my sister, if you haven't noticed, has a mind of her own."

"Oh, I noticed," Danny muttered.

"But she also knows the possible danger," Logan continued, ignoring Danny's small interruption, "and I just don't think..."

"What? What are you thinking?" Deke asked when Logan's look of worry transformed into pure panic in a blink of an eye.

"I just thought of something, and it makes sense."

"Share it with the group, Sheriff," Danny said, his tone emphasizing the word sheriff in an insulting manner.

Logan whipped his head to Danny, his face blank of any expression. "You asked her to go home with you. She told me she would think about it. She said she didn't know if she could leave me."

"Wow, impressive, you're attempting to put doubts in my mind that she won't come home with me," Danny said, shoving his foot against some leaves.

"You're so dense sometimes. I get why. I would probably act that way if something happened to Kat. Listen to my words, Agent O'Rourke. You probably appealed to her by using her memory. Old surroundings and all, her memory will come flooding back. She feels trapped now, rushed."

"Oh, I get it." Deke turned around and eyed the woods that lay in front of them. Colorful leaves hung in the trees, some blanketed on the ground, a slight breeze blowing throughout, knocking the limbs together giving off a mellow sound. "They came out here."

"Aubrey knows I would never bring her out here. Kat sure in the hell isn't going to call me telling me where they're going if that's the case. I have a strong feeling they came out into the woods so Aubrey could get her memories back. She wants to go down into that room." Logan twisted away from them. "Shit!"

"Well, that's one place I don't want my sister going. We

can agree on that," Danny said, staring in the direction Deke had.

Logan slowly glanced back at them. "It's not far from here. Let's check it out and then try to find Bolt. He could need our help."

No one responded except to get back on the four-wheelers for the new destination. Logan grabbed the backpack first, throwing it in the compartment on the back of his four-wheeler.

Danny followed the sheriff, hoping the entire time that Kat and Aubrey were safe. Hoping like hell Aubrey didn't go down there.

KAT SAT on the dirt floor, leaning against the wall near Aubrey, holding her flashlight up at the top of the door, and watched as the smoke filtered in with small waves. A few minutes had already gone by as she contemplated how in the hell she could stop that. Her mind kept telling her it just didn't matter. They were trapped. A fire sat in their pathway to freedom.

She jumped from the slight moan to her right. "Aubrey."

"Kat," Aubrey whispered with a mumble. "What happened?"

Kat helped her sit up and scoot to the wall. "You tripped and fell. You're bleeding, and you'll probably need stitches, well, if we make it out of here, that is. How are you feeling?"

Aubrey reached for her hair and pulled her hand away stained with blood. "I think I'm feeling great."

"Sarcasm is not helpful."

"Did I say it sarcastically?"

Kat looked at her and saw a smile touch her eyes. "We're trapped, Aubrey. Smoke's coming in from the top of the door."

Aubrey glanced at the door and back at Kat just as quickly. "At least I'll die knowing who I am."

Kat's brows raised in astonishment. "Are you telling me that fall knocked some memories into you?"

"Not just some, but all of them. I remember my brother and his undying love and protection. Especially when we lost our parents. His patience and understanding when I acted like a bratty teenager. I can't even tell him now how much I appreciated him being there. I never told him that." Aubrey exhaled a short breath as she took in Kat's appearance. "Why are you sitting here with no shirt on? It's chilly down here, and you're sitting in just your bra."

Kat pointed at the bottom of the door. "I didn't want to jostle you by trying to get your shirt off. I had to take both of mine off, but it's only stopping the smoke from coming in on the bottom."

Aubrey unbuttoned her shirt and handed it to Kat. She only had on a tank top now. "Put this on. It's cold down here."

"Does it matter? No one knows we're here and the smoke will get us sooner or later."

"Just take it."

Kat rolled her eyes and handed the flashlight to Aubrey as she threw the shirt on quickly. Aubrey swung the light around. Her memories were back. Kat couldn't tell yet if that was a bad thing or not. "Are you okay? I mean, stuck down here with your memories back."

Aubrey nodded. "You know, they flash through my mind, but all I see is Logan. His arms around me telling me it's okay and he can't hurt me anymore. It just feels like a bad nightmare and not a horrible memory I endured."

"I'm glad you have Logan. I can see he's been good for you and is helping you in this struggle, but you've also been good for him."

"I'm glad, too. I just wish—" Aubrey paused as she reached for the other flashlight lying by her feet. "Here, hold this light to the ground."

Kat grabbed the light and held it in place like Aubrey suggested. "What are you doing?"

"Do you think the fire will reach us? Do you think the door will keep us safe?"

"I don't know. Hopefully we're dead by then. I don't really wanna burn alive. I'd rather fall peacefully asleep from the smoke inhalation. Shit, I don't even know if you go peacefully."

"Kat, stop. Logan will check on us, maybe he'll figure out we came here."

"And if he doesn't..."

Aubrey started digging into the floor with the flashlight's handle. "Then I'm going to leave him a message, pointing him to the man he needs to arrest. As long as the fire doesn't reach us and burn the message away."

Grayish-white smoke billowed in heavy waves as they weaved their way through the dense woods. Logan gunned the four-wheeler to the top speed as he raced to the fire that sparked near the door that he knew with all his heart held Aubrey and Kat. Derek's four-wheeler sat not far from the door. Derek wasn't here, but he knew Kat and Aubrey had taken it.

Damn it! Kat knew better than to take Aubrey here. He flickered a glimpse at Danny, who raced beside him, Deke hitching a ride on the back. He nodded at Logan as his four-wheeler kept pace.

Logan barely shut the four-wheeler off as he stopped in front of the building flames and jumped off quickly. "Fire extinguisher in the back."

Danny hopped off the machine, grabbed the lid, and glanced at Logan. "And you just happened to have this with you?"

"Backwoods country, Agent O'Rourke, you're prepared for anything. Help is not a minute away out here. Most times you're on your own." Logan rattled the explanation out, shooting his extinguisher at the door's base.

Danny yanked his extinguisher out while Deke ran for Derek's four-wheeler and the fire extinguisher waiting for him. Danny juggled with the nozzle when he saw Deke slow his steps and pull his weapon out of its holster.

"Movement to my twelve o'clock. You guys get the fire, I'll pursue," Deke hollered as he went into a run toward the figure that ducked behind a tree.

Danny and Logan nodded but didn't respond. Danny turned his attention to the fire and sprayed near the big white birch tree close to the entrance. After what felt like hours, they extinguished the fire.

"That's Kat's backpack and Derek's four-wheeler. They're here," Logan said, nodding his head toward the backpack that lay torched next to the door.

"Please tell me they aren't down there." Danny pointed at the door and bristled at the notion.

"Not only do I think they're down there, I think we have more fire to contend with. Smoke's filtering through the door's sides. Do you smell the gasoline? And the canteen lying over there. That's not Kat's." Logan pointed toward the door's left side. Half-covered by a pile of leaves was a camouflage-colored canteen about the size of a dinner plate.

"Do you happen to have a long metal stick to pry open the door? It's probably too hot for us to touch." Danny's sarcasm didn't go unnoticed.

"Yep." Logan was already pulling out a tire iron from the compartment before Danny could finish his question. "Can never be too prepared."

"Of course not," Danny said dryly. "Slide it through the handle. I'll take one end, and you take the other."

Logan did as Danny instructed. They started to lift, awkwardly positioned, exerting with all their strength. The heat slammed into his face, knowing Danny could feel it as well as they both leaned back as far as they could while simultaneously lifting as close as they could. Together they managed to pry open the door. They immediately jumped back as the door slammed to the other side and more white smoke floated into their path with a touch of sparkling orange flames.

They grabbed for their extinguishers and started blowing out the flames. The entrance was too narrow for two large men to walk down side by side. Logan went in first, pausing on the second step. "Grab that third extinguisher, just in case."

He didn't wait for a response. Slowly, he made his way down the steps. The heat coming off the walls burned his throat. God, Kat and Aubrey. What were they suffering through? The fire wasn't given ample time to grow, but that didn't mean they weren't seriously injured. He suddenly wished for the cool, damp air from the last time he ventured down into this pit of darkness. He made it to the bottom of the stairs when his extinguisher started to sputter and wean down to nothing.

"Move, I got it now," Danny said, almost shoving him to the side.

Logan stepped back, trying hard not to touch the walls. He dropped his extinguisher and grabbed the extra one Danny held in his left hand.

They slowly made their way down the darkened hallway, coughing and pounding out the fire each step they took. When the last flame died, their pathway suddenly filled with a swirling smoke that burned their eyes and clogged their throats. They couldn't see a damn thing anymore without the fire lighting the way.

Logan set the extinguisher down and grabbed his phone from his belt, cursing violently that he forgot to grab a flashlight. "Do you have a flash…" Logan coughed, "…light or is the light on my phone all we have?"

Danny threw his hand in Logan's face, coughing roughly. "Got my phone light, too. Let's get 'em and get the hell out of here."

When they got to the door, almost passing it from the swarming smoke, Danny tore off his jacket and jerked the door open. The fire had simmered about 15 feet away from the door, but they couldn't risk the chance the handle was too hot to touch. The smoke rushed in behind them.

"Aubrey!" Danny dropped to his knees by her side, lightly grabbing her head.

"I'm fine, Danny. Just a scratch," she replied, coughing at the same time.

"Kat, are you okay?" Logan pulled her up with one hand and embraced her in a fierce hug.

"Better…much better. Aubrey needs stitches. Get us out of here," she whispered close to his ear.

Logan looked at Aubrey, who gave him a reassuring smile, but made no move to leave Danny's helping arm. He smiled back and gestured his head toward the exit. "Let's go."

Logan took the flashlight offered from Kat and led the way, holding onto her the whole time. Unharmed and safe. He couldn't ask for anything more. Aubrey had a small injury to her head, but what had been flashing through his mind the moment he saw the flames was far worse. The images still wouldn't dissipate.

He wanted so badly to pull her into his arms, but the look on her face, and more importantly, on her brother's face, stopped him. He didn't have the right to, not like Danny did. He could feel himself losing her each step they took.

The moment they breached the fresh outside air, Kat dropped to the ground and had a coughing fit. Logan knelt beside her, rubbing her back soothingly. "You're all right, Kat. I got you."

"Aa-uu-brey," she said between coughs.

Logan glanced over to where Danny helped Aubrey lean against the four-wheeler, her wound piercing to the eyes in the bright sunlight. Her hair was matted against her head, a slow trail of blood running down her ear to her neck and down the side of her arm. Before Logan could tell Danny a first aid kit was in the four-wheeler's compartment, a shot rang out.

Danny immediately shoved Aubrey down to the ground. "Shit, Deke."

Logan glanced in the direction Deke had run off. "You two stay here. Did you see anyone before the fire started?"

Kat tried calming her coughs and reached for her ankle. "No. Nothing. We'll be fine. Go check it out." She pulled a small gun from her ankle holster and flipped the safety off. "We're good, Logan, go."

"Be safe, come back to me," Aubrey said, grabbing Danny in a quick hug, then pushed him away.

His eyes widened, startled, then he grinned before putting his game face on and followed Logan into the fray.

"How come you have a gun?" Aubrey asked, resting against the four-wheeler and glancing over at Kat, who scooted closer to her.

"For this exact reason. What you said to Danny..."

"My way of telling him my memories are back. Probably dumb going into a gunfight, but just in case, you know, something happens. There were a lot of times I hated his job. Still do, actually. We lost our parents in a blink of an eye. One day they were there and the next, just gone. I wasn't prepared to lose him too by some crazy asshole with a gun or a knife or hell, even one time he walked into a situation that had a bomb. I got into the habit of always telling him 'be safe, come back to me.' He's all I have, Kat."

Kat grabbed her hand. "Wrong. You have me, Seth, and seriously, how can you not count Logan? You have all of us. They'll be fine. I should really check that cut on your head."

Kat jumped into a crouch as she made her way to the back of the four-wheeler. The crunching of leaves suddenly sounded from the other side. She put a finger to her lips to signal to Aubrey to keep quiet. Aubrey nodded, keeping a look out in front of them. They would be royally screwed if that happened.

"What do you see?"

Kat flickered a wary eye at her. "We might have a problem."

LOGAN AND DANNY caught up to Deke, who was hiding behind a big tree. He motioned for them to come near him quickly and low to the ground. Logan managed to get behind a large tree to his left while Danny took cover against a tree on his right.

"I have Wayne Barten pinned down behind the crop of trees to our two o'clock. He has nowhere to go but up the hill behind him or straight toward us. He fired one shot at me before hiding. Hasn't moved since," Deke whispered, taking another quick peek toward Wayne.

"What do you think?" Danny asked Deke, giving a questioning eye to Logan as well.

"We come in hot, you two flank to the sides and I'll go straight for him." Deke shifted his head between the two looking for confirmation. "He fired one shot, but if he really wanted a fight, he would've kept on firing. He's either scared shitless or low on ammo."

"Give us a moment to get in position. I'm ready when you are." Logan saw Danny shake his head in approval. He started to turn and make his way to the left when Danny spoke directly to him.

"Don't get shot. Aubrey would hate me."

"Watch it, Agent O'Rourke, you might make me think you like me." With those parting words, Logan continued to his destination hoping like hell nobody got shot, especially Danny. He imagined Aubrey would hate *him* for it. Guess they both were in a rocky boat.

Logan took a straight path for about twenty feet, then

quickly veered to the right making his way toward the hill. He crouched behind a tree at the hill's base and peeked his head around the tree, gun held tightly in his hand and close to his chest. Danny stood directly opposite of him peering from behind a tree about the same distance Logan had taken. He pointed a finger to something. Logan finally made out Wayne sitting against the bottom of a tree staring into his lap. Logan couldn't make out what he was staring at, but he assumed a gun.

He glanced back at Danny, who nodded once, his eyes trailing to Wayne. He nodded back and flicked his eyes over to Deke, who gave him a simple signal and took off at a sprint toward Wayne. Logan and Danny followed just as quickly.

The sudden sound coming from all directions had Wayne lifting his head and shifting to find where the noise was coming from.

"Sheriff's Department! Don't move. Drop the weapon," Logan hollered as he continued running straight for him, his weapon out, and aimed for Wayne if he decided to make a move.

Wayne jumped up, raising his gun as he did.

"Drop the weapon. You're under arrest," Danny shouted.

Wayne started to move forward, glancing back and forth between Logan and Danny, completely forgetting about the movement behind him. He brought his gun a little higher and pointed it directly at Logan.

"I suggest you lower that weapon slowly and put your hands behind your back. I don't take kindly to people shooting at me. There's no telling what I might do," Deke said in a calm voice as he held his gun against Wayne's head.

"You pigs can go to hell." Wayne kept his eyes trained on Logan and spit a huge loogie in his direction.

Logan didn't flinch. "The only one going to hell is you, Wayne. Like father, like son."

"Mr. High and Mighty, Logan Caldwell. You think you're better than everyone. You wanna shoot me? Go ahead. You got nothin' on me."

"I have enough. I'll see you go down for touching one hair on her head. In fact, I think if I...you know what? My threatening words won't scare you. So you can either lower the weapon or I'll shoot you."

Wayne laughed heartily. "Shoot me, Sheriff. I'll just shoot you at the same time."

"I've changed my opinion about you. You're just plain dumb," Deke said, pressing the gun harder to his head. "Do you not feel this gun?"

"You won't shoot me. You pigs can't."

"Well, you don't know us very well. You have to the count of five to lower that weapon or I will shoot you. I haven't decided where I will either," Danny said through clenched teeth as he kept focusing on the gun centered on Logan's chest.

Wayne laughed again. "Let me count for you, pig. Because the minute you shoot me, I'll shoot the big bad sheriff." More haughty laughter escaped his lips. "One... two...three...four...fi—"

A lone shot rang out in the air.

Wayne collapsed to the ground, clutching his leg. "You shot me, you bastard!"

Logan grabbed for Wayne's gun that fell from his grasp the moment his downward fall occurred. He checked the weapon quickly, flipping the safety on, and tucked it behind his back.

"Can't call me a liar, that's for sure." Danny grabbed Wayne's arm and hauled him to his feet. Wayne hollered from the pain. "You're under arrest for kidnapping, assault, attempted murder, and yadda yadda yadda. You get the picture, don't you, Mr. Barten?"

"You damn pig. You shot me. I'll have your badge." Wayne struggled to stand and collapsed again from the pain.

"The only thing you'll have is your girlfriend back when the door closes in your face. Did you have a favorite? Any requests for cellmates? How much do you like it up the ass?" Danny taunted him as he cuffed Wayne. He yanked him back to his feet and shoved his arm to start walking.

"You fuc—" Wayne screamed in pain as Deke jerked on his other arm to help him walk a little better.

"Watch your language, Mr. Barten. We don't appreciate name-calling. If I hear the word pig one more time... Oh, and don't forget, you have the right to remain silent. Unless, of course, you have forthcoming information about the kidnapping of Aubrey O'Rourke. Otherwise, I suggest you remain silent. I'd hate for another bullet to hit you," Deke said.

That quickly shut Wayne's mouth besides the frequent moans of pain as they made their way back to the four-wheelers. Logan walked behind them, watching with a skillful eye. Wayne Barten had been a troubled kid with a hot button that didn't take much to set off. He was now a grown man with years of experience in the criminal world. He didn't trust him. And he certainly didn't doubt that Wayne would have shot him. The hatred in his eyes. The same look his father carried.

Logan's mind played the scene over, especially the part where Danny fired his weapon. Shocking, to say the least. He couldn't decipher the why. Was it because the man who took Aubrey stood in front of him? Or because a gun was centered on Logan? He couldn't figure it out and wasn't too sure he wanted to.

Just then, Danny turned his head slightly and shared a look with him. An array of emotions filtered out. Logan nodded once, deciding he'd decipher what those emotions meant later. For now, a simple nod of thanks would suffice.

When they neared their destination, Logan went into a full-on run when his eyes landed on the scene unfolding in front of them.

"Shit. What happened?" Logan asked, kneeling by Bolt where Kat held a wad of gauze to his side.

"I'm sorry, Sheriff, I—"

"Shh, Bolt, don't talk," Kat interrupted. She gestured toward Wayne, who cried out in pain as they dropped him to the ground. "He surprised Bolt and shot him. He's lost a lot of blood already. He needs to get to a hospital."

"All right. Okay." Logan stood up, trying to calm his racing heart. "Let's get him onto a four-wheeler. We'll have to meet an ambulance at the road."

"I already called Derek, and he's on his way with reenforcements and an ambulance." Kat grabbed Bolt's hand and pressed it over the gauze. "Hold this tight to your side. Don't let go of it."

"M'kay, Kat. I can do that," Bolt muttered as his grip loosened somewhat.

"Bolt, hold it tight," Kat repeated, pressing harder, eliciting a deep moan from him. "All right, let's get him up."

Logan went to hook a hand underneath Bolt's arm when Aubrey stepped near them and almost lost her footing. Logan changed tactics and grabbed hold of her. "Sweetheart, you're bleeding, too." Without waiting, he lifted her at the waist and planted her on the four-wheeler right next to them. "You need to get to the hospital as well."

"I'm fine. Bolt needs more help than me."

Logan leaned in close to her lips. "Don't argue with me. Not now. My heart can't handle any of this, especially the blood trailing down the side of your head."

Aubrey nodded, giving Logan the reassurance he needed. He went back to helping Bolt stand up, struggling with Kat to carry him to the other four-wheeler when Danny stepped up and joined in. They managed to get him on the machine. His body, lacking the strength, started to lean over too much, almost falling off. Kat steadied him as she started barking orders.

"Logan, you ride with Aubrey. She needs her head stitched up. Agent O'Rourke, you ride with Bolt. Try to go gentle but fast. He needs a hospital ASAP."

"Who made you the boss?" Danny asked.

Logan had already walked away toward Aubrey. With one hand holding Bolt, Kat leaned into Danny's face. "Bolt needs a doctor, and Aubrey needs you *and* Logan. It makes sense for you two to go. I'll stay with Deke and help guard Wayne until Derek gets here. How about you try not arguing for once?"

"I just noticed how beautiful you look when you get angry." He backed away from her and hopped on the four-wheeler, grabbing Bolt's hand to wrap around his waist. "Hold on to me tight, Deputy. I'll get you out of here as quickly as I can."

"I'll t-try," Bolt muttered as his hand slipped from around Danny's waist.

He repositioned Bolt's hand. "Try harder, Deputy. You're going to be just fine."

Danny briefly looked at Kat before dragging his eyes to Deke, communicating with that quick glance that she had better stay safe. He had enough to worry about, and here he was, suddenly worried about this aggravating woman.

He started the four-wheeler and trailed after Logan as they made their way out of the woods.

18

DANNY PACED in front of the door, his agitated steps sounding throughout the hallway. He paused for a moment and glanced at Logan, who appeared just as agitated, but displaying it differently. Logan sat on a chair, his hands on his face, hiding his expressions from everyone. Not that anyone else could see him in such a disconcerted state. They were the only two people in the hallway. Aubrey sat on the other side of the door with the doctor.

Besides his worry for Aubrey, his mind couldn't get away from the fear he held for Deputy Bolten. It wasn't hard to think about him considering his shirt clung to his back from the blood loss the deputy endured. He had struggled the entire way through the woods, holding him upright. Before they made it to the road, he had passed out, thankfully leaning into his back in a decent position that he hadn't fallen off the four-wheeler. Derek apparently wasted no time calling for help as an ambulance pulled up simultaneously as they emerged from the woods. They loaded Bolt into the back and sped off to the hospital. Logan helped Aubrey to the truck, and they headed to Lucky's clinic where Logan called ahead to prepare the doctor for their arrival. Now they waited. And worried.

And Kat. He didn't want to think about her, especially since he didn't even understand why he cared about her in the first place. She drove him nuts most of the time. But she was safe. Deke had called him not too long ago. So his worry for her turned off. Somewhat.

His worry turned into guilt as he paced the hallway floor. Guilt for thinking the deputy had been involved in harming his sister.

"I'm sorry."

Logan dropped his hands and looked at Danny. "For what?"

"The things I said about Deputy Bolten. I hope he pulls through."

"Yeah, me, too. He gets a little zealous at times, but he's not a bad deputy." Logan dragged his hand over his face and took a deep breath. "In the woods...thanks."

Danny knew what he meant and shrugged. "That asshole had it coming." He resumed his pacing just to stop again. "You know, you make it difficult to dislike you when you're always so damn agreeable. I want to hate you."

Logan leaned his head against the wall. "I could ask why, but I think I already know the answer to that. I get why you hate me."

"See, that's what I'm talking about. I give you fighting words about hating you, and you're all common sense about it."

Logan lightly laughed. "Well, two reasons for that, I guess. First one, I just can't help myself. It irritates you, and I find immense enjoyment out of that. Second reason, Aubrey. I'll do anything not to hurt her. Snapping back at you would only hurt her."

"My sister...she's—"

Logan held his hand up. "Look, Agent O'Rourke, I'm not going to get in the middle of you two. She's your sister. That's all I need to know. You need her right now, and I know she needs you. Doesn't mean I won't miss her like hell."

Danny held his lips in a tight line. "You don't even know what I was going to say. You sound so sure she's leaving with me."

"Maybe I don't want to hear what you have to say. It can't be anything good."

Before Danny could give him a few more choice words, the door behind him swung open. Dr. Matthews stepped out with a smile. "Gentlemen, she's fine. Four stitches, but nothing else to worry about. No concussion, but it would be prudent to watch for the signs just in case. Dizziness, disorientation, severe headache, nausea, that sort of thing. Keep her wound clean and dry. And a good amount of rest."

"The smoke..." Logan started to ask as he stood up from the chair.

"Her lungs sounded good. Her throat is a bit sore and dry, but nothing to worry about. I think you two probably inhaled more smoke than they did. Perhaps I should take a look at both of you. Agent O'Rourke, is any of that blood yours?" Dr. Matthews asked, eyeing the large red stain covering his shirt.

Danny reached to touch it, then stopped himself. "No. I'm fine, Dr. Matthews. I just want to see my sister if I can."

"I suppose you'll deny me as well, Sheriff. You can go in there. It's about time I finally was able to see her again. Not how I wanted to see her, though."

"I tried, Doc. She didn't feel comfortable coming in, and

I hated making her. I know you would've made a house call whether we liked it or not," Logan said with a small smile.

"You know me well, Sheriff. I would have. I want to see her next week for a checkup. No negotiating. Either bring her in or I'm coming to the house. Let me get a prescription ready for her, and then you can take her home." Dr. Matthews walked away.

Danny walked into the room first, grabbing a hug from Aubrey without asking. "You do some of the dumbest stuff sometimes. Why do you make me worry like that?"

"Gotta keep you on your toes," she whispered, hugging him tightly.

He chuckled in her ear at the familiar words. So many times, she said that same exact thing after a reaming or two from him for one of her youthful escapades.

"I missed you, Danny. I'm so sorry."

He pulled away, holding her cheeks gently. "You have absolutely nothing to be sorry about. Not about what happened, not about your memory loss, just nothing. If anyone should be sorry, it should be me. None of this should've happened."

"It's not your fault, Danny. Not mine either." Her eyes left his and landed on Logan, who stood a few feet away, his expression indiscernible. "Logan...any word on Bolt yet?"

"Not yet." He took a few steps forward. Danny was kind enough to back away so he could grab a hug. "Are you okay, honey?"

"I'm fine, Logan. Really, I am. The bump on my head helped."

He pulled away in the same fashion Danny had, except

he grabbed her hand instead of her cheek. "What do you mean? Your memories are back."

"Yes, they are. All of them. That man...in the woods...he hurt Bolt. He's also the one...who hurt me."

"We found his backpack. Your necklace was inside of it. The one Mom and Dad gave you. We know already. We don't have to talk about it now," Danny said softly.

"But there's more, Danny." Aubrey squeezed Logan's hand hard, but she couldn't look at him. "It's about Richard."

"That bastard was involved. Is that what you're saying, Aubs?"

"I don't know." She shook her head as she closed her eyes to keep the tears at bay.

A soothing hand cupped her cheek. She leaned into the comfort, opening her eyes to Logan. "You're safe, honey. Whatever it is you want to say about him, just take your time."

She grabbed his hand from her cheek and placed it on her lap, fiddling with his fingers. "I don't know if he's involved with...with my abduction, but I'm pretty sure he's involved in some sort of criminal activity." She hesitated, not sure how to formulate the right words.

"Like the sheriff said, Aubs, take your time."

She glanced at Danny and gave him a wry smile at him calling Logan sheriff still. "A few days before it happened, I overheard him on the phone. It wasn't a happy phone call and the things he said confused me. I don't think he knew I heard him, but when he got off, he suggested we eat, and he would go grab some food around the corner. I didn't argue. The minute he left, I ran to his office and started searching through his stuff. I suddenly had a bad feeling about him and was trying to dispel my horrible thoughts. I was trying to prove myself wrong with what I heard. He hadn't been acting himself for the last month or so before that call. My mind just suddenly thought the worst of him."

"What did you hear, honey?" Logan asked softly after she stopped talking.

"I don't know. Just bits and pieces. Something about he was trying to get more and was having a hard time. It was all so confusing. It made a little more sense when I found a cell phone in one of his desk drawers. It kind of looked like a burner phone or something, I don't know, but I do know it wasn't his normal phone he used. That thing is glued to his hand. Anyway, I started fiddling with it and saw some text messages. All of the messages were in code, but I've been around you and Deke enough talking about work that I had an inkling what they were. I think he was talking about drugs." Aubrey still hung on to Logan's hand like a lifeline, but she couldn't look at him. Her attention centered on Danny.

"The good doctor involved with drugs. What kind?" Danny asked.

"Please, Danny, forgo your nasty attitude. I know you never liked him. Trust me, I don't like him anymore either."

"Sorry, Aubs. What kind of drugs do you think?" Danny asked again.

"I have no idea. I said the messages were confusing. I faked a stomachache when he got back and left right away. I went home wracking my brain trying to figure it out when it clicked with me. You remember that charity ball about a month before...before I..."

"Yeah, Aubs. I remember. I actually showed Sher...Logan a picture from that night and that's how we figured out Wayne Barten was involved. What about it?"

"I don't remember seeing him there." Aubrey pierced

her brows in contemplation, trying to think back to that night. "Anyway, I do remember hearing Dr. Roberts talk about some drugs going missing over the course of a few months. I don't remember what kind or anything...I am making no sense. I keep saying I don't know."

She hung her head down, the tears finally finding release. Utterly useless. She wanted to sink into the floor and disappear into hell. Even with her memories back, she couldn't provide proper information. I don't know, her favorite mantra, still spilling out of her mouth as if she knew no other words in her vocabulary.

Logan's soft hand slipped from hers. Then a warm embrace wrapped her up in a comforting cocoon. "Honey, please don't cry. You're doing just fine. I know where you're trying to go with this. And we don't need to talk about it anymore right now."

She couldn't respond. Her tears turned into sobs as Logan hugged her tighter, yet gently soothed her by delicately rubbing a hand up and down her back.

DANNY COULDN'T HELP but watch and think that it should be him comforting his sister, not the sheriff. Always the sheriff taking that job away from him.

Logan turned his head to Danny with a soft voice. "You had some agents pick him up for questioning, correct?"

Danny nodded and pulled his phone out. "No call yet. Maybe they called Deke."

"I suggest you call them and add a bit more information into the questions they should ask. Based on what Aubrey was saying, I'm going to guess he was stealing from the hospital and maybe supplying drugs to someone." Logan took a moment to kiss the top of her head and offer a few more soothing words. "You know, when I was going through Wayne's record, he had quite a few drug possessions and distribution going on. That could be the link on how he and Richard know each other."

Danny held a quick finger up for Logan to give him a second and continued to rapidly type away on his phone. "Just sent Deke a text. And I agree about Richard and Wayne. That's probably the connection. But why would Wayne be at that charity ball? He's not a man who fits that scene."

"Well, we can ask him now. Provided he tells us the truth, which I sincerely doubt. It's probably best I don't question him."

Danny glanced at Aubrey. Seeing her pain made his pain fresh and deep. He almost couldn't stand to see her like this. Yet, the good ol' sheriff looked nothing but calm. It made him wonder how often he comforted his sister in this same fashion. But the conversation was steering into territory he didn't want to have in front of her. "I have an idea why that's probably a good idea. Let's get Aubrey home. She needs her rest."

"Come on, sweetheart. Let's go home," Logan whispered as he scooped her into his arms and walked out of the room.

Danny followed closely behind, wondering what home Aubrey would choose in the end.

SETH KNOCKED ONCE on the door, then stepped back. Space. Except, no amount of retreating steps would give him the space he truly needed. He blew out a breath as he swiped a nervous hand through his hair, then tapped his foot in an agitated pattern waiting for the door to open. When it finally swung open, he had to resist the urge to throw a fist forward.

"Seth. What are you doing here?" Evan asked, holding onto the door.

"Can I come in?"

Evan shrugged and walked away with the door wide open. Seth took another breath and stepped inside, closing the door with more force than necessary.

"So I take it this isn't a social call?" Evan said, walking into the kitchen and grabbing a beer from the fridge. "Want one?"

"What I want is for my best friend of nineteen years to tell me what he's hiding, not a damn beer." Seth clenched his fists and forced himself to unclench as he waited for an honest answer for once.

Evan popped the cap and flicked it onto the counter with a twist of his wrist. "Guess you can leave then if you don't want a beer. Can't give you the other thing since I'm not hiding anything."

"Will your brother tell a different story?" Seth asked with a bit of cockiness.

"Is *your* brother the one who shot him?"

"Wayne shot Bolt. He's fighting for his life right now because he lost so much blood. He tried to kill Kat and Aubrey. Tried to burn them alive." Seth took a few steps forward and stopped before he fully entered the kitchen. "Why are you protecting him?"

"I'm not, you dickhead. Why can't you get that in your thick head? I'm sorry about what happened to them. Especially Kat. I know how you feel about your family."

"Do you remember when we were kids, and we took

your dad's shotgun out and did some target practicing in the woods?"

"Yeah." Evan looked surprised by the question for a fraction of a second.

"Do you remember when we got back, and you put the gun away just exactly the way your dad had it positioned before we took it out? And how he walked in just as we stepped away from the glass case?"

"Yep. Hard to forget. What's the damn point, Seth?"

"I'll never forget what your dad said right before he smacked you across the face. 'Boy, you can't lie to me. Your jaw ticks every time.' Right now, Evan, your jaw is ticking like a time bomb. Do you still wanna lie to my face?"

Evan's jaw tightened, making him look more menacing. He took a swig of beer and set the bottle on the counter. "You know where the door is, Seth. I suggest you leave."

"I'm not leaving until you tell me the truth." Seth crossed his arms. The longer he waited, the more Evan's muscle ticked in unison to the time spreading before them.

"Fine. I'll give you a truth. I love Stacy. I have for a long time."

"Did you sleep with my girlfriend?" Seth croaked out. Damn it, his worries had been right. He always thought he saw a spark in Evan's eyes when Stacy was around.

"She's not your girlfriend anymore. But no, I've never touched her. Why?" Evan grabbed his beer with a tense hand and took a long swallow, slamming it back on the counter. "Because you're my best friend and I would never do that to you!"

"Some best friend you are. Standing here in front of me telling me you love my girl—ex-girlfriend—just to dodge what you're hiding about your brother. You can't shift this conversation. You can't hide the fact you're lying. What is it?

I'll understand if Wayne threatened you. Come on, man. I know what kind of asshole he is."

"So, does that mean I have permission to ask her out?" Evan asked with a small smirk.

"You almost remind me of Wayne and your dad right now. A worthless, piece of—"

Seth went down hard when Evan's fist connected with his face. Seth touched his eye for a moment before he shielded another blow with his forearm. Evan pulled his arm back for a third punch, giving Seth enough time to wind his own arm and throw a punch back. Evan stumbled back but had a better grip on his stance and tried hitting Seth again. Seth moved his head just in time and threw another fist in Evan's face, this time, enough to get him off balance. Seth rolled his body and jumped on Evan, throwing another punch. Evan took a few before he got another blow across Seth's face.

They rolled around on the floor a few minutes, dodging blows, taking punches, and fighting like two strangers in a bar fight. Seth was the first one to scramble away and stand up, his fists hanging in the air, waiting for another attack. His heavy breathing mirrored that of Evan's as they stared each other down.

"I'm done fighting with you. In fact, I'm just plain done with you. Enjoy Stacy all you want, you asshole." Seth dropped his fists and walked away with a limp, slamming the door on the way out.

THE KITCHEN TABLE acted as a lifesaver in a mellow river, hoards of papers scattered all over its wooden body. Danny stood staring at a picture with glazed eyes when Logan walked into the kitchen.

"What's going on here?" Logan asked, eyeing the mess.

Danny dropped the picture. "How's Aubrey?"

"She's fine...I guess. Her head hurts, and she's tired. She just fell asleep, and I thought I'd check on what sort of progress we have. Do we have any progress? What is all this?" Logan walked closer and picked up the picture Danny put down. He stared in confusion at Aubrey in the picture. She was walking on the sidewalk, her phone pressed to her ear and a smile on her face. She looked happy.

"Well, this half is the stuff we were piling over this morning," Deke said, pointing to the papers on the left side. Then he gestured to the right. "This stuff we found in one of the pockets of Wayne's backpack. It looks like he was following Aubrey a few weeks before he grabbed her. That picture you have was taken around the corner from where she lived."

The picture fell from Logan's hand as if it burned him. "Did we hear anything back about Richard yet?"

Danny shoved a hand through his hair. "Yeah, he screamed like a little baby once our guys put a slight amount of pressure on him. It probably helped that they searched his car when they picked him up and found a bottle of oxycodone. Not prescribed, of course. They talked to Dr. Roberts, the same one Aubrey mentioned earlier, she heads the hospital's administration. She checked the supplies, and surprise, surprise, some oxycodone was missing."

"What did he confess to?" Logan asked.

"Stealing drugs from the hospital and supplying one of the gangs in the area. The Cheetahs. Talked to one of the guys in the drug division who said the Cheetahs are one of the fastest growing gangs in the area. I think they were trying to be funny when they named themselves because they take pride in the fact they are the fastest in the industry. Quick supply of drugs to even quicker distribution," Danny said, rolling his eyes at the lunacy of it all.

"And Richard, a doctor...what kind of doctor?" Logan asked.

"A cardiologist. Thinks he's a damn genius," Danny said.

"Fancy." Logan couldn't keep the sarcasm out of his voice. "So Richard, a prestigious doctor, takes to stealing drugs and supplying a gang. That makes no sense. Why would he risk his career over something like that? He doesn't sound like a dumb man."

"He's not. But he had a friend who needed painkillers and couldn't get them. Severe back pain, but his doctor cut him off. So he went to Richard, who wrote him a few prescriptions. Then Richard cut him off because he got a little nervous writing out illegal prescriptions. So his friend found the Cheetahs. He had a big mouth and mentioned Richard and how he would write him the prescriptions. Like Danny said, the Cheetahs pride themselves on a big turnaround with the drug supplies. They gotta get them from somewhere. So they paid Richard a visit, and he caved pretty quickly to write out prescriptions and steal oxycodone from the hospital. I guess a gun to the head can be pretty persuasive," Deke said with a shrug.

"I'm guessing the conversation Aubrey overheard was him trying to weasel his way out of getting more drugs for them," Logan said.

"Yeah, he's been trying for a while. Our guys asked if he knew Wayne. He said Wayne was one of their little lackeys they put on his tail to make sure he didn't veer off his job. Aubrey probably didn't see Wayne at the charity dinner that night because he wasn't there long. He showed up to put a little fear into Richard because he was late on his delivery. After Aubrey took that picture, Richard turned around and saw him. They stepped outside where Wayne had a few choice words and left. Richard delivered the next day." Danny glanced back at the pictures on the table, his eyes squinting in frustration.

"Did he confess to being involved with Aubrey's abduction?" Logan asked.

"No. He denies any involvement. He didn't start confessing about the drugs until our guys threatened charges of kidnapping, accessory, and all that good stuff," Deke said, leaning back in his chair. He waved his hand around the table, pushing some of the photos. "My theory is that Wayne saw Aubrey that night and something clicked with him. If you look closely, this photo here of Aubrey at the charity dinner, her hair is a darker brown with some highlights."

Deke grabbed the photo and handed it to Logan. Then he picked another one up and handed him that one as well. "This photo was taken a few days after the charity dinner. She got her hair done a day or two after the charity dinner, dyed it a lighter brown. All these pictures of her, her hair is the lighter brown. That's when he started following her around. These photos suggest to me that she became an obsession."

"Did he say anything at the hospital? Is he still there?" Logan asked. His main concern had been Aubrey. He hadn't left her side once since he brought her home from the clinic. And he was afraid to leave her alone. Afraid her memories would become too much. Afraid his time with her was slipping away.

"Besides calling us pigs and cussing like a sailor, nope. He asked for a lawyer. His dad showed up and started calling us pigs right along with his son. Said he was going to get the fanciest lawyer he could find, and his son would be out in no time. He had to be escorted out of the hospital because of his loose tongue. Wayne is currently spending the night. Another set of agents will escort him back to Florida tomorrow. He'll be wishing soon that Danny shot him dead," Deke said, glancing at Danny.

"Should've, that bastard," Danny muttered as he glanced down the hallway where Aubrey lay sleeping.

"I'm guessing that has something to do with the Cheetahs," Logan said.

"He dropped them without a word good-bye. They don't take kindly to that sort of thing. He let his obsession with Aubrey go too far. The minute he walked away from them, he signed his death warrant. I'm sure once they hear he's back in town they'll make a move on him. I can't say I really care," Danny said, sharing a look with Logan. Nope, he didn't care either.

"So, we don't need to do anything else? Case closed. I'm sure there are tons we could try to interrogate out of him and what he did to Aubrey those three months, even the reason why. But honestly, I don't want to know. I only want to know if she tells me, and only because it'll help her move on. That's all that matters. Who wants a beer?" Logan said, dragging his feet to the fridge.

"I'll take one. So will Danny. I think we all need to unwind and just enjoy this victory for what it is," Deke said as he started to grab all the photos and papers strewn across the table.

Danny took the beer offered from Logan's hand. He just twisted the cap off when the front door opened and slammed just as quickly.

"What the hell happened to you?" Logan set his beer on the counter and took a step toward Seth.

Seth waved him off and went straight to the fridge, pulling a beer out. He gently rested it against his eye for a brief moment, then twisted the cap and took a long swallow. After downing half the beer, he shut the fridge and turned around.

"What's all that on the table?" Seth asked, avoiding eye contact with Logan.

"Your eye is black and blue, your lip has a cut, and I'm pretty sure I saw a slight limp. So, I repeat, what the hell happened to you?" Logan said, his voice conveying no argument would be had.

Seth finished his beer in another long swallow and set the bottle on the counter with more force than necessary. "I saw Kat. She was upset. Derek reamed into her for taking Aubrey out in the woods. She told me everything that happened out there. I tried to stay and talk to her, but she kicked me out of her house. I have no idea what Derek said to her, but she was pretty upset...and hurt."

"Why would he be that upset? I can't imagine your sister did that to you. Did Derek for some reason?" Danny asked.

"Maybe you haven't had a chance to notice, but Derek likes my sister. He probably let her have it because the thought she could've gotten hurt scares the hell out of him. I know how he feels." Logan picked his beer back up and took a sip. "But I know Kat didn't bust up your face and neither did Derek."

Danny gave Logan a funny expression, but wiped it from his face before Logan could decipher what it meant.

"I had a chat with Evan. This is how it went." Seth turned around and grabbed another beer from the fridge.

Before he could twist it open, Logan's hand covered the

top. “Getting piss ass drunk isn’t going to solve whatever the hell is going through your mind. How in the world did you get into a fistfight with Evan?”

Seth shrugged Logan off and rotated the bottle in his hands. “He’s still lying to me about what happened to Aubrey. He’s still denying he knew something. We went back and forth, words got heated, and he punched me. I’m done with him.”

“Seth, we have nothing to suggest he had anything to do with it. Maybe he’s not lying,” Deke said cautiously.

“Have you talked to Wayne?” Seth asked, glaring at Deke. “Because I know when my friend is lying to me. I’m not an idiot.”

“Wayne’s not talking right now. If, or when he does, I’ll let you know if it turns out Evan’s lying to you or not. How long have you guys been friends?” Deke asked.

“Long enough to know when he’s lying.” Seth looked at Logan. “He admitted to loving Stacy. He’s the other guy. He’s the reason for all our problems, but he said he never slept with her. I believe him.” Seth looked back at Deke. “But I don’t believe a damn word when he denies knowing something about what happened with Aubrey.”

“Seth, I’m not condoning anything Evan said about Stacy, but I wouldn’t say he’s the reason for all the problems between you and her. I’ve told you before you need to be more open with her. You both are at fault in that relationship. Why don’t you just stay away from Evan for a while? It sounds like you both need a breather,” Logan said.

Seth’s hand tightened around the bottle. “Oh, I’ll be staying away from him because I’m done with him. Don’t talk to me about Stacy. I don’t want to hear her name ever again. You’re one to talk. You talk to Aubrey yet?”

Logan backed away as he set his beer on the counter. "About what? Because, yes, I do talk to Aubrey."

"Whether she's staying or not?" Seth demanded.

Logan resisted the urge to look at Danny as he took a short breath to calm down. "I can see you're still looking for a fight. I'm not going to indulge you, Seth. I'm not having this conversation in front of her brother. That's not even fair. Go home."

SETH WATCHED as his brother walked out of the kitchen, eyes straight ahead with no glance at Deke, and especially Danny.

"I don't have a huge problem with the sheriff like Danny does here, but that was a low blow, even I have to admit that," Deke said, as he took another sip of beer.

"Yeah, I know. I seem to do well at hurting my brother lately." Seth set his beer on the counter and started to walk out of the kitchen when he stopped in front of Danny. "Maybe he hasn't said it, but I will. He doesn't want her to leave. I've never seen him with any other woman like I have with Aubrey. He loves her whether he chooses to tell her that or not. Don't be an ass just like I was. Let her make her own decision whether she wants to stay." He continued toward the door, closing it with a quiet click for the first time that night.

Deke picked his beer up, taking another swallow. "He has a good point."

"Shut the hell up, Deke." Danny grabbed his beer, downing it in the same fashion Seth had as he glanced down the hallway with the weight of the world on his shoulders.

19

SHE INHALED the sweet aroma that she attributed to Logan and curled into him. His arm tightened around her waist and stroked the skin between her underwear and shirt.

"How are you feeling, honey?"

She tucked her head under his chin. "Better. My head doesn't hurt as much. How long was I out?"

"A few hours. Rest is good for you."

"Did you stay with me the whole time?"

"No, I stepped out for a bit. Richard's been arrested for stealing drugs and handing them over to a local gang in Tampa. Same gang that Wayne worked for. He hasn't said anything, but we have enough to arrest him for what he did to you. He can't hurt you anymore."

"I never worried he could. Not when I'm with you." She brushed a finger across his chest. "So it was just Wayne involved? He's the only one I remember walking into that room. I don't remember who grabbed me. It was so fast. One minute I was walking, and the next, I was grabbed from behind and knocked out. I woke up inside a trunk. I hate the dark now, Logan. I can't stand it."

"I know, sweetheart. It's not dark in here," he said, pointing to the bathroom where the light shined brightly, filtering into the bedroom. Then, he gestured toward the bedroom door. "Door's wide open. You're safe. Not confined. Never again."

"Any word on Bolt?" She traced another path across his chest, smiling at the slight shiver that erupted from him.

"He lost a lot of blood, but he survived surgery, and the doctors are hopeful he'll pull through."

"Good. I'm so glad to hear that." She circled another path on his chest, then stopped. "Are you mad at me?"

He grabbed her hand and pulled it up for a kiss. "Never. I know why you did it. I hate that you felt like you had to do it without me. I'm sorry I never even entertained the thought. I just have a hard time seeing you in pain like that. I'm glad you're okay."

"I was nervous that you were. Is Kat okay?"

"She's fine. Seth said she was upset with Derek because they had some words, but she'll be fine. I don't know about Seth, though."

"Why? What happened?"

"Are you sure you don't remember anyone else coming into that room? It was just Wayne?"

"Are you asking about his brother Evan?"

"Yeah. I am."

"He was never there. I saw a picture of him on Seth's phone, and I didn't recognize him. Will Seth be okay?"

He kissed the top of her head and caressed her hand. "Yeah, I think he will be. I worry because I can't help myself."

"Anything else you're worrying about?" she asked softly. "I don't like you worrying about anything."

Logan let her hand go and cupped her cheek as he

pulled her in for a kiss. She immediately pressed closer to him as her tongue swirled in unison with his.

She broke the kiss, murmuring against his lips. “I want you, Logan.”

“The door’s wide open, but I want you just as badly.”

She looked at the door, then stretched her neck a little more to give Logan better access to pepper kisses all over. “Close it, then.”

He nibbled on her ear. “Your brother’s at the end of the hallway. I will not risk his wrath by closing the door. I shouldn’t even risk what I’m doing now. The man doesn’t have a fondness for me.”

She pulled away from him and jumped out of bed.

LOGAN FROWNED. Just great. Without much effort, he upset her. She turned toward him when she reached the bathroom, a huge smile on her face. “I think I need help, Logan.”

“Help with what?” Maybe he hadn’t upset her. What was with the naughty gleam in her eyes? It wasn’t something he’d ever seen before. Perhaps this was her true personality coming out, her memories resurfacing and all.

“You’re the sheriff. It’s your job to find out what and then provide the help,” she said, raising her eyebrows deviously.

He hopped out of bed giving a quick peek at the doorway and followed her into the bathroom. She closed the door and flipped the lock, then put her back to the wall and grabbed his hands, pulling him into her body. “Your touch, since the first moment you ever touched me, soothes away every pain imaginable. No one else has that power like you do. Soothe me, Logan.”

He brushed a sweet path with his hands from her arms

to her cheeks, lightly kissing her on the lips. "If your brother—"

She kissed him hard. "He's been overprotective of me since the day I walked into his life as his dependent and not a sister. These last ten years, he's been more of a father than a brother. I won't lie. I haven't made it easy on him. If he has any gray hairs, they're because of me. But I won't let him get in the way of what's in front of me. No matter how hard he will try, he can't take this pain away. Only you can. You're making me a little worried here."

"About what? You have nothing to worry about. Of course, I want you. I always will. It just feels...a little wrong to do this with him in the house." He rested his forehead against hers, his breath a sweet kiss on her lips. "He hates me. I really don't want him to. I don't want there to be any tension for your sake."

"You make me worried that you won't fight for me. You said at one time that once I was in your arms you would never let go. It feels like you're letting go."

"And I feel like I'm losing you. I'm afraid of you walking out the door."

"I haven't walked out yet. Help me with this dilemma, Sheriff," she whispered, her lips brushing against his.

Logan grabbed the hem of her shirt and pulled it up. His hands slid down her arms, caressing the sides of her breasts as he trailed to her underwear, hooking his fingers on the band, and pulled them down in one sweet stroke. He grabbed a kiss, pressing into her as he ached to be inside her.

Her words tortured him. He never wanted her to worry about his feelings for her. He'd show her exactly how he felt. Lay his brand on every inch of her body. Although, he swore he already had. Except, he figured, the one thing that could sear into her heart.

He shoved his pants and boxers down, never once breaking the kiss that spoke volumes. It consumed him, tore at his heart at the deep frenzied need he sensed from her. He felt her pain, and each time his tongue touched hers, he zapped a bit of it away.

"I don't have any condoms in the bathroom. They're in my room."

She kissed his lips. "It's okay. I don't want a barrier between us anymore. Do you?"

He picked her up and gently eased her down onto his hard shaft. The moment he felt himself fully wrapped in her softness, he broke the kiss and held her completely still to savor the feeling of being committed to her in such an intimate embrace. He held her gaze as he pressed deeper inside her.

"Never worry about how I feel about you. I will never let you go. Ever. I did say that and I meant it."

He gently pulled out and back in as she grabbed him tighter around the neck and moaned in his ear. "You promise? Because that's not what it felt like."

"I was trying to be reasonable and fair. I'm done doing that. I'll never survive if you leave me." He started rocking her faster, deeper. "I love you, Aubrey."

She threw her head against the wall. He saw the slight pain etch across her face, obviously forgetting that she had a head wound. Bending his lips to her forehead, he tried to soothe her pain away as best as he could.

The ache slowly dissipated as he watched her eyes gloss over into bliss. He curled his lips into the charming smile he knew she enjoyed, bringing them to newer heights as he thrust in and out with complete abandon. He would remember this moment for all eternity.

When he saw the exciting, pulsating tingles of pleasure about to erupt, he crushed his mouth against hers to block out the scream that wanted to escape. He eased the rough kiss into a warm tangle of lips as they both came down from the harmonious high. "I love you, Aubrey."

"I love you, Logan. I definitely think I will need a lot of *help* in the future."

He smiled. "I am the sheriff, I aim to help."

"Do you ever wear an expression that doesn't look like a glare?" Kat asked as she leaned against the porch railing and stared at Danny. His eyes were glued to the front door even though Deke was shoving their bags into the car and he should've been helping him.

"Do you ever mind your own business?"

"No."

He looked away from the door to see her smirking at him. "I'm not going to miss you."

"You wound me. And here I thought you would be pining over me," she replied, placing a mock hand on her chest as if in pain.

"I will if you want. Hell, I'll even throw in a goodbye kiss," Deke said, joining Danny near the steps and giving Kat a devilish wink.

"Sure. I like kisses." Kat bounded down the stairs and offered her cheek to Deke. He laughed, planting a soft kiss on her cheek. "I think I might actually miss you, Kat. You are one hell of a woman. A guy could drown quickly in your presence."

"Yeah, sure. That's why my door is flooded with tons of men falling at my feet." She glanced at Danny, his expression wiped clean of any emotion. "You don't have to worry. I know, I know, you will anyway. She'll be fine here."

"It's impossible not to worry. I haven't been away from my sister like this in...shit, since I left for the academy when my parents were alive. I am worried. Deathly worried." Danny turned around and took a few deep breaths, hating the sheriff more and more as each minute passed.

"It's called a phone. And vacations and airplanes and visits. It's not like you'll never see me," Aubrey said as she grabbed his shoulder.

Danny turned around and pulled her into a hug. "I can't help it. Are you sure you want to stay, Aubs?"

"I love him, Danny. Please try to understand and be nice to him. He's a good man if you give him a chance. I'm a big girl. I'm twenty-five. It's time I spread my wings a little."

He stepped back and tried to smile for her sake. He just found her and the pain in his heart felt like he lost her all over again. He glanced down at her hand. "What's that?"

She held up the carefully wrapped bags and handed one to him and one to Deke. "Goodie bags. I made some cookies the last few days while you guys wrapped everything up with the case. And a few more things I saw in the pantry that I thought you might like for the plane ride. I wanted it to be a surprise. I never made you cookies before, so I hope you like them."

He grabbed another hug from her. "I'm sure I'll love 'em. I'm going to miss you."

"I'll miss you, too. A phone call away, remember."

"Let's go, man. We'll miss our flight if we don't hit the road," Deke said, clapping him on the back. He walked toward Logan and held his hand out. "Sheriff, it's been a pleasure. Take care of Aubs for us. I trust you'll do a fine job."

Logan shook his hand. "I will. I'm sure we'll see each other again soon. Aubrey needs to take care of her apartment, so I see a road trip in the near future."

"I still can't believe you kept my apartment this whole time," Aubrey said to Danny as she shook her head in disbelief. "I mean, where did you get the money to keep up my rent?"

"It's nothing for you to worry about. Take your time. Make sure this is where you want to be. Your rent's paid up for the next few months."

"Danny..." Aubrey said with veiled patience.

"Yeah, yeah, I'm giving him a chance. Can't you tell?" Danny took a few steps toward Logan and held his hand out. His friendly smile didn't fool Logan as he leaned into the shake. "You hurt my sister in any way and I'll kill you. I know many forms of disposing of a body."

"Funny. Me, too," Logan said with the same friendly smile. "I love your sister. It's the last thing I would ever do."

Danny held his grip on Logan's hand, exerting a certain amount of pressure to get his point across. The longer he held Logan's stare, the more he saw how much he didn't need to worry about Aubrey. He saw the love the damn sheriff had for his sister. It pissed him off for some reason. "You think you'll have it easy with her, you're wrong. Just wait until that demon comes out. She's more of a rebel than you know."

"I look forward to it. I love every part of her." Logan glanced at their hands. "Can I have my hand back? The threat was enough to get your brotherly point across."

Danny let his hand go and glanced at Kat. "Bye, Kat."

"See ya, Danny boy." She laughed as he cringed at the nickname.

Danny and Deke grabbed one more hug from Aubrey and walked to the car. Deke climbed into the driver's seat, but as Danny almost slid into the passenger side, Seth pulled into the driveway. He had been scarce the last few days, so his abrupt presence was a bit of a shock to Danny. He didn't expect to see him again. Seth got out of his truck and headed straight for him.

"Safe trip, Agent O'Rourke. It was nice meeting you. I have to say, I'm happy to see Aubrey standing by my brother."

"I'm still making a judgment call about that. I took your words into account. I'll be gunning for you first if he hurts her."

"Sure, whatever, I'll take the first hit for my brother. It's the least I deserve. He'll never hurt her, though."

"Yeah, he better not. See you around, Seth. Stay out of trouble. Your brother has enough to worry about with Aubrey."

Seth turned around and glanced at them, a sweet smile on Aubrey's face. "I'm not sure what you mean. Aubrey's a sweetheart."

Danny climbed into his seat and laughed. "Yeah, she is. Until she gets a mind of her own and doesn't feel like listening to you. You'll see." He shut his door and gave a slight wave as Deke backed out of the driveway.

SETH SHUFFLED HIS FEET, then turned around and walked up to the rest of the gang. He put his hands up and shrugged innocently. "I acted like an ass...again, and I'm sorry." He combed a hand through his hair, scratching down to his neck, and rubbed nervously.

"You look like shit," Kat said, pointing to his eye that still held an ugly discoloration.

"I love you, too, sis," Seth said with a smile, bringing his eyes to Logan. "I didn't mean to put my foot in my mouth. I said I was sorry, Logan. What else do you want me to say?"

"I just want to know you're okay. You haven't been around the last few days. I already forgot about that mess. Let's move on. It doesn't matter anymore." Logan walked up to him, pulling him into a quick hug with a small pat on the back. "We're good, Seth."

"Good. Thanks, Logan." Seth gave Aubrey a charming smile. "How are you? I'm so glad you decided to stay. Logan's a lucky guy."

Aubrey curled into Logan's embrace as he threw an arm around her. "I like to think I'm pretty lucky as well. I'm fine, Seth. Each day is a better day. Some memories I'm trying to forget, and thankfully I'm surrounded by wonderful people who are helping with that."

Kat clapped her hands together. "Great! Let's play some cards."

Logan and Seth instantly groaned as Aubrey squealed with excitement. "Can I pick the game? I love War."

"Ugh, you always win at that game. Fine, but then I pick the next one." Kat started up the steps, glancing at Logan and Seth, who stood frozen. "It's not going to kill you two to play one game."

"You're a maniac when you play. I haven't heard good things about Aubrey either." Seth looked at Aubrey with a tender smirk as she deviously smiled back. "All right, I'm in for one game and that's it."

Seth followed Kat into the house while Aubrey grabbed Logan's hand and tugged on it. "You're going to play, right?"

"I seriously hate playing with Kat. The last time I watched you play, you were almost as ruthless as her." Logan chuckled as he walked up the stairs with her.

She stopped him, planting a hot kiss on his lips that melted him to the bones. "You promised you would play with me. You still haven't delivered on that."

"I was thinking more of a private game, where we make it interesting. Something along the lines of...I don't know, strip poker," Logan said, kissing her lips again as he trailed a soft hand down her back.

"I like that idea. Maybe we could kick Kat and Seth out," Aubrey said, leaning in for another kiss.

"You know we can't do that. We can, however, kick their butts at cards, then kick them out."

He tangled his tongue one more time with hers, pulling her closer as her tiny moan made him ache for so much more. Pulling away, he kissed down her neck and back up to her ear where he took a nibble as she moved to the beat of his kisses. "Aubrey...you have no idea how much I love you. I'll show you every day of my life just how much."

"I'll hold you to that. I've always felt lost in life. I feel like I've truly been found for the first time. Don't ever leave me. I love you too much."

He wrapped her in a hug, letting the peace that settled in his soul make itself at home. "Never. You're in my arms, and that's where you'll stay."

For Danny & Kat's story
Dangerous Memories
A Lucky Town Novel, #2

Has the nightmare returned or is this a darker threat?

Agent Danny O'Rourke's greatest wish is for his sister, Aubrey, kidnapped months ago, to finally come home. Though he couldn't save her then, he'll do whatever it takes now to help her heal and bring her back into his life. Except one thing is standing in his way—the Caldwell family.

When a new case links to the Caldwells, he's determined to find answers, even if it means facing off with the alluring Kat Caldwell. Though he tries to hate her, Danny can't deny the intense attraction burning between them.

As the body count rises, Danny has the chilling realization that Kat is the target of this twisted predator's obsession. Haunted by the failures of his past, he'll risk it all to protect her. But one question remains: is the danger they're facing now linked to Aubrey's disappearance...or is an even more sinister force at play?

As Danny follows the clues down a rabbit hole of lies and depravity, there's only one thing he knows for certain: losing Kat is not an option. As their passion flares white-hot, the killer's trails turns deadly cold, and Danny must confront his greatest demon to rescue the woman he loves...before she's taken from him forever.

For Seth & Pepper's story

Stolen Memories

A Lucky Town Novel, #3

Some secrets are worth killing for...

Seth Caldwell has always been the family troublemaker, but he's ready for a change—starting with his best friend Evan. But before he can talk to him, Evan goes missing and his boss turns up dead. Despite the lies between them and Evan being the prime suspect, Seth knows he's no killer. Now, in order to find him, Seth is forced to turn to feisty new deputy Pepper Wilson for help.

With her razor-sharp instincts and ability to unnerve him like no other, Pepper quickly becomes a temptation he can't resist. But Seth senses she's hiding her own secrets behind that alluring smile. As the danger grows closer and they spiral deeper into a twisted web of deception, one truth becomes clear—some will go to brutal lengths to exact revenge.

Grab this enthralling thrill ride that will leave you gasping for more today!

For Deke & Charlotte's story

Deadly Memories

A Lucky Town Novel, #4

Love is scary...death is terrifying.

Deke Sumnter only has casual sex. Anything beyond that, he's not interested. Until Charlotte. She's smart, sexy, and something he's always craved. But one time was all he could give her. He should've known it wouldn't be enough. Now, she won't even talk to him. He'd take just being friends over the silent treatment.

When trouble starts brewing again in their small town, this time targeting the woman he swears he doesn't love, he won't let anything stop him from protecting her, even if everything inside of him says he needs to stay as far away from her as possible.

Captivating suspense and electric romance unite in this emotional thriller that will leave you breathless. One-click now to start reading today!

For Bolt & Cherry's story
Forgotten Memories
A Lucky Town Novel, #5

She isn't looking for trouble...

Despite being a city girl, Cherry Chapman could get used to the small-town life. Not that she's welcome in Lucky. She only wants to meet her half-sister, Pepper, and get to know her, not stir up a hornet's nest. So far, the only person welcoming her is Deputy Bolten, and at times, she feels even he doesn't trust her. The way things are going, she's going to need more than just his kindness. She's going to need his help. But if he doesn't trust her, how can she trust him with the problems that followed her to town?

While the past year has been a rough one, Bolt is trying to move forward. When Cherry comes crashing into their town with her sweet and innocent nature, he can't help but be wary—and attracted to her. The more he gets to know her, the more he wants to help her. He knows something is going on, but no matter how hard he tries, she won't confide in him. He's failed before—getting shot is proof of that—but he vows not to fail again. He'll protect Cherry at all costs, even if that means being on the opposite side of his friends.

With high tension, suspense, and smoldering romance, dive into the danger and desire with the final book in the ***Lucky Town series*** *today.*

ABOUT THE AUTHOR

I'm a *USA Today* Bestselling Author that loves to write contemporary romance and romantic suspense novels, although I am partial to romantic suspense. I even dabble in paranormal. Honestly, I love anything that has to do with romance. As long as there's a happy ending, I'm a happy camper. And insta-love...yes, please! I love baseball (Go Twins!) and creating awesome crafts. I graduated with a Bachelor's Degree in Criminal Justice, working in that field for several years before I became a stay-at-home mom. I have a few more amazing stories in the works. If you would like to learn more about me and my books, head to my website by scanning the QR code. Thanks for reading!

www.ingramcontent.com/pod-product-compliance
Lightning Source LLC
LaVergne TN
LVHW091025080826
845145LV00002B/360

* 9 7 8 1 9 5 5 8 8 6 0 0 0 *